ADMIRAL REMAR LOOKED GRIMLY
AT KISSINGER

"Last week I got my first live-fire demo. They put fifty-seven thousand grenades into an area no larger than a football field in under a minute.

"I'm telling you, John, this is heavy duty ordnance you're dealing with. If you or Hal are connected with the people charged with tracking down whoever stole the prototypes, you're going to have your work cut out for you. But I think I can help."

"That would be appreciated," Kissinger replied. "And you're right about our people. If they have to go up against any force of considerable size, it's my responsibility to arm them with the proper tools. That's their only chance for success. I need to get my hands on some of those weapons."

"Fight fire with fire."

DON PENDLETON'S

STONY

AMERICA'S ULTRA-COVERT INTELLIGENCE AGENCY

MAN®

MAELSTROM

A GOLD EAGLE BOOK FROM

W®RLDWIDE®

TORONTO • NEW YORK • LONDON
AMSTERDAM • PARIS • SYDNEY • HAMBURG
STOCKHOLM • ATHENS • TOKYO • MILAN
MADRID • WARSAW • BUDAPEST • AUCKLAND

First edition August 2005

ISBN 0-373-61962-6

MAELSTROM

Special thanks and acknowledgment to
Jon Guenther for his contribution to this work.

Printed in U.S.A.

MAELSTROM

For Mr. William Fieldhouse—mentor, colleague, friend

PROLOGUE

Adelaide, Australia

He watched the puffs of smoke rise into the air as the weapon cycled through sixteen 40 mm grenades at the rate of four per second.

Wallace Davidia knew the shells were nonlethal—their noses packed with iridescent orange powder versus high explosives—but they weren't the object of his attention. The mechanism of delivery was what took center stage. That weapon, and the others like it, being demonstrated at the fifth annual Defence Science and Technology Organisation Land Weapons Conference, was what had brought the Resurrected Defense League to Australia. It was this technology that he wanted—no, *had*—to possess, and the reason the men with him now sat and waited patiently, professionally.

Davidia lowered the binoculars and looked at the shadowy figures seated near him, illuminated only by the small opening in the side of their shelter. The fourteen-foot moving truck stunk of sweat mixed with anticipation and fear. Davidia knew those scents well; he'd known them from his adolescent years growing up in the heart of Brooklyn. Those had been the hardest times of his life. He was the youngest son of Jewish parents who barely escaped the Holocaust only to find another war for survival going on in their own neighborhood. Nonetheless, he'd done his part for his country, serving four years in the Marine Corps, including a stint in Operation Desert Storm, and returned to New York afterward to become a police officer on beat patrol in his old stomping grounds. Life hadn't always been easy, but he'd been happy until called off shift early one morning to have the police chaplain tell him a surprised burglar murdered his wife, a burglar whose attorney got him off on a technicality by proposing that the police had discriminated against the man because he was Palestinian.

Determined to right a wrong, Davidia joined the Jewish Defense League and even spent a short time with a radical Jewish activist group conducting underground operations in New York City, but one too many protests in the streets, one too many acts of violence, eventually led to a demand for his resignation. Davidia didn't go quietly. He found his wife's murderer and put a bullet in the guy's head before renouncing his citizenship and fleeing America. Eventually, Davidia founded the Resurrected Defense League. He trained his mind and his body, honing the military skills Uncle Sam taught him and the terror tactics gleaned from membership in the Kach-Kahane

Chai to a sharp edge. It had all led up to this day. This would be the day that he would reveal his abilities for the first time since his self-imposed exile. The RDL was about to make a statement the world would never forget.

Davidia nodded with assurance to his lieutenant before raising his voice just loud enough. In Hebrew he said, "We move in two minutes. Weapons check."

They had timed the operation down to the final second, laid out every part of the demonstration grounds to the last detail. His men knew every corner of this area and they were familiar with every street in Adelaide. They had spent months visiting the area, mapping various escape routes and planning for every possible scenario. They had to do this to insure the success of their mission and secure escape. Davidia knew the weapons he sought were prototypes, but the RDL's engineers were waiting at a secret location far from here, a location known only to him and his lieutenant, Boaz Rasham. If something happened to one of them, the other could still accomplish the objectives. If both of them bought it, the mission was terminated and the men were under clear orders to cover and conceal, and escape by any means possible. Capture or surrender was unacceptable.

His organization wasn't large, maybe 150 in membership with about triple that in financial supporters, but it was a force big enough to implement Davidia's plans. Years before, the Kach-Kahane Chai had attempted to utilize a technological device to effectively end the conflicts on the West Bank once and for all.

Unfortunately the plan had failed, thwarted by Mossad agents and Americans from an unknown organization. Davidia left the Kach-Kahane Chai and took his staunchest supporters with him. He knew that ending the war between Israel and the Palestinians would never truly stop the oppression. No, the only way to stop their sworn enemies was to utterly eradicate them. Davidia's plans called for the total extinction of those vermin, and the most ingenious part was that the nations of the world would do most of the work—starting with America.

"Thirty seconds," Davidia announced as he stored the binoculars. The terrorist leader then checked the action on the mini-Uzi, putting the weapon in battery before letting it dangle at his side by its strap. Davidia then swung one leg over his seat and positioned himself comfortably on the seat of the four-wheel ATV.

The sound of ATV engines being started echoed loudly inside the confines of the semi-trailer. There were twelve ATVs in all, each one manned by the very best of Davidia's soldiers. These were the cream of the crop, the most experienced members of the RDL's strike teams. Davidia had handpicked the crew for this mission, given its importance. The success of their action now would set the stage for the rest of his plans and he couldn't afford to let anything go wrong. These men were his first, best insurance policy against any eventualities. They would succeed—God was with them.

Davidia nodded to Rasham, who would stay behind with the truck and prepare for the return of the men and their spoils. The man grabbed the door release and heaved. The sunlight nearly blinded them as the door rolled upward and Rasham kicked out the ramp. The ramp dropped to the ground with a clang that was drowned by the roar of the first ATV engine as its rider rolled out with a pop of the clutch.

Davidia revved the engine of the ATV and anxiously waited his turn to exit the trailer. It was time to make history.

CHAPTER ONE

His name was David McCarter, and he was team leader to some of the most dangerous men on earth.

The fox-faced Briton turned to study the profile of one of those men now. Just the way the man held his tall and lanky form betrayed his readiness, and his sharp, brown eyes intently searched their field of fire. In all the years McCarter had known this man, he'd come to respect his professionalism and integrity, not to mention his skills in the heat of action. This guy could hold it together in the toughest situation. He was a first-rate soldier.

Calvin James cast a sideways glance at first notice that McCarter was watching him, then turned his head fully and grinned at the Phoenix Force leader. "What?"

"Just thinking," McCarter replied, turning his attention back to their assigned watch.

"Well, if you like what you see, I'm free Saturday night," James cracked.

"You're not my type, mate," McCarter said, grinning. Then the smile disappeared. "Actually, I was just wondering when Hal sent us out on this bloody mission if you might have been thinking the same thing I was."

James shrugged and scratched his chin. "What, that this is a waste of resources? Much as I hate to admit it, any decent security team could have handled this. We should be out chasing down bad guys, not baby-sitting a bunch of tight-assed military contractors."

McCarter chuckled and said, "You got to start saying how you *really* feel about stuff, Cal. You hold back too much."

"Well, I can't believe you disagree. Say it isn't so."

"Maybe a little," he admitted. "But remember that Hal sent us here to get a feel for these new weapons systems. Kissinger has him convinced they'll be useful in the field for future operations."

James nodded toward the field. "Yeah, and Cowboy's down there right now in the firing area with a ringside seat to this circus. We should be down there with him instead of standing on the sidelines and feeding peanuts to the elephants."

John "Cowboy" Kissinger was the top weapons smith for Stony Man Farm, America's premier counterterrorist organization, and one of her best-kept and most effective secrets. It was Kissinger who had convinced Harold Brognola, chief of the Stony Man operation, to let the members of Phoenix Force accompany him to Australia for their first look at the weapons of the future. Naturally, Phoenix Force was on call at a moment's notice at all times, ready to be dropped into anything, at anytime and in any place. Nonetheless, all of its men were consummate professionals who had taken the job without complaint, and McCarter couldn't have asked for more. Still, James was right—this was a waste of talent.

McCarter chuckled. "You're beginning to sound as cynical as Carl."

Before James could reply, McCarter keyed up the wireless transceiver attached to his belt, which was no larger than a standard pager. Phoenix Force had recently decided to go with one of Akira Tokaido's latest inventions—a communications system for the team to use during sensitive or covert operations that might require distance between them, thus splitting up one of the world's most effective counterterrorist units. This system was quite different from the one they'd used in the past, since these transceivers sent microwave signals. Under normal circumstances, such transmissions would have required line-of-sight, but with a satellite linkup there was no such limitation. A programming algorithm designed by Tokaido to control the burst-rate provided the security. This system had a range comparable to Los Angeles County, and all of those factors made it much more effective and reliable for the team.

"All units check in," McCarter said.

"Red team's clear," came the voice of Gary Manning, indicating he and Rafael Encizo, positioned at the other end of the field, had things well under control. McCarter detected the boredom in Manning's voice, but he didn't let that bother him. Both the men in red team were as dedicated to their jobs and Phoenix Force as James.

"Blue team's clear," echoed T. J. Hawkins, who had partnered with the liaison of the parade ground security chief.

Leaving the youngest and newest member of Stony Man on his own with a much less experienced man hadn't been McCarter's first choice. After one look, the Briton could tell that the security chief was nowhere close to being as experienced or seasoned as Hawkins. Still, McCarter knew Hawkins was the best choice, since blue team was working the bleachers where the military observers were seated and the younger guy was "best fit" to act as an active Army soldier. Hawkins, a former member of a Delta Force team, had immediately taken to the role since it allowed him to put on the uniform once more.

McCarter nodded with satisfaction and was about to kill the transceiver when Hawkins added, "Gold team, check that last comm. Looks like trouble in grid six."

McCarter checked that direction. It was a large open space comprised of mostly tall, dry grass, scattered trees and the occasional boulder that separated the demo field from a busy uptown street. However, it was a fairly open space and it didn't make a whole lot of sense that someone would launch an attack from that direction. It wasn't until he saw the dozen or so ATVs racing toward the demo field that McCarter changed his mind.

McCarter keyed the transceiver. "Red team, move

to defensive posture. Blue team, stand post and watch for alternates in case this is a diversion. First to targets calls the ball."

As both teams acknowledged his transmission, Mc-Carter and James burst from their position and sprinted down the slight grassy knoll bound for the center of the demo field. It was long odds they could make it in time to implement a fully effective defense, but what had the Briton more concerned were the intentions of these new arrivals. It was possible they were just a group of crazies who wanted to stir the pot, but Mc-Carter didn't buy it. They were attired in desert camouflage uniforms and the Phoenix Force warrior was certain he'd seen light reflecting off gunmetal. Kids weren't so brazen and showy, and they certainly didn't congregate in those kinds of numbers. McCarter smelled nothing but bloody trouble.

And he didn't like it one damn bit.

RAFAEL ENCIZO and Gary Manning spotted the group on ATVs at the same moment Hawkins reported them, and the pair of Phoenix Force warriors immediately bolted into the fray.

"First to targets calls the ball," McCarter had said. Well, Encizo knew exactly what the hell that meant. While the Phoenix Force leader was charged with all final decisions, it sometimes made sense to let whoever was closest to the enemy direct the action. After all, a field soldier's report of troop movement and direction was much more accurate than that delivered by some armchair quarterback in the rear. Encizo's and

Manning's position put them much closer to the approaching ATVs, and that meant they would likely reach the perimeter of the demo field before James and McCarter. In that event, Encizo would take the lead.

The two men reached the demo field and sprinted for the fence line. Encizo could hear Hawkins shouting at somebody from the bleachers, but he didn't bother to risk a backward glance. The young Texan was probably yelling at the Aussie security team to clear the field of all nonessential personnel. Those weren't soldiers seated in those stands, they were officers and defense contractors who were slow and well stocked on doughnuts. And the guys by the weapons were nothing but engineers, thereby incapable of putting up a fight with their prototype weapons, except of course Kissinger.

Phoenix Force would handle this.

"Definitely hostiles…at least ten…well armed," the Cuban reported to them as he breathed heavily from the exertion. "We're engaging."

Encizo produced the MP-5K he'd concealed beneath his jacket, and in his peripheral vision he noticed Manning had already drawn a SIG-Sauer P-239 with an extended 8-round magazine. The big Canadian preferred not to indulge in compact machine pistols like the MP-5K, finding them too bulky for a mission of this type. However he was no less deadly with a semiautomatic pistol than Encizo with a machine pistol.

Encizo was the first to demonstrate that fact as he stopped near the fence, knelt and steadied his sights on the first target. He'd set the MP-5K for 3-round bursts, and the first trio of rounds took one of the ATV riders in the chest. Blood stained the man's shirt as the impact lifted him from his ride. The ATV careened toward the fence, spinning only at the last moment, the two left wheels striking the fence, which held firm despite the weight of the vehicle.

Manning missed once in his opening salvo, but round two caught another rider in the gut. The driver keeled over, and his ATV slowed considerably as the man clutched his abdomen. Even from that distance, Encizo could see the agony on the guy's face. The driver looked up in time to see that he was going to hit the fence and he tried to avoid it, but the ground was still damp from rains that morning and the ATV slid into the fence. The rider was hurled face-first and the impact twisted his head at an odd angle. Encizo could tell the guy was dead from a broken neck before the body hit the ground. The warrior looked for his next target, but McCarter's voice interrupted the action.

"Incoming!"

Manning and Encizo threw themselves to the ground in time to avoid the whistling projectile that passed only yards above them. A moment later the ground shook as a blast erupted. Encizo risked a glance long enough to determine the source of the attack. A few of the ATV riders had stayed back and were providing covering fire utilizing CIS 40GLs. The Singapore-made grenade launcher was almost identical in design to the M-203—it fired 40 mm grenades with a maximum effective range up to 400 meters.

"That's some heavy shit we're up against here," Manning muttered.

"Tell me about it," Encizo replied.

"Get some cover," McCarter advised even as the two Phoenix Force commandos were on their feet and converging on their position. "We'll lay down some fire for you."

"Roger," Manning answered through his transceiver.

The sounds of James's and McCarter's MP-5Ks resounded through the air as they laid down a full-auto onslaught against the enemy troops. Encizo knew there was no way they could hope to repel an attack of this kind, and that the fence would serve only as a minor barrier.

The best bet was to evacuate the innocents and hope some window of opportunity opened.

JOHN KISSINGER WASN'T exactly a warrior, but he knew how to take care of himself. Unfortunately he'd been serving in the capacity of VIP to the weapons demonstration and, being that close to the prototypes, he wasn't allowed to carry a firearm.

Not that it really mattered. A pistol was no good against high-explosive grenades anyway—at least not when the grenadiers were at the range they were. Staying alive seemed a bit more important to Kissinger and he saw it as his duty to keep the weapons operators and engineers that way, as well. After all, they were fellow gun junkies, and Kissinger watched out for his own kind. Besides, the men of Phoenix Force could take care of themselves. The best he could do was to get the innocents out of the way.

"Move!" he told the engineers and operators. "Go for that cover over there!"

Kissinger waved them in the direction of a low-slung building that ran parallel to the bleachers. It was made of heavy concrete and steel, with a small open-air observation window that provided a full view of the field. It was actually a bunker-style observatory, designed for inclement weather and to provide some relative protection during demonstrations similar to this one.

One of the operators tripped and Kissinger reached down and hauled him to his feet. He practically dragged the guy as he rushed toward the cover of the observation building. They had just reached the door as the second grenade struck the bleachers and sent an explosive blast of sharp, superheated aluminum shrapnel in every direction. A pang of fear stabbed at Kissinger's heart even as he pushed the operator—whose name he remembered was Randy Wallis—through the door of the building. The armorer turned his attention toward the bleachers and breathed a sigh of relief when he saw they were already empty.

HAWKINS HAD BEEN the first to spot the team of ATV riders approaching the demo field, and he knew immediately they weren't an Olympic cross-country team just out for some fun. He'd started screaming orders at the surprised military observers and contractors. A couple of the generals in the crowd had at first acted as if he were nuts, giving Hawkins stern looks that signaled he was violating military protocol. The explosion of the first 40 mm grenade a mere twenty-five yards from their position turned annoyance into pandemonium, ending any further doubts the observers might have had about Hawkins's maintaining a military decorum. People scrambled down the five rows of bleachers, moving toward the bunker-like building in the rear under the direction of Hawkins and the head of security, a young and inexperienced lad named Thaddeus Kornsby. What the youth lacked in experienced he made up for in enthusiasm and steadiness under fire. His handling of the situation was admirable.

Which is why Hawkins felt anger wash over him when, halfway to the building, he turned at the sound of the second explosion that blew apart the bleachers and toppled Kornsby, who was now short his left arm. The young security officer stared blankly into Hawkins's eyes, oblivious to the sound of the woman pinned under him, who was screaming and kicking. Hawkins realized something the woman, covered in the gore that had erupted from the stump of Kornsby's wound, didn't. He'd sustained his injuries throwing himself on top of her to save her life.

Hawkins turned and rushed to retrieve both of them before the situation could get any worse. Although he really didn't see how that could be possible.

McCARTER AND JAMES went prone about the same time they'd warned Encizo and Manning to grab cover. The

Phoenix Force leader watched helplessly as a 40 mm grenade sailed over the demo field in a lazy arc and came to land about thirty meters on the backside of where they had set up the new prototype weapons. Less than a minute passed before there was a loud crack and a second grenade landed in the bleachers, although it appeared Hawkins and Kornsby had already cleared the spectators.

McCarter also noticed that Kissinger had managed to gather the weapons operators and engineers away from the hot zone. With innocents out of the way, it would make it easier for Phoenix Force to do its job.

McCarter keyed the transceiver. "Blue team."

"Go," came Encizo's voice.

"We've lost sight of you, mate. Are you clear?"

"We're in the range building."

McCarter scanned the grounds and quickly found the location. The range building was, in fact, a small wooden structure dug into the earth, its roof and about two feet of uprights actually aboveground. McCarter had seen many like it. It was designed for range cadre to mark distances during live-fire exercises and call back the data to weapons operators. McCarter had familiarized himself with the process long before, when competing in pistol matches all over the world. But that had been a lifetime ago, when he was still with the SAS. Now the enemy seemed to have the advantage.

McCarter meant to change that.

"Red team, what's your status?"

"We're inside the observation building," Hawkins replied.

"Do you have a clear line of fire?"

"We did...until they blew up the damned bleachers. Now there's too much smoke."

"Hang tight, mates," McCarter said, hearing the tension in his teammate's voice. "We're coming for you."

McCarter and James got to their feet and continued charging toward the demonstration grounds. The group of ATV riders was now inside the fence line and headed straight for the prototypes. The Briton got within what he deemed was a reasonable distance, then knelt and steadied his MP-5K. He delivered another sustained burst, with James following suit. Another rider's body flipped sideways off the ATV and his machine caromed off that of one of his partners before rolling onto its side and stopping, one handlebar leaving a gouge in the soft dirt-sand mix of the demo grounds.

James entered the fray, capping one of the several hardmen in a group that had reached the prototypes. Rounds from the MP-5K slammed into the rider's back as the man dismounted from his ride, and he pitched forward violently and landed face-first.

McCarter could now see the winking of muzzles from the open slit in the range building. It looked as if Manning and Encizo had them in a cross fire. The Briton grinned. That pair was performing admirably, despite the overwhelming odds. Phoenix Force was neither heavily armed nor prepared for this kind of an assault. They weren't packing any spare clips, heavy weapons or explosives of any kind. The enemy had every advantage here.

As if in response to the thought, McCarter heard the unmistakable sounds of two grenade launchers being fired. He yelled at James to get clear as he got to his feet and sprinted toward a large boulder. The natural terrain here was rocky, comprised of heavy dirt and sand. There were plenty of boulders like this around, especially in their area, which is why McCarter had chosen it as strategic for observation. That decision was probably going to prove to be one that saved his life and the life of his colleagues.

When the grenades struck, he'd managed to get far enough away. The only consequence was the shower of dirt and rocks—the direct result of his proximity to the explosions. As the last of the debris settled, McCarter risked exposure by glancing at the area over the boulder. His heart sank into his stomach when he saw the motionless form of Calvin James lying close to the smoldering impressions left by the twin blasts.

"I've got one down," McCarter said into the microphone of his transceiver.

Then he left his cover and rushed for his friend.

IMMEDIATELY FOLLOWING McCarter's transmission, Hawkins made it a point to find Kissinger so they could discuss their options.

"This isn't good," Hawkins said.

"That's an understatement," Kissinger replied. "You're the pro here. What do you want to do?"

"Our first mission is to protect these people," Hawkins said in a hushed tone. "I can't very well leave you alone with them, and if I try to get to David, I'll get my ass shot off."

"I can stay here with them."

"And do what?" Hawkins asked with disbelief. "You're not packing. I've got the only weapon, and it's just a pistol. And if we don't get out of here very soon, Kornsby's going to bleed to death."

"Yeah, we really got caught with our pants down on this one," Kissinger replied. "But I think we'll be okay without you. I think whoever the hell that is out there is after the prototypes, and nothing else."

"Maybe," Hawkins replied, gritting his teeth. "But I just can't take that chance."

ENCIZO AND MANNING could barely see through the haze and smoke left in the wake of additional grenade explosions. This didn't account for the smoke that was filling up their position. It stung their eyes, causing them to choke, and it wasn't dark or thick, which told the pair that they were the victims of CS gas. The enemy was stealing the prototypes and there wasn't a damned thing either of them could do about it.

Encizo couldn't remember the last time he'd felt this helpless.

As Manning wiped tears from his face, he said, "I hope Cal is all right."

"I'll tell you what," Encizo said, one muscle twitching in his cheek. "If he's dead, I'll hunt down every one of those bastards and kill them barehanded."

"Let's not jump the gun, Rafe," Manning said quietly. He cleared his lungs with a fit of coughing and then continued. "We don't know if he's dead or not dead. David just said he had one down. We don't know what that means."

Encizo's eyes were as haunting as his expression. "I know what it means."

Manning decided not to argue with his teammate; partly because he didn't see any point and partly because he knew it didn't much matter. The roar of the ATV engines and subsequent fading as they moved away from the demo grounds told the whole story. Their enemy had escaped with their booty and Phoenix Force had been unable to stop them. The reasons no longer mattered, that was just the way the chips had fallen.

One thing was certain in Manning's mind. This wasn't over. Not even close.

CHAPTER TWO

Stony Man Farm, Virginia

The unlit cigar nearly fell from Harold Brognola's mouth as he sat forward in his chair.

"Say that again, please?"

Barbara Price, the Farm's mission controller, had just walked into the big Fed's office and set a cup of coffee in front of the man. She took a seat in front of his desk. Price immediately observed the knuckles of Brognola's hand turning white. He was clutching the phone and furrows were forming above his eyebrows. That wasn't a good sign. It meant the Stony Man chief was stressing, his anxiety building to a point that would one day either cause him a stroke, heart attack or some other fatal ailment. He already suffered from digestive problems.

"Okay, I'm sure we'll hear from our people shortly. Thank you for calling, sir. I'll keep you informed."

Brognola dropped the phone into the receiver.

"Hal, what is it?" Price asked.

"That was the President," he said, looking her in the eye with a granite expression. "The Secretary of State just notified him that there was what the Australian government described as an 'incident' at the conference."

"What happened?"

"Apparently a dozen or more heavily armed men, which by the way have not yet been identified, attacked during the middle of a demonstration and began shelling the area with grenades and automatic weapons fire. Security teams responded, including Phoenix Force, but apparently there were some casualties. One of them was identified as a black man belonging to a, quote 'private security detachment assigned to the conference,' end quote."

"Calvin."

"There's no confirmation of that yet," Brognola reminded her with a stern look and a wagging finger. "And there have also been no reports of any deaths, so let's not jump to any conclusions until we know what the hell is going on."

"Well, why haven't we heard from Phoenix yet?"

"I'm not sure," Brognola replied. "It may be that if one of them was injured, they're getting medical attention first. I'm sure David will contact us when he can."

As if on cue, a buzzing sounded on Brognola's phone. It was a unique signal that indicated the call was coming from the internal voice and data communications network that connected the farmhouse with the Annex, a new underground facility that housed highly advanced centers for communication, cybernetics and security to support all of Stony Man's operations.

"Brognola," the Stony Man chief barked into the phone. "They are? All right, we'll be right there."

Price wasn't sure she'd ever seen him move so fast. Brognola was out of his chair and hurrying toward the electric car that ran nearly a quarter-mile underground between the farmhouse and the Annex. Price followed him with all of the same vigor.

The big Fed flipped a switch and the car obediently surged toward the Annex. "That was Aaron on the phone. He says that David's called in."

"Did he say how he sounded?"

Brognola shook his head. "I don't think Aaron knows yet that there was even trouble."

"Well, if I know David, he knows now."

They arrived at the Annex and a minute later they were standing outside the Computer Room, their way blocked by a burly guy with a wrestler-like body that was, unfortunately, confined to a wheelchair for life. Still, that fact had never broken the mind or the spirit of Aaron "The Bear" Kurtzman. The indomitable technology genius greeted them at the door and raised a cautionary hand.

"Everyone's okay," Kurtzman reported. He fixed Brognola with a gentler expression and added, "Including Calvin."

Price felt the anxiety ebb from her and she could literally see the tension dissipate in Brognola's shoulders. She thought it odd that she could read her boss, even from the rear, but the tension in his posture had been so evident that the relief could only be equally so.

Kurtzman turned and entered the Computer Room, followed by Brognola and Price.

Brognola said to strategically placed speaker phones, "David, you with us?"

"Yes, and you bloody well kept me waiting long enough here, Hal."

Price couldn't help but smile. She winked at Brognola when he looked at her and smiled triumphantly before saying, "Report."

McCarter sighed. "We took some pretty bad hits. This has to be one of the worst security gigs we've ever done."

"I just got off the phone with the Man, and he tells me the Australian government was hedging when briefing the SOD."

"That's a mild understatement, " McCarter replied. "They had just completed their fourth demonstration and were about to move on in the presentation when it all hit the bloody fan. Aggressors were dressed in standard desert camouflage fatigues, carrying a variety of automatic rifles and machine pistols, and launching high-explosive grenades into the area like it was free."

"How many are we talking here?"

"A dozen, give or take. We managed to bring down about half before it all went to hell."

"Were you able to determine origin?" Price interjected.

"No, but there wasn't exactly time to ask them

where they were from, and none of us got close enough to tell. They were definitely thorough. They not only got the weapons, but they managed to round up their dead."

"Obviously looking to avoid any type of identification," Price concluded.

Brognola nodded at her, then asked, "What's Calvin's status?"

"He'll pull through. The bugger took a bit of shell shock. The concussions from their HE grenades damn near knocked us all batty. We had to get him and all of the civilians evacuated first before I could touch base with you. We're at our hotel now and this is the first chance they've given us to contact you."

"First chance who's given you?"

"Investigators from the Crown," McCarter replied in a sour tone.

"They have no right to hold you under *any* circumstances," Brognola replied. "I made sure your credentials granted you diplomatic immunity. I'll make a call and get you released."

"Well, make it quick, will you? We're in a foul mood here, and the rest of the blokes are about to vote on making a break for it and shooting our bloody way out of here. Can't say as I blame them, and I might just do it anyway."

"Don't cause any trouble. Just hang tight and keep a low profile. I promise I'll have you out of there within the hour. In the meantime, give me whatever else you can."

"Well, I can tell you this was no ordinary terrorist attack."

"How so?"

"Our friends here had a particular goal in mind. They came with the intent to steal the new prototypes from Stormalite Systems, and that's just what they did. It didn't seem like they were interested in taking hostages or murdering innocent civilians."

"So they weren't looking for shock value," Brognola said. "Go on."

"It also seems obvious they knew exactly what they were doing, Hal, and they got away with it. Their tactics were ingenious and unfamiliar. I don't think I've fought against a group quite like this. Very methodical and calculated."

"You said there were maybe a dozen or so?"

"Yes."

"Okay, so that means just a small group was trained for this operation. And given they knew what to hit and how to hit it, I'd have to guess very specialized in these kinds of operations. I agree with your assessment. This was no ordinary terrorist attack. This was a military operation."

"Or at least an attack by a group well-versed in military tactics," Price added.

Kurtzman shook his head with a disbelieving expression. "Mercenaries?"

"Possibly," Brognola replied. "It would explain the theft of these prototypes."

"Well, I managed to get in a few words with the blokes from Stormalite before reinforcements showed up. Thanks to Cowboy, I managed to glean the inventory that was stolen. I've got it here on our transceiver if you want me to send it."

"Do it," Brognola said, nodding at Kurtzman.

The computer wizard did a one-eighty in his chair through a single motion from his powerful arms and raced over to a communications console. He got to the nearest keyboard, which consisted of nothing but a flat rubber base with soft-touch keys, and quickly entered a fifteen-character alphanumeric code. A moment later tones similar to a fax-modem resounded through the room in bursts. The data transmission took less than thirty seconds.

"Bear, did you get it all?" Brognola asked when the tones ended.

Kurtzman checked the large, flat-panel LCD monitor at a nearby workstation and nodded. "You bet. Looks like there's a full inventory here of everything they had, plus schematics. Very nice work, David. But how did you get all of this in such a short period of time?"

"I downloaded from one of the engineer's notebooks."

"That's good work," Brognola said, and they knew he meant it because the Stony Man chief wasn't one to toss compliments lightly. "That's *excellent* work, as a matter of fact."

"So, what do you think this mysterious new group might be planning?" Price asked.

"I was hoping you might have some ideas about that," McCarter replied. "We've talked among ourselves here about it already, and the consensus seems to be that this group plans to build additional weapons from the prototypes."

"Agreed," Brognola said. "There's no way this group could do much with the prototypes. While these weapons are powerful, there aren't enough of them in circulation to be effective during a terrorist operation."

"There's something else we have to consider," Price said.

"What's that?" McCarter asked.

"Well, it's possible this group doesn't plan to use the prototypes at all. Up to this point, we've assumed they have some purpose or use with them, but maybe they just stole them and plan to sell to the highest bidder."

Brognola nodded. "That would fit more in line with the mercenary theory."

"We considered that at our end, and immediately dismissed it," McCarter replied. "They went to some considerable risk to get these weapons. They had it planned to the last detail. If an outside party hired them, then they gave the group a lot of privileged intelligence. Much more intelligence than I would think such a group would have."

"David has a point," Price said, nodding in agreement.

"Well, we can sit around on our duffs and debate this for the next ten years, or find out who this group is and what they want. With that information, I think we might have enough to figure out where they're going."

"We're already working with the Australian security team that was charged with this here. Our contact is a guy named Tad Kornsby. He's a pretty good chap. Even though the Aussie's federal agencies are ready to jump in, they're still hedging until asked for help. Right now, we have to rely on local and state police authorities to investigate and it's taking them for-bloody-ever."

That made sense. The Australian Security Intelligence Organisation was responsible for gathering intelligence and producing information that would alert Australian officials—particularly the Department of Defence—to any threats against national security. However, the ASIO was a last resort, and it was natural that local police agencies, operating under the jurisdiction of South Australia's Minister of Justice, would want to keep control. This would remain in the hands of state authorities until such time it was determined that this attack was actually a terrorist attack, or that the prototypes had been removed from the country. Thus far, it didn't sound as if there was any evidence to support either of those scenarios, and so the ASIO would naturally not become involved until such proof surfaced.

"I'll see if I can get the President to nudge this up a bit, David. In the meantime, I'll definitely get you freed up. If this group plans to smuggle those prototypes out of the country, I want to be able to put Phoenix Force on their trail at a moment's notice."

"The sooner, the better, Hal," McCarter replied.

Price said, "You mentioned something about an angle you were working with the locals. What's the story there?"

"This group attacked us using four-wheelers. They

left a few of them behind, so the SA's Justice Technology Services are going over every inch of them to determine their origin. They also apparently have video surveillance tapes that might have captured pictures of one or more of the players. We're hoping we can get our hands on them."

"You know, Bear," Brognola interjected, "if any of those tapes have pictures of our people, we're going to have to make sure they disappear."

Kurtzman sighed. "Yeah, and that's going to take some time. But I'll get our contacts working on it. I'll also see if I can glean some information from the tapes once we have them."

Brognola nodded, and then said, "We'll start digging in here and see what kind of intelligence we can get you, David. It's going to take us a little time, but I'll make this everyone's top priority. I'll also get the Man briefed on your situation there. Expect to hear from me within twelve hours."

"I hope we have that much time," Price said after the call was disconnected.

Brognola didn't reply.

Adelaide, Australia

JUST AS BROGNOLA promised, federal officials contacted South Australia's Ministry of Justice. They were ordered to extend all diplomatic courtesies to Phoenix Force, and every member of the team was free to move about the country as necessary. That trouble resolved, Phoenix Force was able to solicit cooperation from

men working under Tad Kornsby, and the SAMJ officials assigned to investigate the attack at the demonstration grounds.

Their first order of business was to view the tapes.
David McCarter and Rafael Encizo met up with Kornsby's second in command, Anthony Halsford, at the
Justice offices in downtown Adelaide. When they were
finished viewing the tapes, Halsford turned off the television monitor and then sat back on the table and folded
his arms. He was a burly fellow, with a shock of reddish
hair. He had thick sideburns, beard and a mustache that
were reminiscent of the type worn by many officers
during the American Civil War. Thick, aromatic smoke
curled from an ornate pipe clenched between his teeth.

"So…what do you think?" Halsford asked. His Australian accent was heavy and his voice a rich baritone.

"I think we're dealing with terrorists, mate," Mc-
Carter replied.

"I agree," Encizo added. "Those guys were definitely more than mercenaries. If they look like terrorists act like terrorists and move like terrorists, they're
probably terrorists."

Halsford pulled the pipe from his mouth and eyed
the Cuban warrior with a mix of interest and suspicion.
"Kornsby tells me you're a private security detail hired
by Stormalite Systems."

"That's right," Encizo said in a congenial tone.

"For a security group, you seem quite well informed. And from what I saw of your movements on
those tapes, I'd guess this isn't the first time you've
been in these kinds of circumstances. Am I correct?"

Encizo smiled but kept the tone in his voice cool. "It's probably best you don't ask any more questions like that. Nothing personal."

Halsford studied Encizo a moment and then shook it off with a shrug and a grin, stuffing the pipe back in his mouth. "It's nothing to me. We've got the go-ahead to cooperate with you mates in whatever way we can, and as I understand it, that came straight from the prime ministers office."

"Tell me something, Mr. Halford. What do you know about those four-wheelers recovered by your people?"

"Our technical people are still examining them. We believe they were purchased from several local dealerships throughout the city, as well as some surrounding areas. The blooming things aren't exactly uncommon here. The locals have been swearing to hundreds of sales daily."

"So they won't be so easy to trace," Encizo finished for him.

Halsford frowned. "I'm afraid that's true."

"What about these tapes?" McCarter asked. "How many people have seen these?"

"Aside from yourselves, only I have—and my immediate superiors."

Encizo stepped forward, slid an arm around Halsford's shoulders and patted the guy's arm with camaraderie. "I don't suppose you could keep it that way for a bit longer. Could you?"

Halsford shrugged. "I don't believe it would hurt anything, as long as I can get some cooperation from you in return. How would you make it worth my while?"

"Well, let's talk about that," McCarter said. "Your federal boys don't know anything about these tapes yet, right?"

Halsford nodded.

"That means they don't necessarily *have* to know about it. And if our people can get a look at those tapes, then maybe, just maybe, we could make sure whatever information we get we share with you."

Encizo smiled and whistled. "That would look awfully good on you and Kornsby, huh? You'd be the first to crack the case. I'm already picturing it—press releases, newspaper headlines, CNN interviews."

"Not to mention the commendations and promotions," McCarter said, adding some additional fuel to Encizo's already roaring fire.

"Did you say promotions, mate?"

"You bet," Encizo said. "We're talking at least captain, maybe even major."

There was a long silence and the two Phoenix Force warriors could tell from Halsford's expression that the wheels were turning. Of course, they didn't have any real control over that stuff, but a word from the Oval Office could make a little go a long way. And they certainly wouldn't leave Kornsby's people hanging on this. They would find some way to make good on it without actually promising anything. Stony Man's connections ran wide and deep, and touched members of the highest governmental circles in nearly every foreign government.

"Very good, then," Halsford finally said. "As the Americans like to say, 'We have a deal.'"

And the trio shook on it.

CHAPTER THREE

Brooklyn Heights, New York

Carl "Ironman" Lyons was angry, and with good reason.

Yeah, it bothered him when innocent people died, but when they died because of their skin color, that *really* riled him. In fact, it put him in a damn foul mood, and when he got feeling like this, not even his longtime friends and brothers-in-arms liked being around him. Still, neither Hermann Schwarz nor Rosario Blancanales would have thought even a moment of abandoning Lyons—not in a million years.

So Lyons decided to hold his temper in check until they could get the gist from New York City's finest. In fact, he was all smiles as he questioned the lead detective while Schwarz and Blancanales maneuvered their way through the broken glass and twisted metal of storefronts, stooping to look into the faces of the Arabic victims who owned the variety of shops and eateries along Atlantic Avenue.

"So explain this to me again," Lyons said.

"It's just like I said, sir," the detective replied. "Everything you're seeing here is corroborated by the stories we've gotten so far from witnesses. We're still canvassing, but I don't think anyone we talk to from here out will have much to add. It just happened too damned fast."

The detective was a guy from the neighborhood, a third-generation Lebanese assigned to one of the local boroughs. He'd introduced himself as Elmore Nuri. Lyons didn't know if that was his given name, but it didn't much matter. The guy seemed pretty knowledgeable about the area, and he was acting as though the devastation now before them was nothing new. Nothing behind Nuri's dark eyes betrayed he was the least bit surprised by the carnage. It was a whole new world.

Lyons looked around him again. The scene was gruesome.

At approximately 1545 local time, a school bus stopped in front of a group of shops on Atlantic Avenue where it borders Cobble Hill. Witnesses claim at least fifteen men and women, dressed in combat fatigues and armbands emblazoned with the Star of David, and toting assault rifles, jumped off the bus and lined up in front of the shops. Moments later, they simultaneously opened fire on the commercial area that was chock-full of citizens from a variety of ethnic backgrounds, although predominately Middle Easterners and Asians. The butchery continued for nearly a full minute as the terrorists periodically reloaded their weapons and each delivered at least two full magazines worth of wanton violence and destruction.

It had all occurred less than two hours earlier, and apparently it hadn't ended there. A pair of transit cops who had just emerged from a subway station apparently tried to evacuate nearby citizens in an orderly fashion when the terrorists spotted them. Several members of the terror group turned their weapons on the officers—the transit cops never stood a chance. Several witnesses also said that they watched helplessly from alleyways or behind cars as the heavily armed assailants then entered several of the shops and polished off any possible survivors of the barbaric attack. Less than two minutes had elapsed when the terrorists got back on the bus and it fled the scene well before the first squads arrived.

As soon as the first of it went out over the airwaves, computers at Stony Man Farm alerted Kurtzman and his team. Able Team had been on its way back from a mission via chopper when Price called and ordered them to detour to JFK. The details had been sketchy at that point, and even now they didn't know much more than they had when they arrived. Nonetheless, Price had told them they had authorization from the highest levels and to use their standing credentials as a special task force of U.S. Deputy Marshals with the Department of Homeland Security.

"What can you tell me about this area?" Lyons asked, turning his attention back to Nuri.

The detective shrugged. "What do you want to know?"

"Let's start with the neighborhood. Is it mostly Arabic?"

Nuri half coughed, half snorted. "You're kidding me, right?"

"Look, Detective, I don't have any time for games," Lyons replied with a scowl. "So let's cut this small-talk shit and stick to facts."

"Yes, sir…sorry, sir. Mostly, it's a pretty mixed neighborhood. This part of the Heights is older and we've got a pretty good mix. There's a section of Russians, French and even Hispanics, but it's primarily Arabic."

"Any Jewish population?"

"You bet," he replied with a nod. "In fact, the population concentration in this part is Middle Eastern. I'm talking Iraqis, Iranians, Pakistanis, Jews, Indians. Hell, there's practically every known representation of the Fertile Crescent here. And for the most part, everyone's always gotten along. Brooklyn Heights just isn't known for these kinds of hate crimes. I mean, this was some serious shit."

"Yeah, there's a lot of that going around lately, guy," Lyons told him. "Thanks for your help. I'm going to go take a look-see with my partners now. I may have some more questions, so don't get lost."

"Oh, don't worry," Nuri replied. "I've got the feeling I'm going to be around here for quite a while."

Lyons nodded and then turned on his heel and went off in search of his comrades. The Able Team warrior found "Gadgets" Schwarz first inside one of the small Mediterranean restaurants. He was kneeling over the body of a little, dark-haired girl who couldn't have been more than six or seven. There was a large, gaping wound in her forehead, and the prone corpse of woman—the back of her bloody coat shredded—covered the better part of the girl's frail form.

"Probably her mother," Lyons said quietly. "Looks like she was running for cover with the girl when the shooting started. She bought it, girl got pinned beneath her and then one of the bastards came in and finished the job." Lyons pointed to his forehead for emphasis.

Schwarz looked at him with a gaunt expression and Lyons saw something dangerous in the man's brown eyes.

"Easy there, pal. You look like maybe you want to lose control."

Schwarz stood and took one lasting look at the girl. "I'm cool, Ironman. We need to find these bastards— and quick."

"Okay," Lyons said, stepping forward and clapping a firm hand on his warrior friend's shoulder. "But let's find Pol first."

They found Blancanales in a nearby clothing shop, where there was more glass on the threadbare carpet than blood. Most of the blood spatter had soaked into the many garments hanging on the crowded racks, some of which were now in cockeyed positions. Obviously the place had been flooded with autofire, just as the other shops and eateries. The decimation and horror of it was almost surreal.

Rosario Blancanales, known as the "Politician" for

his amazing ability to remain suave, cool and diplomatic under even the worst conditions, put his hands on hips and shook his head.

"I don't know about you guys, but this was no ordinary terrorist attack."

"Since when is any terrorist attack ordinary?" Schwarz asked.

"That's not what I meant," Blancanales replied quietly, fixing his teammate with a level but questioning gaze. He then looked at Lyons and continued. "Look, there was something much more behind this. Call it another purpose, an ulterior motive, or whatever, but I'm telling you there's something real funky going on here."

"Explain," Lyons said, stepping closer to his friend.

"Well, for one thing, it seems strange that all of the players in this were wearing Jewish symbols. I mean, come on, the usual mode of operation for most terrorist groups is to claim credit after the fact, and Jewish terrorists are no exception. If this were the Kach-Kahane Chai or a violent offshoot of the Anti-Defamation League, we'd be standing here with our thumbs up our collective asses, wondering who the actual perpetrators were."

"And we'd finally hear two or three days from now who was actually responsible," Schwarz interjected.

Lyons nodded in agreement. "That never occurred to me. That's insightful thinking, Pol."

"I won't expect any medals," Blancanales replied, waving the compliment away and grinning his usual, disarming grin. "But thanks for noticing."

Lyons sighed deeply. "Okay, so if these weren't Jewish terrorists, who were they?"

"I'm not saying they weren't Jewish terrorists," Blancanales reminded him. "I'm just saying that there must be a reason they made it so obvious. I think if we figure that out, we'll also figure out who's behind it and—"

"Excuse me. Deputy Irons?"

The threesome turned to see Nuri standing in the doorway of the shop.

"What is it?" Lyons asked.

"A report just came over the radio. Apparently that bus was sighted and there's a chase on."

"Where's it headed?" Gadgets asked.

"Uptown Manhattan."

The trio exchanged looks and each could tell he'd reached the same conclusion as the others.

"Let's move!" Lyons ordered.

Able Team left the shop and sprinted for their government SUV. Blancanales got behind the wheel, Lyons took shotgun and Schwarz jumped into the back seat. Seconds later they were speeding away from the crime scene and headed for the posh, uptown section of one of New York City's nicest districts.

Schwarz reached behind the back seat and retrieved a bag of toys that Stony Man had arranged to be waiting at JFK when they landed. They were already wearing shoulder holsters with pistols—Blancanales a Glock Model 19, Lyons a .357 Magnum Colt Python Elite and Schwarz a silenced Beretta 93-R—but those would hardly be enough against a dozen or more terrorists armed with assault rifles and machine pistols. It was time for heavier hardware.

Schwarz loaded a 10-shell box magazine into the well of an S&W Assault Shotgun and passed it to Lyons. It was an AS-3, an automatic shotgun originally developed for the U.S. military's Joint Service Small Arms Program. Similar to the Atchisson, the more modern AS-3 could easily fire 3-inch Magnum 12-gauge shells of Lyons's favorite combo of No. 2 and double-aught shot in single, 3-round burst, or full-auto modes. Its cyclic rate of fire was about 375 rounds per minute at an effective range of nearly a hundred meters, and it was a room broom in the hands of an experienced user.

Schwarz next turned his attention to an MP-5 A-3, a variant of one of the most efficient and widely used submachine guns in the world. Manufactured by Heckler & Koch, the MP-5 A-3 had an extending metal stock that could reduce or increase the overall length of the weapon in a heartbeat. It was chambered for 9 mm Parabellum rounds and considered one of the most precise weapons of its kind.

After passing the MP-5 A-3 to Blancanales, Schwarz procured his own weapon of choice, a 5.56 mm FNC manufactured by Fabrique Nationale Herstal SA. He had grown fond of it for its durability and versatility. While classified as an assault rifle, the FNC was a compact and powerful weapon, built on the popular rotating-bolt standards of its H&K competitor. It had a folding stock, a 30-round detachable box magazine, and fired about 700 rounds per minute, but it was still as light and manageable as nearly any sub-machine gun.

Schwarz reached into the bag and withdrew a po-lice scanner equipped with an earpiece. He turned it on, punched in the UHF channel range of the New York City police department's bandwidth and then donned the ultrasensitive earpiece. He reported the situation to his comrades as they raced toward uptown Manhattan.

"Doesn't sound like the situation's all that good," Schwarz said. "The bus was spotted by a police chop-per. Apparently the cops thought it suspicious that a bus that should be taking children home from school was instead sitting in a forest preserve on the edge of the city."

Lyons couldn't argue with that, and he hoped that NYC would see to it the cops in that chopper were dec-orated for being so sharp and alert. Having been a cop in Los Angeles for many years before joining Stony Man, Lyons had nothing but respect for the men and women in blue. They had a tough job, and most of them performed admirably in the line of duty—espe-cially those serving in *this* city.

"What's happening now?" Blancanales asked.

"They apparently converged on the bus, the driver panicked, and they're chasing him through Manhattan. In fact, right now they're trying to clear the road ahead. I guess the driver's not being too careful about what he hits and doesn't hit, and there are already half a dozen injured bystanders. I'm also hearing there's a foot pursuit and sporadic shootouts between the cops and those that managed to get off the bus before it split."

"Okay," Lyons said, "I think what's going down in Manhattan should take the priority."

"Agreed," Blancanales said, keeping his eyes on the road. "More bystanders."

"And more potential for it to get out of hand."

"May have already," Schwarz replied. "Just got word the chase has stopped and they've got the bus trapped between their squads and a street closure."

"Sounds like our terrorist friends are planning to make their last stand right there," Blancanales said, casting a sideways glance at Lyons.

"Sounds like your 'sounds like' is right," the Able Team leader quipped.

"How far away are we?" Blancanales asked, his gaze flicking to Schwarz's reflection in the rearview mirror.

"I'd say another five or ten minutes unless traffic gets backed up," Schwarz replied.

Minutes later the trio emerged from the SUV and double-timed it in the direction of the standoff.

WHEN ABLE TEAM finally arrived, they found the police had the entire block cordoned off, and a wall of blue was the only thing keeping back a pressing crowd of curious onlookers.

"Come on, folks," one cop was telling them. "Just move along. We don't want anyone else to get hurt."

Lyons could tell the cop was about to lose his cool and he decided to redirect the man's attention by shoving his forged Homeland Security credentials under the man's nose.

"Irons, U.S. Marshals Service."

"Should I be impressed?"

"No, but you should watch your mouth," Lyons growled. "What's going on down there?"

The cop eyed Lyons suspiciously for a moment, but the ice-cold blue eyes, grim stare and amount of heavy-duty hardware seemed to put him in a suddenly more cooperative and respectful mood.

"We've got about eight or nine terrorists pinned down on a bus. We think a few of them have managed to get off. It had been a vehicle pursuit, but I guess the bus took a turn a bit too wide and flipped onto its side. Beyond that, I don't know much, sir."

Lyons nodded, then jerked his thumb in the direction of the line of flashing lights where the police had parked their cruisers nose-to-tail to block access to that part of the city. "Who's in charge down there?"

"That would be Captain Roberson, sir," the cop replied.

The policemen let Able Team past the barricade and then went on about his business of keeping back the growing crowd.

The trio was jogging down the center of the street when the sound of automatic weapons fire suddenly erupted. The cordon of police vehicles shielded the SWAT team and patrol officers as they returned the fire with a volley of their own. Able Team reduced its exposure to possible stray fire by moving to the sidewalk under Lyons's lead, and continuing toward the police line. They were within about ten yards of where a group of officers were cloistered behind one of the SWAT vehicles when someone noticed them and raised a shout.

Lyons managed to produce his badge just as a half dozen of the rear security members from the SWAT team trained AR-15s on the Able Team warriors.

"U.S. Marshals!" Lyons replied.

A tall, dark-haired N.Y.P.D. policeman wearing the rank insignia of a captain raised his arms and called, "Stand down!"

Once Lyons had verified it was safe to approach, Able Team joined the small crew huddled around a makeshift field table set up behind the SWAT truck. The officer who had called off the SWAT team wore a nametag that read I. Roberson. Decorations and meritorious service ribbons galore donned the left breast of the uniform, including the Medal for Valor, one of the highest awards rendered in the department. Lyons offered his hand and the Roberson took it.

"Now what the hell brings the U.S. Marshals Service to the Big Apple?" Roberson asked.

"We're a special detachment from the Office of Homeland Security," Lyons recited. "We're here to assist you."

"No offense, Deputy—?"

"Irons."

"Yeah, Irons. Okay…no offense but I think we got this pretty much under control," Roberson said.

"And no offense to you, sir," Blancanales said, stepping forward. He knew Lyons would explode if he didn't intervene, and Lyons knew that he knew, so he let Blancanales take the wheel on this one. "But exactly *what* control?"

"Complete control," Roberson replied. "There are about six terrorists inside that bus, and we think some of them are wounded. We've got them pinned down to no more than one city bus, and I have two SWAT detachments clearing civilians out right now. They've got nowhere to go."

"Okay, fair enough," Blancanales replied. "But what intelligence do you actually have? Do you know, in fact, whom you're dealing with? You have any idea who these people are, or what they want?"

"Well, er, ah—"

"That's what I thought," Lyons muttered.

Blancanales threw his teammate a cautioning look, then returned his attention to Roberson with the friendliest grin and calmest tone he could muster. "Listen, Captain, we're not here to step on your turf."

Roberson looked at his men, his face flushing, then said, "My people here agree that they're either militants or religious fanatics. One of them tried to escape from the bus when it flipped, and we shot him dead." Roberson turned and picked up a bloody armband from the table. He held it up and added, "The suspect didn't have any ID on him, but he was wearing this."

"And that's exactly why we're here. We don't think these are either militants or religious fanatics. We don't have any solid evidence yet, but we do have experience, and we think maybe we have some information you might not have."

Roberson's expression hardened some. "And just what is that? You guys just got here. How could you possibly know more about this than we do?"

"You'd be surprised what we know," Schwarz said.

"Look, we just came from that slaughterhouse over in Brooklyn Heights," Lyons interjected. "From what we saw there, we have reason to believe these are terrorists trying to make it look like some nut-group's behind all of this."

"Now what the hell reason would they have for doing that?" Roberson said, cocking back his hat and scratching his head.

Lyons jacked the slide on the AS-3. "Let's go ask them."

CHAPTER FOUR

Rosario Blancanales converged on the bus in a cover-and-maneuver drill he'd practiced countless times before. He'd act as point while Lyons and Schwarz covered him by taking firing positions at the corners of opposing rooftops. The rest they could only watch play out and react accordingly. While it was possible Roberson's intelligence was sound, and the good guys did in fact have the upper hand on the terrorist group, Able Team had no intention of taking unnecessary risks. They planned to play this one by the book, and they also had to account for maintaining appearances. Their alleged "covers" as U.S. Marshals had to hold up to any scrutiny.

Blancanales reached the rear of the school bus and knelt with his back to its belly. He yanked an AN-M83-HC smoker from the satchel on his hip, pulled the pin and tossed the bomb overhand in front of him. He retrieved a second one and let it fly.

Lyons couldn't see the grenades from where he

laid—the fixed sights of the AS-3 trained on the area just above Blancanales's head—but he heard them clank and clatter along the side of the bus. A moment later he could barely pick up the faint sounds of them dropping through the open windows and the subsequent shouts of the occupants. Those last sounds caused him to smile. Naturally the terrorists wouldn't know whether they were dealing with smoke or CS; for all they knew, it was poison gas. Regardless of what might be going through the terrorists' minds, the grenades produced the desired effect.

Only a few moments elapsed before bodies emerged from the windows of the bus. Lyons and Schwarz began shouting for the terrorists to surrender. The group apparently figured it was better to stand and fight than to risk capture and interrogation. Only a couple of the terrorists went prone on top of the bus, others not bothering to get cover of any kind, and all of them began to spray the area with gunfire.

Lyons ducked behind full cover and quickly keyed his microphone. "Guys, we need to take at least one of them alive!"

The Able Team leader couldn't tell if either of his teammates had received the response over the sudden cacophony of weapons reports, both that of the terrorists and the SWAT teams. Lyons cursed under his breath—this was no good! Roberson had promised he'd show restraint, but the guy's word apparently meant nothing. Instead, he was letting his people shoot at will, and every round meant one less chance of taking a prisoner.

Lyons switched channels and cut into the N.Y.P.D. frequency. "Dammit, Roberson, tell your people to shut it down! Now!"

He got no reply, but after a few more seconds, weapons reports coming from their AO went silent. There were some scattered shots from the terrorists now on the bus, but there were no more return shots from the SWAT team members.

Lyons had a perfect view of the terrorists that had exposed themselves, and took a quick head count: seven. Okay, so that wasn't too bad at all. He leveled the shotgun sights on the closest terrorist, took a deep breath, braced the shotgun tightly against his shoulder and squeezed the trigger. The AS-3 roared as the first specialty load rocketed from the muzzle and took one of the terrorist's full in chest. The terrorist dropped the AK-47 as the heavy shell flipped him off his feet. The force of the blast landed him on his back and his butt crashed through one of the few unbroken windows.

Schwarz got the terrorist next to Lyons's target a few moments later with a well-placed 3-round burst from his FNC. Two of the 5.56 mm NATO rounds punched through the terrorist's throat and the last split his skull wide open. The guy's head exploded in a grisly spray of blood and gray matter, and his body spun awkwardly. He dropped off the edge of the bus and disappeared from view.

The terrorists turned their attention in every direction above their heads, probably in realization they were no longer taking their fire from ground level. They began spraying the area with fresh autofire, and

Lyons moved back as a few of the rounds chipped away plaster and stone from the edge of the parapet. As soon as there was a lull in the firing, Lyons returned to his position, sighted the next target and delivered another shell blast. This time, though, Lyons was gunning for a prisoner. The special shotgun load did a number on one terrorist, blowing out a large chunk of the guy's knee. The terrorist dropped with a scream that sounded like combined pain and surprise to find he was suddenly unsupported by both of his legs.

BLANCANALES KNEW his chances of staying alive in this environment wouldn't last. His mission had been to smoke the terrorists into the open, and he'd done that. Now it was time to get the hell out of the line of fire before the terrorists realized he was immediately below them and posed an easy target. The Able Team warrior yanked the Glock Model 19 from his shoulder holster, jumped to his feet and rushed for a corner drugstore with a square, brick support in front of it. He made it to the thick support just in time to avoid a hail of slugs fired at him by several of the terrorist goons. Blancanales waited until the firing stopped, then risked exposure in tracking for a target, pistol held in a Weaver's grip, forearms braced against the support.

It didn't take him long.

Blancanales quickly found his target and squeezed the trigger successively. Both 9 mm rounds reached flesh, the first punching through the enemy gunner's stomach and the second cleanly detaching his left ear. The terrorist dropped his weapon, one hand clutching his gut while the other attempted to stop the sudden, violent flow of blood from his head. The terrorist dropped to his knees and began to moan, but it didn't appear to Blancanales that either shot was lethal.

SCHWARZ WATCHED the terrorists fire on Blancanales as his friend sprinted for cover. The Able Team warrior found it interesting that they would focus all of their energies on one man. That wasn't the typical discipline of terrorists, especially when they were the ones being terrorized. Then again, now wasn't exactly the time to worry about it.

He listened for any further signals from Lyons, but the Able Team leader—his blond hair visible even in the twilight—wasn't showing any sign of letting off the pressure on the terrorists below. He watched as Lyons took another one with a head shot. Schwarz followed suit. He aimed at one of the terrorists focused on killing Blancanales and squeezed the trigger. A trio of rounds rocketed from the muzzle of the FNC and drilled through the terrorist's shoulder, continuing onward to blow out a good part of his chest wall.

The body of one of the terrorists they had wounded began to convulse and jerk. It took Schwarz only a moment to spot the reason for it. A lithe, shorter terrorist had managed to squeeze clear of one of the rearmost windows. A cascade of dark hair protruded from under the terrorist's cap. The terrorist was a woman, her body lithe and shapely, even beneath the coveralls she was wearing.

Schwarz keyed his transmitter. "We've got one female party killing our wounded, guys!"

"Acknowledged," Lyons replied. "Take her out."

Schwarz nodded, sighted his target and squeezed the trigger. Milliseconds before fire from the Able Team trio reached her, the woman turned and dropped off the back edge of the bus. Schwarz was in motion even as he noticed movement from Lyons in his peripheral vision. His headset crackled with a burst of static and the sound of Blancanales's voice, but he couldn't make out the words.

He keyed his transmitter as he reached the fire escape. "Say again, Politician…I didn't copy."

"I said, 'she's headed eastbound on that side street.' She'll be closest to you, Gadgets."

"Copy."

"We'll have to hold our position here, buddy," Lyons replied. "You'll be on your own on this one, so watch your ass."

"Understood," Schwarz replied as he slid down the ladder, then began to descend the steps of the fire escape three at a time.

It took him only twenty seconds to reach the sidewalk and he made it in time to see the woman duck inside a large club half a block down. Schwarz launched himself in the direction of the club, trading his FNC for the Beretta 93-R on the fly.

The Able Team commando came low through the club entrance, pistol tracking quickly and smoothly. It was comparatively cool to the muggy, outdoor air. He cleared the vestibule of the club, which was decorated with muted blues, grays and purples, and then proceeded into the main area. It was a pretty decent club, typical for middle-class clientele. The place was crowded, not surprising since it was a Friday and it was happy hour, and Schwarz kept his pistol low and behind him as he maneuvered between the tables. He smelled booze, food and cigarettes, and he also detected the fearful odor of his prey; she was very close.

So close that he nearly got his head blown off.

The female terrorist emerged from the shadows of an alcove Schwarz hadn't seen and unleashed hellfire from her machine pistol. The Able Team electronics genius rolled to avoid being hit, came up near the bar and prepped to take his target. But pandemonium erupted after the shooting started and too many people scrambling for the exit made the job a bit too risky. One young woman caught a bullet that dropped her on the floor and left her screaming and writhing with pain.

Schwarz waited until the firing ceased with a click of a bolt locked back on an empty magazine, then exposed himself long enough to rush the felled bystander while simultaneously laying down a hail of fire in the terrorist's general direction. It was meant more as a play to keep the gunner's head down than to actually hit her. Besides, they still needed to take one of the terrorists alive, and Schwarz had no idea if any of the ones they'd wounded in the initial play at the bus were still alive after their cohort had turned her weapon on them.

Schwarz reached the wounded club-goer and

dragged her behind a heavy, overturned table. She wasn't moving and her eyes were closed. He checked her carotid pulse—it was strong and regular—and a quick check of ear to nostrils confirmed she was breathing. Okay, so she'd passed out from the pain, which was sure as hell better than being conscious for it.

Schwarz waited for a lull in the firing and then decided to take a risk. He had to neutralize this woman and fast. He reached to his belt and latched on to a flash-bang grenade. He pulled it from the belt with a quick turn of the wrist. A pop and snap followed, indicating the special mechanism he'd rigged to his belt had broken the plastic strap designed to prevent inadvertent dislodging of the spoon and simultaneously removed the pin. He jumped into view and hammered the area where he estimated his target had taken cover. While firing to force the terrorist to keep her head down, Schwarz released the grenade in a light overhand toss.

The electronics whiz went flat, opened his mouth and plugged his ears. The grenade went off a moment later, then he was up and moving. He vaulted the table he'd been using as cover, Beretta in one hand and FNC in another. He quickly found his opponent writhing on the floor, her eyes and ears discharging watery blood. Schwarz holstered the Beretta and reached for her, but the terrorist surprised him with a judo circle throw.

Schwarz landed hard on his back, sucking down air to replace the wind knocked from him. He blinked several times and in one of those saw his opponent suddenly loom above him, her hands raised over her head as she wedged his skull between her thighs. Something kicked him into high gear and he brought both arms up in a cross block. Having stopped the combat knife from being buried in his chest, he then reached around and snagged her wrist. A quick sideways jerk and she landed on her right shoulder, facing him. He landed a rock-hard back fist punch on his adversary's forehead and she dropped the knife, cried in pain and then lapsed into unconsciousness.

The Able Team commando rose, a bit winded from the encounter, but a quick physical inventory said he was still in one piece. He snapped riot cuffs on the terrorist, then returned to aid the bystander. He found the gunshot wound, a clean hole through the fleshy part of her thigh that exited the other side. He'd seen much worse and he knew she'd survive the physical scars, although the mental ones would have a more lasting effect. She was just becoming conscious as Schwarz removed two field compresses and bound them on the entrance and exit wounds, securing them with his belt.

She looked at him, a haze in her eyes.

He smiled at her. "Just relax. You're going to be fine. The ambulance is on its way."

"What happened?"

"Someone will explain it to you soon enough. For now, you've been shot and I want you to lie still."

"I've…I've been shot?" Her eyes widened.

"Yes, but it's not fatal. You're going to pull through just fine."

"How would you know?"

"Because I've been shot plenty of times," he said with a chuckle, pouring on the charm. "I just know. Will you trust me?"

"I guess," she whispered, smiling at him a little before she passed out again.

Schwarz sighed.

"Gadgets!" called a familiar voice.

He turned toward the entrance in time to see Lyons and Blancanales enter the club, weapons drawn and held at the ready.

"Over here," he reported tiredly.

They quickly rushed to his aid.

"You hit?" Lyons asked.

He shook his head, then pointed at his patient. "She took an in-and-out in the leg, but I've controlled the bleeding. She's got some shock, but I think she'll be okay."

Blancanales helped him to his feet as Lyons quickly scanned the room. His eyes came to rest on the terrorist. "Is she dead?"

Gadgets scowled with a negative shake of his head. "Dreamland. She nearly impaled me with this, though." He held up the knife.

Blancanales gingerly took the knife from him and whistled. "Looks like she was planning on some Schwarz-ka-bobs."

"Very funny," the electronic expert deadpanned.

SHE CALLED HERSELF Magdalene Darmid from Israel, but a quick fingerprint analysis said she was Deborah

Babbit from Kansas. Able Team settled on the second name as the most believable.

"Although she's got a great accent going there," Carl Lyons told them just before they entered the interrogation room.

Because she'd lied, they decided a hard approach was the best kind.

Blancanales started. "Listen, Deborah—"

"My name is *not* Deborah!" She was irritated because everyone coming into and out of the room in the last hour had been saying "Hi, Deborah" and "Would you like something to drink, Deborah?" and "Deborah, that's such a pretty name." Needless to say, that had her frazzled and angered enough to tell the Able Team commando where to stick it.

"You're not making things easy on yourself," Lyons warned her when she tried to spit on Blancanales. He easily sidestepped the offense, which only seemed to anger her more.

"I'd listen to him," Schwarz added, jabbing a thumb at Lyons.

Lyons's voice went quiet. "Maybe that beating you threw her wasn't good enough, Deputy Black."

Schwarz looked at him straight-faced a moment, then said, "Maybe you're right. Maybe I need to do a more thorough job."

"Now that you mention it, your work has been sloppy lately," Lyons replied with a curt nod.

"Hey…wait a minute." Blancanales raised his hands in mock innocence and said, "She's now under the protective custody of the U.S. Marshals Service.

You two can't just start beating the hell out of her. We'll *all* lose our jobs!"

"Calm down," Lyons replied, waving at him casually as if he had it all under control.

"Yeah, really," Schwarz jumped in. "What are you getting all backed up about? She just killed a bunch of innocent people. You think we should give a shit about her? Who's going to complain?"

Lyons stepped forward and grabbed the woman by the throat, transforming her smug look into one of terror. "I'm sure after some neck-wringing we'll put her into a spirit of cooperation."

The woman managed to emit a squeal of outrage and pain before Lyons closed her trachea with one squeeze, immediately depriving her of oxygen. With her arms cuffed behind her, she had no way to defend herself. She tried to kick at him, but the proximity of her chair to the table made the attack ineffective. A moment later it stopped being an act of defiance and started to become an act of desperation. Her lips began to turn blue and her ears reddened.

Blancanales stepped forward and cracked a fist down on the brachial-cephalic nerve area of Lyons's arm. The blow looked real enough, although Blancanales insured he was actually an inch off the actual nerve bundle. Lyons let go of Babbit's throat with a mock yelp. The hulking Ironman turned on the Politician, but it was Schwarz who got in between them.

"Knock it off!" he said, trying to sound like the voice of reason.

"Yeah, but did you see what that fu—"

"I said, knock it off!"

The room went silent as Schwarz and Lyons squared off on each other for nearly a full two minutes. It was finally Blancanales with his calm voice and lax demeanor who became the voice of reason.

"Hey, we shouldn't be fighting with each other," he said. He pointed to Babbit and said, "She's our enemy."

"Yeah," the two men chorused.

Blancanales turned back to Babbit and said, "What you have just seen is a test. This is only a test. If this had been an actual emergency, I would have just let him strangle you to death. Now, do you want talk to us? Or should we just skip the formalities, take you out into a public square and shoot you dead?"

"You're crazy! All of you are fucking crazy!" She began to scream and shout additional obscenities. "You can't just take me out and kill me!"

"Well, actually, we can," Lyons said. "You see, you're not an American. You're a foreigner who has entered this country and committed a terrorist act. Under the new laws enacted by the *Homeland Security Act,* the things you and your friends did today are considered crimes against humanity and acts of war, and as such that means you are subject to the rules of war."

"He's right," Schwarz said. "You have no rights as a civilian, since you're not a citizen of this country."

"In fact, you're not even in the country legally," Blancanales added.

That did it.

"Yes, I am! I am! My name *is* Deborah Babbit. I live in Kansas City, and I went to high school at Monroe High and I can tell you anything about my life you want. But I'm an American citizen and you can't execute me!"

"We couldn't execute you anyway," Lyons said with a shrug, and started to walk toward the door, Schwarz on his tail. "Summary execution of a POW is a violation of Geneva Convention rules."

Her eyes reverted to Blancanales's who was now seated across the table and studying her with a broad grin. "Let's start from the top."

CHAPTER FIVE

Stony Man Farm, Virginia

"So that's the story," Carl Lyons finished, his voice resounding through the speaker.

Hal Brognola sat back, folded his arms and chewed thoughtfully at his unlit cigar. For a moment nobody said a word. Price and Kurtzman stared at Brognola, waiting with anxious expressions. They didn't wait long.

Brognola grunted and said, "All right, let me see if I heard you right. You're saying that these Jewish terrorists aren't really Jewish?"

"Right," Lyons said. "Maybe one or two originally hail from Israel, but the one we got to roll said she's from Kansas, and the N.Y.P.D.'s computers confirmed it from her prints."

"Did this Babbit give you any explanation for her being an American?"

"Nothing other than she was hired to do the job by

parties unknown. They went to a secret training camp stuck in some part of the Louisiana backwater for two months. Claims she has no idea where because she was blindfolded along with the rest of her comrades and nearly beaten and starved to death during the first week."

"Sounds like your standard, run-of-the-mill mercenary training," Price remarked.

"Maybe and maybe not, but in either case it doesn't matter," Brognola said. "Even if we could find this camp, I don't think it could tell us much more than Babbit has. What's your recommendation, Carl?"

"I say we stick with our current information. I think she's telling the truth, and she's already agreed to help us in return for leniency. She got into this for the money and nothing more, which she says was real good by the way."

"It seems strange that someone would pay them to do this," Brognola said. "Why hire a group of Americans to dress as Jewish radicals and waste a bunch of innocent people in front of God and country?"

"Well, they obviously want to start a street war," Price offered. "Maybe stir hatred for Jewish radical groups."

"I can buy fueling the fire for a street war," Lyons said. "I just talked to our liaison with the N.Y.P.D., and he said this incident has already started riots in three separate areas of the city. The cops are calling in everyone they can find to help out."

Kurtzman sighed. "Great."

"But that second part about stirring hatred up for Jewish groups just doesn't wash, Barb," Lyons continued. "In fact, Babbit told us how this one guy kept telling them they were fighting for the Jewish cause and to think how nice it would be to secure their country from the Pakistanis, the Arabs and so forth. She was adamant about what he said, and we all agree here that she's telling the truth. She said this guy preached pure hatred of them."

"Like it was personal," Price said, looking at Brognola.

Brognola nodded. "Carl, you said something earlier about this group that I found interesting. Something about arm bands they were wearing?"

"Yeah, the witnesses canvassed by the uniforms where the massacre took place consistently referenced arm bands with the Star of David."

"Wait a minute!" Kurtzman snapped his fingers. "We just received the first transmissions of the tapes from David McCarter. Those terrorists they went up against were wearing arm bands just like that."

Price inhaled sharply. "These two incidents are connected, then?"

"Let's not get ahead of ourselves yet," Brognola said. "Although I think we'd better consider that as a possibility."

"What happened to Phoenix Force?"

Price gave him a quick overview of the situation, skipping most of the minutiae. When she was finished explaining, they all agreed that the similarities and the timing were more than coincidences. There *had* to be a connection, and it had now become Stony Man's number-one priority to find out what that was and to predict the group's next action.

"Like I said before, this Babbit's willing to help us," Lyons concluded. "She says she has some sketchy details of other plans this group might have. If we grant her immunity, she'll deal."

"You know our policy, Carl," Brognola replied. "We don't 'deal' with terrorists."

"I understand that, but we may not have any other choice. If David and the rest can't make a connection there, then we'll have to work it from our end. She's the one lead we have, Hal, and I want to exploit that to our advantage."

Lyons was right, of course, and Brognola knew it. Sometimes the rules had to be bent. That was the name of the game, and it was fortunate that Stony Man had the freedom to conduct operations as they saw fit, as long as they kept the President apprised.

"All right," Brognola conceded. "I'll arrange for her to be cut loose and remanded to your custody. See where she leads you. But whatever you do, keep her alive. You're right. She's our only link to whoever's behind this."

"Understood," Lyons said, and he disconnected the call.

ONCE THEY HAD concluded their call with Lyons, Price and Kurtzman began working on their intelligence, performing keyword searches and investigations into the backgrounds of Babbit's deceased associates. It didn't take long to figure out that most of them had ended up at the remote training camp in Louisiana after responding to an ad in a mercenary magazine. An anonymous caller took out the ad by contacting one of the magazine's copy editors, faxing the three ambiguous lines advertising paid mercenary training, and paying for the job by money order mailed without a return address. The caller had given a fake name and the address and telephone number turned out to be that of an elderly woman who had two weeks before been admitted to a long-term nursing facility.

"They call themselves the Resurrected Defense League," Barbara Price told Phoenix Force.

McCarter's face filled the computer screen in the Communications Center of the Annex. John Kissinger—on a charter flight back to the States—was also on the conference line via his cellular phone, but he had no video feed.

"Sound like a nice bunch," Kissinger interjected.

Price talked about their conversation with Lyons, then said, "We're convinced these two incidents are connected, and we're also sure these won't be the last."

"You have any luck with those tapes we sent?" Encizo's voice cut in, although Price couldn't actually see his face.

"Bear and Carmen are now working with facial recognition software to see if they can identify any of the dead and tie them to any of the members Able Team neutralized in New York. We're also analyzing the prototypes data you sent to see what connections we can pull from that."

"What else do we know about this group?" McCarter asked.

Price frowned. "Not much. They're relatively new to this game."

"Couldn't prove it by us," T. J. Hawkins said. "This attack was well planned and coordinated. They were obviously practiced and ready for any eventuality."

"They managed to take us by surprise," Gary Manning said.

"Only the fact we were separated saved our hides," Calvin James added. "If we'd been together when it went down, we probably wouldn't be having this conversation right now."

"It's good to hear you're back to your old self, Calvin," Price said, smiling into the camera.

James's grinning countenance suddenly filled the screen, pushing McCarter slightly out of view. "Thanks, Barb, because it damn sure feels good to be alive."

McCarter took back center stage and with a cocksure grin and sideways glance, said, "You can play nice-nice later, mate."

The line erupted with laughter.

"Okay, enough with the court jester routine," Price said, although she knew they weren't taking her that seriously. She was happy to know everyone was still breathing. The morning's news had really worn on her.

"What about the prototypes, Barb?" Kissinger asked. "Is there anything you think can help us there?"

"Possibly, but I'm not sure how far we can go. As you know, although Phoenix Force may not have been told, we were first alerted to this from a Pentagon connection of Hal's. There's a Navy man who spent considerable time consulting with the design and development engineers at Stormalite's headquarters near Lake Victoria. His name is Kendall Remar, a rear admiral with the Naval Air Warfare Detachment at NAF Key West. What I need you to do, Cowboy, is to divert there. He's expecting you. He has a wealth of additional information he can provide, which we then need you to forward to us and the field crews."

"No problem," Kissinger replied.

"What about us?" McCarter asked.

"I think I can help out there," Kurtzman replied, wheeling up next to where Barbara Price stood with her arms folded. "I have Carmen sending an upload to you now. We connected two of those faces with a photo capture by a camera posted at the airport. We don't have positive IDs on either of these guys yet, but we have confirmed they're both players you went up against at the conference."

"Where are they headed?" McCarter asked.

"Well, we can only guess as to final destination, but the plane they boarded was headed for Spain."

"Seems like a strange place to go," Gary Manning interjected.

"Not really," Price replied. "There is significant support in Spain for a wide variety of terrorist organizations. We've known this for years, actually, but because of very stringent laws and Spain's influence in both the UN and the European Union, we've never really considered the risks of operating there worth the potential costs in U.S. foreign relations."

"Of course," McCarter said, snorting. "We wouldn't want to upset those protecting terrorists. That would be a bloody shame."

"I know the politics are something that sticks in your craw, guys, but you know there's little I can do about that," Price said.

Price was very empathetic to the teams. Walking the line they had to walk was difficult. It certainly wasn't something she could have brought herself to do; her political convictions were a little too strong for that. But the members of Able Team and Phoenix Force had to temper those convictions and maintain some level of neutrality. Still, it didn't stop them from bitching about it, and Price saw no reason to begrudge them being able to verbalize. Most of the time, it was just a way to blow off steam.

"So where do we go from here?" James asked.

"Well, I just spoke with Jack and he's waiting for you at Adelaide Airport. He's fueled and ready to go. The plane that carried our two terrorists landed in Madrid less than twelve hours ago, so you're not far behind."

"Far enough," Encizo pointed out.

"Listen, we've already got every operative in Spain on this," Price said. "As soon as we know something, I promise we'll let you in on it. We also have to consider that where two of these terrorists go, more are likely to follow."

"Seems to me we ought to account for the possibility this pair is just a decoy," Manning said. "Barb's right about Spain being a terrorist group haven, but we could be headed on a wild-goose chase."

"I agree," Encizo added.

"Well, it's not a bloody democracy here," McCarter said, "and that means we'll go with Barb's plan. If we're chasing our tails, then we'll damn well find it out soon enough."

"It's a risk, but it's one you'll have to take," Price said. "I'm sorry, but it's the best lead we have right now and we should pursue it."

"I'll get you the information as quickly as I can on these prototypes, David," Kissinger added. "That should at least help you be better prepared."

"Having been close enough to see the abilities of those weapons firsthand," Hawkins announced, "I can tell you we don't stand a chance against this Resurrected Defense League if they decide to turn even the prototypes on us."

"Then we'll have to make sure we don't give them that chance," McCarter replied.

All of the Phoenix Force warriors nodded in agreement.

Cartagena, Spain

WALLACE DAVIDIA KEPT one eye on the door leading from the shipping warehouse and the other on his men as they unpacked the crates containing the prototypes for repackaging in new boxes.

Once they made their escape from Adelaide, they traveled to a remote location, quickly disassembled the weapons using specifications purchased from a former employee at Stormalite Systems, and then smuggled them as various parts of the ATVs. Triggers and firing mechanisms were stored in drained fuel tanks, barrels concealed in hollowed tail pipes. The electronic firing chips were removed and stored inside the instrumentation and the nonessential material was destroyed. Their engineers in Madrid could refabricate those parts. The ATVs were then sent to distributors throughout the city, and forged paperwork and purchasing documents called for them to be shipped to Cartagena by plane and boat. Originally, Boaz Rasham had suggested they ship the prototypes straight to Madrid, but Davidia disagreed. The more time wasted and false clues they threw any potential pursuers, the more difficult it would be for their enemies to pick up the trail. Thus far, Davidia's plan had been successful, and he was proud of that.

But pride cometh before the fall, Davidia reminded himself.

"Wallace, I have to protest one more time my concerns about your plan," Rasham said, intruding on Davidia's introspection. "This is *not* efficient in any way. We're wasting precious time. The sooner our engineers get these prototypes, the sooner we can move forward with this."

Davidia turned, smiled and placed a firm hand on Rasham's shoulder. "You are like a brother to me, you know this, but you have this annoying quality about you that tries me at moments. You need to learn patience."

"I have tolerance," Rasham replied. "And tolerance is an adequate substitute for patience. You've said so yourself."

"True, but I've said that in the context of training others in our ways," Davidia reminded him. "During an actual operation, patience is a preferable and admirable quality."

Rasham waved as if shooing away an annoying insect. "Either way, our goal is to get results. I haven't seen any."

Davidia's eyes swept the small warehouse, one of many that dotted the shores of Cartagena's wharf district. "We successfully escaped with the prototypes and at an acceptable loss. You don't consider those results?"

"I won't split hairs with you, Wallace," Rasham said. "And I won't draw lines in the sand. I am a man of truth and candor. You know that about me, as much as I know it about you. I will always speak my mind."

"And this is what I admire most about you," Davidia replied. "But I was elected the leader of our group, and you seem unwilling to accept my plan."

"If blind obedience is what you expected when we elected you to lead us to the remembered glory of our nation, then you accepted your nomination under misguided pretexts and arrogant assumption. After all, you're an American."

Davidia smiled, but he lent no warmth to it. "You're coming dangerously close to crossing a line with me now, my friend. I've neither said nor done anything to suggest my men should follow me blindly. However, we should not forget that obedience to orders is a part of military discipline. The outsiders call us terrorists, and that's their opinion, but I consider us soldiers for a cause. Soldiers don't follow their leaders blindly because of some idealism, Boaz. They follow them because they know it's a matter of discipline, and they'll expect the same courtesy from their subordinates one day when they're tasked to carry on our fight."

Davidia paused for effect. "So please, don't presume I've lost my objectivity by suggesting I've gone through some twisted process of self-deification. Like you, I'm human and bleed, and like you, I've suffered at the hands of others. So I leave the god complex to the fanatics of history. I'm just a soldier who happens to be a leader of soldiers. My past and my lineage have nothing to do with that. I'm in the here and now."

Rasham smiled and shook his head. "That was quite a speech, and I still disagree with your plan. However, I cast my lot with you, so I will stay faithful to our cause and follow you to my death."

Davidia threw his arm around Rasham and kissed his cheek. "I will make sure it does not come to that, brother. I would prefer that none of us should die, but I know this is the cost of war. You know it, too."

The matter now behind them, Davidia and Rasham turned to the packaging activities. If all went as planned, they would be able to transport the weapons to Madrid by no later than the following afternoon. They could have started shipping some of it by truck tonight, but they had to wait for two of their people to arrive in Madrid and make preparations.

A sleeper group awaited there, including the engineers they had hired to manufacture copies from the prototypes, as well as a rather large guard unit. The

RDL's largest difficulty in the operation had been funds. Fortunately, splinter group supporters in America as well as those from small Kach-Kahane Chai units had helped the cause in that light. The operation was expensive. Obtaining weapons and other material at rock-bottom prices had been the easy part—it was financing the forged passports and shipping manifests, bribes to customs agents all over the Middle East, Europe and North America, and payments to the technical people, that had cost them a significant amount of money. That was one of the reasons that Davidia was taking his time. He wouldn't rush the operation simply because he *couldn't* rush it. Some of his investors were quite powerful people in the international community of terrorism and he had no aspirations to lose his head over this. Careful planning was the key; strategy and stealthy movements were the mechanisms to carry out the plans. He'd accounted for everything to the last detail.

Once they had the weapons, Davidia planned to split the group into two teams: one would go to the United States and the other to Israel. Reports and rumors were already coming in that their first attack in New York had been successful, although there was talk that they had lost the group to N.Y.P.D. tactical units. That was fine. Davidia had considered the possibilities and the risks that they might encounter. Their instructions had been clear: do not be taken prisoner.

They still had other cities to hit. Davidia had managed to catch a television report of the New York massacre and that there was now looting and rioting going on in a number of areas in the Big Apple heavily populated by Arabs and Jews. That was excellent news. Before it was over, they would find the same kind of trouble in Chicago, although Davidia's unit was there only to scratch the tip of the iceberg. He planned to bring the prototypes with him and start a major war himself.

They had considered hitting other major cities, but the cost had become too great. By attacking just the major Arab-Jew population centers, word would spread like wildfire and there would be fallout in other cities sufficient to take eyes off of the RDL and its real goal. Terrorist alerts would rise, naturally, but by making it look as if this were a local problem and not one instigated on a global scale, the U.S. government would shift focus toward handling the domestic problems and make less consideration of any international fallout.

It was all just part of the plan. Davidia wasn't worried about anyone discovering what was really happening. And even if they did, by the time anyone could muster a response, they would be well on their way toward reaching their goal. He predicted that within a month, RDL would have gained enough support to hold the Arab world at bay. Citizens in the Middle East would be afraid to come out of their own houses for fear of reprisal and the Israeli people would finally have the upper hand.

Yes, the Jews had been oppressed quite long enough. Once the Arabs were under control, RDL could then turn its attentions to the fascists, the Neo-

Nazi and Skinhead movements. At last, the Jews of the world would stand united and unchallenged in accomplishing their goals. Jews everywhere could stop being afraid, because the Resurrected Defense League would become a veritable army of freedom fighters so powerful and massive that not even the superpowers of the world could oppose them.

And no one would ever steal from them again.

CHAPTER SIX

Boca Chica, Florida Keys

John "Cowboy" Kissinger stepped from the small, commercial jet and sucked in a breath of salty, humid air rolling in from the Atlantic. Formerly designated a naval air station, the NAF of Key West was not only the premier training facility for naval aviators, but also shared a tactical interagency relationship with Howard Air Force Base in Panama. The Overseas Highway connected Key West with Miami, traversing the clear, emerald waters where the Atlantic Ocean met the Gulf of Mexico.

More than five thousand personnel were assigned to Key West, about one-quarter of them active duty or reservists, while the remainder were family members or civilian support workers. Units included the U.S. Army's Special Forces Combat Divers School, Joint Interagency Task Force-East and the U.S. Coast Guard Group Key West. There were also a half dozen annexes spread across five separate bases that supported the Caribbean Regional Operating Center, VF-101, Naval Security Group Key West, and more Marine and Navy testing facilities than anyone probably cared to count. In short, the place was a significant representation of U.S. military might by sea, air and land.

And it was a great place to be sent under the circumstances. Kissinger couldn't help but think it nothing more than dumb luck at being directed here by Stony Man. He considered maybe staying a few extra days after the assignment was complete, or returning here for some R & R if he found himself having to go back to Stony Man for any reason.

A muscular, black man wearing the rank of lieutenant commander and wearing a nametag that read D. Paxton greeted Kissinger with a perfunctory salute. He then identified himself as Remar's personal aid and offered to take Kissinger to Area Bravo III where Remar was waiting. After Kissinger advised Paxton he wasn't Navy and preferred not being saluted, he squeezed his tall, lanky body into the Hummer and they were off.

At first, it didn't seem like Paxton was all that chatty, but was naturally gregarious. It only took the Cowboy a minute to get Paxton to open up, and in a short time he'd learned Paxton was married with two kids, had been stationed here for the past year, and that his first name was Delmar.

"This is great," Kissinger said. "I could get used to the weather here."

"Is this your first time in Key West, sir?" Paxton asked.

Kissinger admitted it was.

"It's quite a place," Paxton replied. "Since I've been here, well, at least since I've worked for Admiral Remar, I've really enjoyed it."

"What's your home of record?"

"Cleveland, sir."

"Then this must be quite a change for you."

Paxton shrugged and said, "I guess so, sir. My first duty assignment after I graduated college and completed OCS was in Hawaii, so I've grown rather accustomed to this climate."

"Think you'll go back to Cleveland after all of this?"

Paxton smiled and said, "I doubt it, sir."

"I wouldn't, either."

"I figure to go career. I like the Navy."

Kissinger nodded although he didn't say anything. In a lot of ways, Paxton reminded him of Calvin James. He had that charming grin and likable personality that made it seem easy to talk to the guy. He was also built like James, and it was apparent he kept in shape. He was still a pretty young guy, though, and he didn't possess that dangerous something that was ever-present in Calvin. The black badass from Chicago carried an edge with him everywhere and into every situation. It wasn't really anything obvious; it was just something that *was*.

"How do you like working for Admiral Remar?"

"He's a good man, sir, and a fine officer," Paxton replied.

Kissinger didn't detect either hesitation or trepidation in Paxton's tone. That showed conviction, which meant Kissinger could probably count on Remar to be a straightforward type. That was good, because the Stony Man weapons smith knew how important it would be that he get good, technical information to Kurtzman and Phoenix Force. The RDL terrorists were well organized and particularly dangerous, and Kissinger didn't have time to battle with the territorial politics sometimes present in military environments.

In about ten minutes, they arrived at Area Bravo III. Paxton showed Kissinger to a cool but cramped office in one of the annex buildings, and after Kissinger declined his offer of something to drink, Paxton went away.

Kissinger studied the walls and shelves, trying to get a better feel for Remar. He didn't really know what to expect; there hadn't been time to have Stony Man send him a dossier. He did get a basic rundown of Remar's career, which had turned out quite impressive. Remar had entered the U.S. Navy in 1966 at age seventeen as an enlisted man, and in three years attained a Petty Officer Second Class rating. Following action in Vietnam as part of a small support boat crew operating for a Marine recon unit, Remar returned to the States and was assigned to the Navy Yard in Washington, D.C.

On a couple of occasions, Remar had expressed his interest to superiors of applying for OCS in the hope of becoming a Navy SEAL, but the enlisted men among the ranks scorned his desire to be an officer. However, a lieutenant assigned to his unit took a special note of the young Remar's abilities, and the officer used his diplomatic pull in Washington to get Remar into the Navy War College in 1977. He graduated with high honors and was promoted to ensign. His high marks and astute observations brought Remar to the attention of an officer serving under the Secretary of the Navy. The officer had been one of Remar's instructors, and he remembered the young Kendall with the remarkable insights and intuition for oceanic air-warfare. The officer recommended Remar for assignment to the Naval Air Warfare Center, where Remar had served ever since with distinction. Over the years Remar had seen promotion after promotion and was now a two-star rear admiral.

The bang of the door being opened snapped Kissinger out of his catnap. He was a little ashamed, but it had been a pretty long flight and his study of all of the material on the Stormalite weapons had prevented him from getting much sleep on the plane. A hot shower, a meal and a few hours' sleep was something he'd have to consider in short order.

Kissinger stood and turned toward the door. Kendall Remar was hardly what he'd expected. The man was short—*very* short—and had no air of authority whatsoever. He was actually a stumpy character with thinning hair and an ill-fitting uniform. In fact, it looked as though he'd barely made the Navy's height requirements. His eyes were shifty and gray, eyebrows thick, lips full and pale.

Kissinger cleared his throat, but before he could say a word to recover his surprise, Remar stepped forward and offered him a hand. Kissinger was shocked to find Remar had a very firm handshake, dry palms and deep voice.

"Mr. Jones, a pleasure to meet you," Remar said.

"Pleasure's mine, Admiral Remar," Kissinger replied. "And please call me John."

"John Jones?" Remar raised an eyebrow and smiled knowingly, but before Kissinger replied, the officer shrugged and said, "Okay, John Jones it is.

"Are you hungry?" Remar asked.

"I'm famished, actually."

Remar looked at his watch and said, "Well, it's not quite yet time for lunch, but I'd be willing to bet I could have the master chief at the officer's mess whip us up something a little early. If you'll follow me, it's just across the street."

Remar did a snappy about-face and walked out of the office. Kissinger fell into step behind him. There wasn't enough room to walk side by side in the narrow hall, but once outside Kissinger was able to move alongside Remar. The Navy officer immediately struck up a conversation without a bit of prompting.

"Hal tells me you flew here straight from the Stormalite demo in Australia."

Hal? Kissinger almost tripped over his own feet when he heard Brognola's name mentioned with such seeming familiarity. Price had told him that Brognola had dealt with Remar, but he didn't realize it had consisted of any intimacy. Now Kissinger didn't know how far to go—that last little statement had thrown him for a loop.

"You, um, sounds like you know him well."

"Who? Brognola?" Remar chuckled. "I've known Hal since I was a student in the Naval War College. I can tell from the look on your face that you're wondering just how much else I know."

Kissinger shrugged. "It's really none of my business, Admiral. I'm simply here in information-gathering mode."

"Yes, but you're wondering all the same."

"It had crossed my mind, yes," Kissinger replied with a nod. "But you're considered the resident expert on Stormalite Systems and their new weapons, and that makes what you know very valuable in light of some recent events."

Remar stopped at the entrance outside the officer's mess hall and said, "You're talking about the attack in Adelaide. Let's get some dust out of the way up front. I know more than you might think I do. For example, I'm sure that Hal doesn't only work for the Department of Justice, and I'm sure that your name isn't John Jones."

Kissinger didn't reply, but it was obvious Remar had a much higher security clearance than he'd first understood. He would have to be sure to let Barbara Price know that such information would have made the entire process a little easier. Still, he listened out of his newfound respect for the man who was jabbing a stubby finger at him even in the shadow of Kissinger's towering form.

Remar continued. "But out of respect for Hal and our friendship, I've never pressed him on his business and he's never pressed me on mine. Not that he couldn't, since I know he's got the ears of some our mutual friends in Wonderland, and I know if he asked me anything about what I do that I'd have the clearance given to discuss with him by making a single phone call.

"Now that we've settled that, let me tell you what I *do* know for sure. Some group of fanatics has got a real hard-on for us and they've shown it by stealing the prototypes. So now we have a snafu. I haven't got a clue as to how much you already know about those weapons, but I'm sure you know enough to realize we're in the shit. The only thing we've got going for us is that whoever stole those things probably doesn't know crap from Crisco about them. So maybe we have a little time and maybe we don't. In either case, you can bet that these terrorists will get the prototypes in the hands of someone who *does* know something about them in short order, if they haven't already."

"So we've got a lot of work to do."

"Yes," Remar replied as he opened the door. "And I'd love to give you the time to clean up and rest, but I don't think we can spare it. So let's get a bite and then I'll take you to the TRC. What you see there will knock your socks off."

TRUE TO REMAR'S WORDS, Kissinger was indeed impressed by what he had to see. It was more revealing than the technical schematics he'd reviewed of the weapons during his flight. In fact, Remar had an entire library of video taken by Stormalite Systems' staff

members at various internal live-fire exercises. Some
segments Kissinger had seen during the joint briefing
he'd attended with Phoenix Force prior to their depar-
ture for Australia.

Still, nothing compared to some of the things he
was seeing for the first time. The features of a number of the weapons hadn't even been demonstrated at
the conference in Adelaide, which meant that Phoenix
Force was up against much more than they'd originally
bargained for. It was a simultaneously eye-opening
and awe-inspiring experience.

"All four versions of their small-arms prototypes
fire between two hundred-fifty thousand and one million rounds per minute," Remar said as the video ran.
Kissinger was seated in the Technical Research Center building, which occupied a large part of Bravo II,
which was adjacent to the Naval Air Warfare Detachment headquarters building.

"How come we haven't seen this kind of capability in previous specifications or videos?"

"It's highly secretive," Remar replied. "Everyone
from the Defense Advanced Research Projects Agency
to the NSA have dollars invested in Stormalite Systems, and the thing's been need-to-know like nothing
I've seen in all my years with secret warfare. The last
demonstration for DARPA was photographed, and
only ten seconds of the actual two hours filmed was
released for public view. This isn't next-generation
weaponry we're talking about, John. I believe it won't
be commonplace until the grandkids are *my* age."

Kissinger nodded and said, "Okay, so lots of money

involved. What can you tell me about the technical aspects I may not know?"

"So far they've perfected firing mechanisms for 9 mm, 5.56 mm, 40 mm grenades and 80 mm mortar rounds. Recently there's been a shift to seven7.62 mm and .45 calibers.

"There's only one handgun version, the 9 mm, but the 5.56 mm includes a machine pistol and assault rifle."

"I believe I heard one of the onsite engineers at the demo state they also had multibarrel versions of the .45 caliber. These were stolen, as well."

"That's probably the pods, he was talking about."

Kissinger furrowed his eyebrows and said, "Pods?"

"They were designed for guard emplacements," Remar said with a nod, "like at embassies or road checkpoints. Very mobile and very versatile."

"Sounds like these pods are interesting variants."

"Indeed," Remar replied with a cluck of his tongue. He clicked his remote and the live-fire video was replaced by a computer-drafted schematic. The graphic ran through statistics and a listing of vital components as Remar lectured. "All of the weapons utilize a solid-state electronics firing system, which Stormalite claims they developed for three reasons. First, it eliminates the need for moving parts. Second, it allows users to deal with misfires by simply firing the next round. Finally, it facilitates triggering of the weapons using computer-based technology."

"Interesting," Kissinger interjected.

"That's only the half of it. If you think about it on

a larger scale, there are significant applications for this kind of technology. The only moving parts in the weapons are the rounds themselves. They stack the rounds in the barrel and separate them with a propellant charge. This allows them to fire each round contained within a low-temperature, low-pressure environment."

"Okay, so they don't have to account for gas blowblack operation or a feeding-and-ejection system."

"Precisely!" Remar appeared to be getting excited as the discussion ensued. "In addition to that, the propellant load that fires the first projectile keeps the one behind it locked in place until load two ignites, so there's no need for a breech opening."

"I would assume that this is why they're not worried about misfires?"

Remar nodded. "Each propellant load is fired in sequence. So let's just say I've fired four rounds and at round five I misfire. The next propellant load takes care of ejecting the misfired load *and* propelling my objects to target."

Kissinger couldn't help but shake his head with disbelief. "That's brilliant. What about the solid-state firing system tying to computer operation? I mean, I can understand how you'd want it, given these stackable projectiles, but I'm not sure the reasoning behind creating such a system would tie to computer systems. Are we talking about remote-access firing here?"

"That's *exactly* what we're talking about. Take a weapon that literally cannot jam and cannot misfire. Now add to that a solid-state firing system with electronics that can be tied to a computer. This not only means you could trigger one or more of the weapons with a computer, but you could hook that computer up to a network and trigger the weapons using anything from remote-access servers to networking protocols. More than that, you could fire them utilizing wireless technology."

"Holy shit," Kissinger breathed, suddenly realizing the impact of this revelation. "With enough of these things, terrorists could trigger weapons and unleash destruction like nothing ever previously witnessed with small arms, and they could do it from hundreds or even thousands of miles away."

"Even if these terrorists didn't plan to use the weapons in this fashion, they would still be a formidable force. Let's say you take twenty crack troops and issue each of them a conventional assault rifle and a semiautomatic pistol. On the other side of the line, you've got twenty men with an equivalent of these new weapons. Statistically, you can assume that in the initial volley at least three of the good guys are going to have misfires or jams, and that's probably being too optimistic. Meanwhile, twenty bad guys are pouring down fire rates of a million rounds per minute *each,* and that's just the pistols. This isn't good news."

It was unfathomable the kind of horrors imagined by the human mind. Kissinger was no philosopher, but history spoke for itself. From the first catapult to the first atomic bomb, man had shown an uncanny ability to develop newer and better weapons for waging war. The only problem was that these weapons were also proving more and more capable of unleashing violence and bloodshed at a magnitude unparalleled in human history. The more death and carnage a weapon could deliver, the quicker organizations would fork out dollars to possess its secrets. That seemed to be the philosophy of the purveyors of warfare, including those from America.

Kissinger didn't like it, but he understood it.

"I'm curious to know something, Admiral," Kissinger finally said after a long silence. "How is it you happened to get involved with this? I mean, you work for the Naval Air Warfare Center, but these weapons seem geared toward ground forces."

"Not entirely," Remar said with a conspiratorial smile. "Some of this information is still classified, but it doesn't matter since I'll spare you details. A few years ago, I was appointed to begin procurement options for the Unmanned Combat Aerial Vehicles Program, first started by DARPA.

"I served as an adviser to DARPA during the initial bidding process. At that time, I was on TDY at the Pentagon. I was attending a dinner party held for perspective contractors when I happened to strike up a friendly conversation with one of the representatives of Stormalite Systems who was assigned to a local office they'd set up in Virginia. When I asked him about the possibility of applying their weapons technology to the UCAVP, he jumped at the chance. He also told me that he'd suggested this option to his company, but at the time they turned it down due to inadequate funding. Well, it turns out this guy I talked to also served with the Royal Australian Air Force for many years, so he had some expertise. When he went back and told his company of my interest, they jumped at it. Last week, I got my first live-fire demo of 40 mm shells from four separate pods on a low-altitude, high-speed pass. They put fifty-seven thousand grenades onto an area no larger than a football field in under a minute."

Kissinger whistled his surprise and Remar nodded in response.

"I'm telling you now, John, that this is heavy ordnance you're dealing with here. If you or Hal are connected with the people responsible for tracking down whoever stole the prototypes, you're going to have your work cut out for you."

"We already figured that much," Kissinger replied. "What I need to know is everything else you can tell me about these things. And if you think there's any possibility this connection of yours could help some friends of mine get their hands on other prototypes that exist."

"You're looking to give your people every advantage," Remar replied. "I can understand that. And I think I can help."

"That would be good," Kissinger said. "And you're right about our people. If they have to go up against a force of any considerable size, it's ultimately my responsibility to arm them with the proper tools. That's their only chance for success."

"You're saying you want to fight fire with fire."

"Yes, Admiral, that's *exactly* what I'm saying," Kissinger said quietly. "From here out, we're under a scorched earth policy."

CHAPTER SEVEN

New York State

It took nearly four hours of bureaucratic red tape, politics and diplomacy before Able Team was able to depart the N.Y.P.D.'s downtown headquarters with Deborah Babbit in tow.

Neither Roberson nor his superiors had liked the idea of releasing their only suspect to federal marshals, but Brognola's influence with the President went a long way. Not to mention the fact that since the terrorist attacks on the World Trade Center, the various federal offices that lent personnel to any joint task force carried the weight of the *Patriot Act* and the Department of Homeland Security behind them. It would have been considered a serious breach of protocol for the N.Y.P.D. to refuse to let Able Team operate with autonomy. All terrorist acts fell within the jurisdiction of the United States government.

Able Team was now headed out of the city, bound for their first target.

"All right, lady, you've got center stage," Lyons said. Babbit was seated in the back seat of the SUV, wedged between Lyons and Blancanales, while Schwarz drove. "What can we expect at this little country retreat of yours?"

Babbit didn't look at him, instead choosing to keep her eyes on the road ahead. "When we came down from this place early this morning, we left behind a small cell of our colleagues."

"How many?" Lyons asked in a no-nonsense tone.

"Fourteen. They were instructed to sit tight and wait to hear from us."

"Were they to wait indefinitely?" Blancanales inquired.

Babbit shook her head. "They were to wait twenty-four hours, and unless they heard otherwise, their orders were to split up and head toward other assigned targets."

"And those were what, exactly?" Lyons said.

"I don't know."

"That's not an answer I'm looking for."

Now Babbit turned to look him in the eyes. "I'm being straight with you, mister. They all had specific assignments and we weren't told what they were. They weren't even allowed to tell each other. All I know is that there were three teams of four each, and each time had its own assignment. There were also a couple of cell leaders."

"Were these 'assignments' in other cities or were they locations within New York?" Blancanales asked.

"I already told you what I know. They didn't give

me any specifics. My group wasn't even told where we were headed until the last minute."

"Well, what if you had to guess?" Lyons pressed.

Babbit appeared to consider his question seriously for a moment, then finally replied, "Probably other cities."

Lyons chewed on that a minute. Okay, so the Resurrected Defense League invested serious cash and risk to train a group of mercenary wannabes in urban warfare and terrorism. They then split the group into smaller factions with the idea of inserting them into a number of U.S. cities, probably to commit similar atrocities as occurred in NYC. Price had suggested that they planned to start a war on American streets, which Lyons believed. What he couldn't accept was that the architect behind this plan would have such a limited vision. It seemed that the massacre in Brooklyn Heights had caused a secondary consequence in the form of riots throughout the city. Without question, that kind of sensationalism would make the news. If similar incidents were realized in other cities, the backlash would spread—a natural trickle effect of the Information Age—and *that* could have disastrous effects for America and her allies.

The only question remaining then was whether this was the intended chaos, or if those behind such an insidious plot had a still darker purpose. Able Team would have to remember that this entire thing was just a decoy and the true intentions of the RDL may yet remain to be seen. The whole thing stunk either way, and that wasn't Able Team's preferred method of operation. Someone else was calling the shots, and Lyons didn't like it one damn bit.

Sooner or later, something would have to give.

THE SUN HAD SET by the time Able Team arrived at the cabin site in Upstate New York. Lyons gagged Babbit and secured her inside the vehicle with metal cuffs, although she adamantly protested his actions. He really didn't give a tinker's damn if she liked it or not. They couldn't risk the possibility she might escape or warn her comrades. For all they knew, she was leading them straight into a death trap.

"This isn't necessary," Babbit said just before Lyons gagged her.

"Maybe not," he said, cinching the knot. "But if you're setting us up, now's your chance to do the stand-up thing and say so."

Babbit didn't move.

Lyons shrugged. "Okay...but don't say we didn't give you every chance."

Schwarz leaned close and added, "And remember, if we bid it farewell, chances are pretty good you'll die of dehydration before anybody finds you."

The Able Team warriors then turned to the task of preparing their weapons. During their wait for clearance to take Babbit, Schwarz had attended to the task of cleaning and checking weapons, and then reloading. He'd also prepared additional magazines. Lyons had elected to trade his automatic shotgun for an MP-5 A-3. Coupled with the one Blancanales carried, their enemies were in for a firestorm. Schwarz had retained his FNC, and all three warriors had their pistols tucked into shoulder holsters. Additionally, Blancanales and Schwarz were carrying satchels filled with HE grenades; Lyons had a standalone M-203 equipped with a pistol grip and folding stock slung across his back.

Schwarz had parked the car about a hundred yards from where Babbit said the cabin stood, and they now picked their way through the dark woods, moving slowly to reduce noise and maintain proper direction. It wouldn't do any good to get lost out here, and they didn't want to alert the enemy to their presence. Surprise was the order of the day.

It took them almost twenty minutes to reach the cabin. They crouched at the wood line, careful to keep themselves spaced at a reasonable distance. The trio communicated by throat-mounted microphones, common devices utilized by special operations groups throughout the world. The cabin was dark, or at least it appeared that way. Lyons activated a pair of night-vision goggles and scanned the large, two-story cabin. A quick but professional study revealed the windows were blackened, with slivers of light escaping from the edges.

"Lights are on and somebody's home, guys," Lyons whispered. "Get ready to move."

Lyons stashed the miniature NVD and retrieved the M-203. The Able Team leader quietly opened the breech, double-checked the high-yield, white-phosphorous grenade he'd loaded and then secured the slide with a definitive click. He quickly settled on a second-floor window in the center of the cabin, aligned the grenade launchers' luminescent leaf sight on it and took a deep breath. He squeezed the trigger. The M-203 bucked with the force of a 12-gauge shotgun, and the Willie Pete hit the window less than a second later. Lyons heard shouts, followed immediately by the popping sound of the grenade, which then caused the shouts to morph into screams.

The intense heat shattered the window and exposed the white phosphorous to a sudden rush of air. Lyons watched with satisfaction as the now-visible curtains spontaneously combusted. Flames licked hungrily at the frame, and the flurry of human movement was evident beyond the window. Lyons loaded a second grenade, and this time he aimed for a window on the ground floor. The second WP penetrated with the accuracy of the first.

Lyons keyed his mike. "Move."

They charged the cabin simultaneously. Blancanales had taken the center line, so he made a beeline for the front door while Lyons and Schwarz split off in flanking positions. The screaming continued, as did the pandemonium inside, but the first target presented itself quickly. The terrorist leaped through a first-floor window in a flurry of glass shards and wood pieces, rolling to a stop on his knees. Schwarz got him through the heart with a 3-round burst from the FNC. The terrorist's body twitched and jerked under the impact.

A second terrorist appeared in the open window frame, apparently unaware of the demise of his com-

rade. His eyes widened with terror and as he opened
his mouth to shout with surprise, Schwarz put a slug
through it. The back of the guy's head exploded in a
gory gray-red spray of blood and bone fragments.

Blancanales took the front door off its hinges with
a front kick just below the handle. He came through
the doorway and went prone immediately. The action
saved his life. Two terrorists had managed to escape
the searing effects of the white phosphorous and taken
defensive positions behind a massive sofa. They fired
a hail of slugs from semiautomatic pistols that burned
the air where Blancanales had been a moment before.
The Able Team warrior got to one knee behind a re-
cliner, reached into his satchel and withdrew a flash-
bang grenade. He waited until there was a lull in the
firing and then hosed the area with autofire to keep
heads down while simultaneously releasing the bomb.
It had the desired effect, disorienting the terrorists just
as they were unloading a fresh volley in the Able Team
commando's general direction. Blancanales stepped
from cover and dispatched both terrorists with controlled bursts of 9 mm Parabellums rounds.

Lyons reached the side of the cabin unchallenged.
He didn't find any entry point there, so he continued
to the back door. He shot up the lock, kicked down the
door and entered the cabin ready for action. He found
himself standing in a wide, sparse kitchen. Instead of
dodging an expected storm of bullets, Lyons found a
set of long fingernails raking toward his face. He managed to avoid their full force, but he took a shallow
scratch on his chin. The big ex-cop spun on his heel,

went low and drove the barrel into the aggressor's solar plexus with an upward thrust. Breath exploded audibly from the female terrorist. She stepped backward, wheezing for air, but Lyons wasn't about to wait. He fired a rock-solid punch that connected with the terrorist's forehead and slammed her into the wall. Her eyes rolled upward as she slid to the floor.

Lyons spun at the sound of movement and caught sight of a terrorist half running, half sliding down the stairwell. The man was short and muscular, wearing a T-shirt and camouflage fatigue pants. He spotted Lyons as he reached the first-floor landing and raised the pistol in his fist, but it was too late. Lyons swung the muzzle of the MP-5 A-3 into action and fired a 3-round burst from the hip. Two rounds caught the terrorist in the abdomen, the third ripped through his sternum. The impact drove him into the wall and the pistol he carried flew from his fingers. The terrorist was dead before he hit the ground.

Lyons whirled in time to see Blancanales come through the kitchen doorway.

"We clear down here?"

"I think so," Blancanales replied. "I haven't seen Gadgets yet, though."

Lyons keyed the throat mike. "Gadgets, report status."

Lyons's response was as the *tap-tap-tap* of autofire from his teammate's FNC. Lyons and Blancanales exchanged knowing looks and then moved out of the kitchen in the direction from which Blancanales had just come. It didn't take the pair long to size up the situation. They could hear Schwarz firing just outside a side window, and the fainter reports of weapons fire coming from somewhere above him. Second-floor residents had the electronics wizard pinned down.

Lyons crossed the living area in three steps and disengaged the window lock. He raised the window and found Schwarz pressed against the wall just to the right of the opening. Sure enough, gunners above had him pinned down and he was exchanging hurried shots. Lyons leaned against the far part of the window frame so Schwarz could see it was him, but he didn't risk exposing his skull and getting his head blown off.

"Need some help?" Lyons quipped.

Schwarz sent one last sustained burst in the enemy's direction for good measure, then climbed through the window with one-armed assistance from Lyons.

Once inside, Schwarz let out a deep sigh. "That was *too* close. Thanks, Ironman."

"Let's finish this," Blancanales said.

Lyons and Schwarz nodded and the threesome headed for the steps. When they reached the stairwell, the electronics genius offered a Lyons a flash-bang grenade, and he palmed it as he positioned himself for point. Blancanales took rear guard. Lyons started up the steps, stopped halfway up, pulled the pin on the flash-bang and visualized a three-count with his fingers. He then tossed the grenade and the Able Team warriors clapped their palms on their ears and closed their eyes. As soon as the grenade exploded, the three charged up the stairs.

They hit the top landing and immediately fanned

out. Lyons went low, Schwarz took high ground with his back to the wall and Blancanales knelt at the top of the stairs to cover the upper and lower landings. Two terrorists emerged from a doorway at the opposite end of the hallway.

Schwarz opened up with short, controlled bursts of his FNC. Lyons took a more radical approach by aiming just above their heads with the M-203 and lobbing another WP shell into the door frame. The chemical ignited and rained white-hot thermite onto its intended targets. The terrorists's clothing erupted into flame and immediately burned through to their skin. They began flailing and dancing about with pain and terror, finally being dealt a mercy burst by Schwarz. Their smoldering corpses hit the floor in the short order.

Able Team stood its ground for a few moments, but no additional resistance appeared. The hallway was silent except for the crackle, pops and hisses of the flames consuming the pair of corpses. Still, the threesome didn't move for a long time. Lyons finally gave a nod and gestured that he was confident they were all clear.

They scoured the rest of the rooms and found four bodies in a front loftlike area that spanned the entire width of the log retreat. Patches of noxious smoke from ashen skin and severe burns in the treated flooring nearly asphyxiated the trio. It would have been impossible to remain in the room, except that the majority of the fumes was being vented through the opening of the broken window. Lyons and Blancanales quickly frisked the bodies for identification while Schwarz went to search the remaining area. The threesome reconnected in the hall a few minutes later.

"What did you find?" Lyons asked Gadgets.

"Nothing of use," the electronics wizard replied. He jerked his thumb in the direction of the pair at the end of the hallway and added, "They didn't have any ID on them, either."

"Something's wrong," Blancanales said. "Babbit told us there were fourteen here."

Lyons nodded. "And we've only accounted for twelve."

"So she was either lying or mistaken," Schwarz said.

"I'd bet neither," Lyons replied. "I'd say that we have two who already split, for whatever reason. I'd guess they got tired of waiting around and decided to head off to wherever they were supposed to."

"Might also be the two cell leaders that are missing," Blancanales reminded them.

"Yeah, that's a good point," Lyons said in a conciliatory tone. "We still need to search the downstairs."

His teammates nodded and they descended to the first floor, spreading out to save time. Schwarz riffled through the drawers and cabinets in the kitchen, searching for any clue as to where the missing men had gone, or what the plans had been for the rest of the group. His search quickly proved to be as fruitless as the one upstairs. Blancanales used his combat knife to rip open seat cushions but found nothing.

"Hey!" Lyons called to them.

The two quickly located him in a small room off the main living area that they ignored when coming in. Lyons was blocking the doorway because he could barely squeeze by the table that took up the majority of the room. It didn't take them long to determine that it wasn't room, but actually a large, walk-in closet. Blank passports and other travel documents and literature covered the table; there was a plastic-coated map of the United States tacked to the wall. Five cities had been circled in grease pencil: New York, Chicago, Miami, Los Angeles and Salt Lake City.

"Holy shit," Schwarz said slowly and quietly, the disbelief evident in his tone. "They weren't fucking around."

Politician nodded. "I can't argue with that."

"We're lucky we found these guys," Lyons said. "If this crew planned to split off and hit all of these cities, then we just stopped something major. What bugs me is that *one* of them may still be a target."

"How so?" Gadgets asked.

Lyons pointed at each city as he talked. "Well, we know the story in NYC, so no point covering old ground there. There's four other cities, but Babbit says there were only three crews left behind."

"Maybe they were expecting one of them to double up," Blancanales suggested.

"That's a thought, although we can't really be sure. Babbit didn't mention it, and we sure as hell can't afford to assume anything. Let's say the three teams left behind here were each supposed to take a city. That covers four cities, which means one's still in the open. I'd be willing to bet that's where the cell leaders are headed."

"Okay, but which one?" Schwarz asked, although it wasn't really a question.

Lyons turned and looked his friend in the eyes. "That's the million-dollar question. We'll call Hal and have him start putting out the feelers."

"Maybe Babbit will be able to help us," Blancanales said.

Lyons frowned. "Maybe.

"Either way, we'll have to be ready to go at a moment's notice," Schwarz said.

The team turned simultaneously at the sound of moaning from the kitchen.

Lyons slammed a fist into his open palm. "Dammit! I forgot about the woman!"

He pushed his way past Schwarz and Blancanales and hurried into the kitchen. They followed him and entered through the doorway in time to see Lyons reach down, grab the woman by the shirt collar with one hand and haul her to her feet. He pushed her to a nearby kitchen table, yanked out a chair and shoved her into it with enough force that it struck the wall.

The woman was dark-haired with large, brown eyes. There was a welt on her forehead where Lyons had punched her. It would take a day or so for the bruise to show, but his knuckle imprints were clearly visible in the dim light. The woman's head spun and then she vomited on the floor.

Lyons knew her body was reacting to the trauma. Despite all of the woman's training, she obviously hadn't expected to go up against the likes of Carl Lyons. The blond soldier waited another minute for her to regain her senses before speaking.

"Welcome to the land of the conscious," he said.

The woman looked up, squinted at him, then cocked her head as if she didn't understand. *"No hablo."*

Lyons shrugged and immediately turned to Blancanales. "Want to help out here?"

Blancanales stepped forward and began rapping at her with a stream of Spanish phrases. The woman still acted as if she didn't understand, at which point Lyons put up his hand to stop the exchange.

"All right, enough of this shit," he snapped. He grabbed the woman's chin and pinned her head against the wall. "Look, lady, I know you speak English so why don't you just knock off the act. We know what you and your little band are planning. So do yourself a favor and start talking, or it's going to get ugly."

The woman's eyes burned with hatred as she looked at Lyons with a smug and defiant look. The Able Team warrior began to apply pressure to the hinges of her jaw while simultaneously challenging her gaze with an ice-cold stare of his own. Eventually the woman snapped her head out of his grasp and looked down.

"There is nothing you can do that will force me to betray my cause," she said quietly. There was an unrecognizable accent to her voice, so Lyons wasn't sure of its origin. She continued, "For the first time, I have a cause to believe in. It is the *only* thing I believe in, and I will not be remembered as the one responsible for its demise, or for those with whom I fight."

"Oh, brother," Lyons interjected, rolling his eyes and looking at his teammates. "What we have here, boys, is a selfless martyr."

When he looked back, he found those soft brown eyes glinting with the light of a pure fanatic. "Call me what you will, but you cannot hope to stand against the Resurrected Defense League. I will not talk."

Lyons couldn't repress a frosty smile as he replied, "That's what you think."

CHAPTER EIGHT

Spain

Dusk approached rapidly as Jack Grimaldi put down the plane in a makeshift airstrip built secretly by the CIA in a rural area just outside of Madrid. It hadn't been an easy trip; Grimaldi'd had to fly below radar once entering Spanish airspace. Still, they'd arrived without incident. One of Stony Man's contacts from the CIA, Andy Roman, met Phoenix Force as the plane touched down.

Roman was tall and good-looking, with neatly trimmed blond hair and a mustache. His eyes were almost a cobalt-blue, his chin strong and, even through the faded blue jeans and flannel shirt rolled at the sleeves, David McCarter could see that Roman kept in shape.

Roman offered his hand to the Briton. "You must be Brown."

McCarter nodded and returned the handshake, impressed with Roman's grip. "I'm guessing our people contacted you."

"That's right," Roman replied.

Jack Grimaldi joined the group and jerked a thumb in the direction of his plane. "Is this thing *really* going to be okay?"

Roman nodded. "It will be fine, I assure you. We had this place under twenty-four-hour observation for months before building here. Nobody comes around."

"And if they do," McCarter cut in, "you know what to do."

Grimaldi nodded, wished them luck and returned to the plane to begin erecting the overhead camouflage.

After introductions all around, Roman led Phoenix Force to a waiting van.

"Your timing's impeccable," the CIA agent said as he drove them toward the city. "This is one of the most beautiful times of year in Spain, particularly in Madrid."

"Yeah, but I'm sure you'll understand if we decide to skip the sight-seeing," Calvin James replied.

"Of course, which reminds me that I wanted you to know I've been briefed on your mission here."

"You have?" Encizo asked, just a hint of surprise evident in his tone.

Roman nodded as his eyes studied Encizo through the rearview mirror. "I'm the agent in charge here. It was my office that was first put on alert for the two men you're looking for. We've been watching every conceivable place in town since we were first notified of their arrival. We also managed to get cooperation from the local authorities, which I have to tell you is nothing short of a goddamn miracle."

"And why is that?" Manning asked.

Roman shrugged. "Well, I don't want it to sound like we don't appreciate the cops here. In fact, they're actually pretty decent. Your average Spaniard cop is generally tough and efficient, especially in Madrid."

"So what's the problem?" McCarter asked.

Roman scoffed noisily and then replied, "The upper brass, that's the problem. This country is chock-full of crazies, fanatics and criminals, and just about every single one of them is either running from something or someone. Hell, even the locals usually have something to hide. But the politics here are unbelievable. The bureaucrats tie the hands of the little guy just trying to survive on these streets. And believe me when I say these are some pretty mean streets."

"That's funny, I always thought of Spain as a rather peaceful place," James interjected.

"Surprisingly, it is," Roman replied. "And the beat cops are generally the ones responsible for keeping it that way."

"Okay, so we have a bit of politics to worry about," McCarter said. "But what about the pair we're looking for. I take it you haven't found them yet."

"Unfortunately we haven't," Roman said, frowning and shaking his head. "We're still going through the surveillance tapes from Barajas Airport now. We've also put out photographs to hotels and businesses. I have to be honest though, guys, and tell you that this will be like trying to find a needle in a haystack."

"We won't hold your feet to the fire," Encizo said.

The Phoenix Force warriors nodded in agreement, and McCarter added, "We know it's next to impossible anyway. We're counting on a bloody miracle at this point."

"Well, if your friends are in this city, I can guarantee you that my people will find them."

"We trust you," McCarter said. "Now that we're here, we can help you in the search. How much do you know about the men we're looking for?"

"Not a lot, which I have to say isn't making this any easier," Roman admitted. "Whoever you're working for must have some serious weight, because we got a call all the way from the top on this one. My boss told me to drop whatever the hell I was doing and start looking for these guys, and everyone under my command was assigned to it, as well. Only trouble with that is, I don't have the first clue who these guys are. I was told it was need-to-know."

Encizo leaned forward and whispered in McCarter's ear, "David, I understand the need for security, but this guy's trying to help us. I think he has a right to know who we're looking for."

McCarter nodded in agreement. "All right, mate, listen up. The two men we're looking for are members of a new terrorist cell called the Resurrected Defense League. Yesterday morning in Adelaide Australia, they stole a set of new prototype weapons that were under spec of the U.S. Armed Forces and DARPA. Several people were injured, and even a few of us almost kissed our bloody arses goodbye."

"Resurrected Defense League, eh?" Roman echoed. "Sounds like a mean bunch. Okay, so it's safe to assume you guys are Delta Force or special ops."

"Maybe we're just mercenaries for hire," Hawkins suggested with a smile.

"No, you don't have the smell of mercs on you," Roman replied. "I've been in the business awhile now. I know black ops when I meet them. Not that that makes a damn bit of difference, mind you. I just don't want all hell breaking loose here."

"Won't be anything like that if we can find these guys and they choose to come along quietly," James said.

"Which may be easier said than done," McCarter reminded him. "Listen, we'll do our best not to ruin your little Spanish paradise here, but we're going to find these guys, and we'd prefer to do it with your help."

"Don't worry about fouling anything up for me," Roman assured him. "You'll have my full cooperation and the cooperation of my people. I don't want any more terrorists operating here than already are, and if there's something I can do to help in that process, you can bet I will."

With that out of the way, Roman told him of their efforts to that point and advised them he'd booked them a room at the Holiday Inn Madrid in the center of the city. Roman explained a little about the city, which had been the capital of Spain since the 1600s.

It was a thriving metropolis known for its around-the-clock festivities, noisy and bustling streets and cafés crammed with partygoers. Madrid was filled with museums, shops and hotels, had a very efficient rail transportation system, and throughout the year sported every tourist attraction imaginable, including the San Isidro Festival held for two weeks each May.

Evening had settled on Madrid by the time Phoenix Force checked in and got its equipment together. They were clustered in a room being shared by McCarter and James, which was doubling as a makeshift HQ, when there was a knock at the door. Encizo opened it and admitted Roman. The CIA guy was wearing a wide smile, which could only mean good news.

"What's up?" Manning asked.

"We just got a hit on your mysterious pair. They checked into a small guesthouse in the village of Almagro."

"Where's that?" McCarter asked.

"On the west side of the city," he replied. "Most of the area's decent, but not where these two checked in. In fact, this guesthouse isn't even a fully fledged commercial area. It's actually in a three-story building that was restored by one of the local historical societies."

"Got a lot of those in Madrid, do you?" James asked.

"A ton, but that's nothing new. Either way you cut it, we've confirmed the identification, so we're ready to go if you are. All I need is for you to give the word."

"The word is given," McCarter said.

The men of Phoenix Force immediately returned to

their rooms and began preparation for the hit. While the others got geared up, McCarter gave it some thought. He couldn't believe it had been this easy. The warrior wondered if perhaps it wasn't a trap or decoy, but he couldn't be sure. The worse part was that they were going to have to try to take at least *one* of the pair alive for interrogation. That wouldn't be easy, especially not and still keep any innocent bystanders out of the line of fire.

The other difficulty was a bit more practical: finding out where the prototypes had been taken. McCarter wasn't even sure how they'd smuggled the things out of Australia, although he was confident they had. Stony Man still hadn't been able to positively identify either one of these men, and nothing had alerted authorities to be suspicious. Even the customs officials at Barajas Airport hadn't remembered the two men, although one of the off-duty officers they spoke with recalled the two men from their photograph, and indicated he remembered they had only carry-ons with two or three days' worth of clothes, plus the usual amenities. Their purpose of stay had been business and they'd cited Australia as their country of origin.

Who they were or what they were doing in Madrid was still a mystery to McCarter. What was clear was that they were two of the terrorists who had almost wiped out his team, and they had some purpose for stealing the Stormalite Systems technology. McCarter meant to take them alive at any costs, unless Phoenix Force was left with no alternative.

When they were all assembled, McCarter began

their briefing. "Okay, mates, you know what these bastards look like, and you know what they're capable of. We should take them hard and fast, but try to take them alive. If everything goes according to plan, we should be able to get in and out without too much problem or noise."

"What exactly is our plan?" Manning asked.

McCarter looked at Roman with raised eyebrows, a signal that it was now his show. "We bribed a college kid who works there as part-time bellhop to tell us they're staying on the third floor. I'm working on getting you some floor layouts of the hotel. Basically, the local police are already sitting on the place and they'll let us know if the targets leave for any reason. The cops have also solicited the cooperation of the locals running the joint, so you should be able to walk right through the lobby unmolested."

"Once we've seen the layout," McCarter continued, "we'll figure out the quickest way in and I'll dole out assignments at that point. We'll probably run with two fire teams and leave one of us with Roman in the lobby."

"And what happens if they don't want to come quietly?" James asked.

"If it comes down to either you or them, then don't bloody well hesitate to put one between their eyes," McCarter replied harshly. "Don't take chances with these guys."

The men of Phoenix Force nodded their understanding, then descended to the lobby of the hotel. Roman urged them that the fastest way to Almagro would be via the Metro rail system, so Phoenix Force agreed to play along. Their cover was quite effective under the circumstances. They were dressed in lightweight nylon pants and jackets, which they wore over their black camouflage fatigues. They'd all donned tennis shoes, but they had their boots and weapons in gym bags. They fit in perfectly with the athletic crowd in Madrid, which was a major home to sports such as basketball and soccer. The cover wasn't the best given the ethnic mix of Phoenix Force, but it would suffice for their short time in the public view.

It took only thirty minutes to reach the village of Almagro. When they arrived in the neighborhood with the guesthouse where the terrorists were hiding, Roman led them to a small, one-story brick structure with a darkened interior. McCarter went on high alert, and he could almost detect the increased energy and sensitivity of his teammates. They were as ready as he was for deception. The Briton still wasn't entirely sure he could trust Roman. Phoenix Force had been deceived before, and it wasn't inconceivable such a thing could happen now.

Despite any reticence on the part of Phoenix Force, they quickly discovered the little brick house had only one occupant whose face wasn't even discernible in what little light spilled in from the street. The man didn't say a word; he just gave Phoenix Force a cursory inspection and then turned back to his vigil watching through a wide, narrow window. The only other barely visible things in the room outside of blocky furniture were Roman's eyes reflecting the streetlight.

"See that building across the way?" he asked them.

Encizo stepped forward and peered across the way. "You mean, with the watcher in front?"

"Yeah, that would be it. Actually, that's one of the local cops playing street bum. He's keeping an eye on the place pending our little party. Hey, Lewis, why don't you close the blinds and turn on the light? Those two dudes aren't going anywhere soon."

The guy called Lewis grunted and then pulled a string or rope or something. A moment later the guest house and the light disappeared from view. A few more seconds elapsed before the room was bathed in a dim but effective glow of red lights. It wasn't overly bright, but it was more than enough light to see things well and to read by.

The room was large, boxy and sparse, with chairs spaced at regular intervals throughout. A long, heavy table took up the center of it. It was covered with everything from maps and coffee-stained documents to soda cans, paper cups, plastic-ware and empty containers from fast-food restaurants and pizza joints. It didn't look any different than any other CIA case house in any other country that the team had ever seen.

"You've got quite a setup here, Roman," Hawkins remarked. "How many on the payroll?"

Roman's smile was genuine, but with obvious reservation. "Let's just say that's need-to-know."

Hawkins shrugged, apparently not feeling it was important enough to press the point.

"Okay, what's the gig?" James asked.

Lewis spread a large blueprint on the table and then

left the room. The group gathered around as Roman explained the layout of the guesthouse and their general position to it. When he'd finished, McCarter oriented them to the building by quadrant lettering, starting with Alpha on the left and moving counterclockwise with the rear designated as Delta.

He looked at the group and said, "We'll stick with the same team designations we had Down Under, except I'm switching you two." He gestured to James and Hawkins, telling James, "You cover rear flank with Roman on the ground floor. Any trouble starts, you sound the alarm."

James nodded.

"Red team," he continued, gesturing to Manning and Encizo, "there are two stairwells. You take Delta side, and we'll enter through the front. Get to the top as quickly as you can and report when you're in position. Other than that, we maintain communications silence unless the shit hits the bloody fan. Understood?"

All of them nodded.

"Let's do it then, mates."

The team zipped out of the athletic clothes, traded tennis shoes for combat boots and then prepped their weapons. All were carrying MP-5 SD-6s except James, who preferred an M-16/M-203 combo. It was just as well, since he would have the rear guard anyway, and if anything went down, the need for stealth would probably become null and void.

Roman got himself ready, disappearing into an adjoining room and returning five minutes later in urban camouflage fatigues and wearing a knife and holstered pistol. He studied the other weapons that were now in Phoenix Force's possession with some interest.

"You guys aren't messing around, are you?"

"We're like the Boy Scouts," Hawkins said. "We like to be prepared."

"I guess."

Once they were dressed, locked and loaded, the team moved out with McCarter and Roman at point, Encizo and Manning in the middle and James bringing up the rear with Hawkins. They moved quietly between the buildings, staying in a single file as Roman led them through a half dozen yards and alleyways until they reached a sidewalk at an alley entrance directly across from the guesthouse.

McCarter quickly scanned the team, who all gave thumbs-up, and then gestured for Manning and Encizo to proceed. The pair moved across the street quickly and quietly, and disappeared into the shadows of the building. They'd agreed on one minute, no more, to make access.

"You sure your guy will have that door unlocked?" McCarter asked Roman.

"We'll hold up our end, Brown," Roman said as he pulled his .40-caliber Beretta Model 96 Centurion from its holster and checked the action and load. "You just make damn sure you don't get anybody killed. If shit goes south, I don't need the whole damn Spanish Constabulary coming down on my head. Got it?"

McCarter nodded. "We'll watch your arse, Roman. Just make sure you watch ours."

"Deal."

McCarter then turned and gestured to Hawkins, who sidled up next to him. The Briton checked his watch one last time and, at exactly sixty seconds, he and Hawkins headed for the front entrance. The watcher Roman had out front checked the immediate area to insure nobody had observed the pair. For all they knew, someone was watching who wasn't even visible to them. Still, they had done nothing to alert the two terrorists, so there would be little reason for anyone to be shadowing the establishment.

McCarter and Hawkins passed the desk clerk, a young, petite girl who didn't even look in their direction. Everyone was playing it cool and McCarter was thankful that at least the girl hadn't freaked out at seeing a couple of weapons-sweeping, mean-looking dudes in black scurrying through her lobby.

McCarter and Hawkins continued to the stairwell and quickly ascended to the second-story landing. The Briton paused and knelt, watching the stairs ahead and above while Hawkins covered their rear flank. McCarter adjusted the earpiece and cranked the volume just a bit to make sure he could hear Encizo and Manning call in their ready signal. Taking the enemy in such a public environment hadn't been McCarter's first choice—he preferred a more direct approach. You find the enemy, you get a plan, then you go in and burn their bloody arses to the ground. Instead, they had to apply these more covert tactics, the circumstances being what they were and all. It wasn't McCarter's kind of show.

"Red team to gold team, we're in position," Encizo announced quietly.

McCarter acknowledged him as he and Hawkins headed to the third-floor landing. They reached the door leading from the stairwell to the hallway. The enemy's room was about midway between the front and rear stairs, so they had agreed whoever reached it first following McCarter's green-light would make entry and the other pair would be support.

McCarter gave the word as soon as he and Hawkins hit the third-floor landing. "Go."

They went through the door and catfooted down the hallway, toward the target room. They reached it only a few seconds behind Encizo and Manning. The Briton nodded at them even as Manning put his foot to the door. They followed immediately behind the pair, pushing through in controlled fashion, their weapons covering flanking positions while their teammates went up the middle at high and low points.

The darkened room came suddenly alive in bright lights and the quartet dived to avoid a metallic storm of bullets. As McCarter hit the floor and rolled to avoid perforation, he heard the words of Calvin James crackle in his ear. "All teams, we've got company."

CHAPTER NINE

Calvin James heard the reports of automatic weapons at the same moment he saw eight men emerge from an alleyway two buildings down from the guesthouse.

McCarter had been right—it *was* a trap. Well, it was his job to cover their asses, and it sounded as though they already had their hands full. He didn't know what kind of fighter Roman was, but he didn't have time to worry about that now. If it turned out the odds were eight-to-one against him, then that's the way it was. Roman started forward to intercept the crew, but James grabbed the lapel of his fatigue blouse and restrained him.

"Not yet," James said.

"But your guys inside—"

"Can take care of themselves, so just wait."

Roman fell silent and James could tell he was watching with bated breath. He couldn't help but grin at Roman's enthusiasm. Yeah, he was concerned about the situation, but if there was a time to stay calm and collected it was now. Panic wouldn't solve a damn thing, especially not when his colleagues were suffering a lot more heat in the moment than they were.

James quickly raised the M-16/M-203 over-and-under to his shoulder and rotated the quadrant sight on the side of the M-203 into place. He adjusted for the entrance, accounting for distance and speed and matching that to the approaching figures. He needed the blast to be debilitating enough that it would neutralize the enemy, but simultaneously he needed it to remain far enough out so there was no chance of injuring innocents inside the lobby or passing in vehicles.

James acquired his final strike point for the grenade, then took a deep breath and squeezed the trigger. The 40 mm HE grenade sailed on a true course and landed where he had predicted it would. The resulting explosion at ground zero devastated the terrorists just as they reached the hotel lobby doors. The concussion threw the first two headfirst through the glass doors. The pair behind them took most of the heat and effects of the blast. One man's face visibly melted under the searing gases and the concussion separated his arms from his body. The other lost a leg and was sent flying through the air to land headfirst.

The remaining four were far enough away to avoid the full effects, but were disoriented at the sudden swiftness and ferocity of the attack. They were obviously also unprepared for the tenacity and resolve of their attacker.

James looked Roman in the eye, his tone grim. "You remember fire-and-maneuver?"

Roman nodded.

"Then let's do it. You take right flank, I'll take left."

James didn't even wait for a reply. He sprinted from the cover of the alleyway and laid down the first volley on the disoriented troops, firing in 3-round-burst mode. Roman began to squeeze off rounds as he sprinted toward the hotel lobby.

The terrorists quickly realized they were still under active attack. James reached a thick, wrought-iron light pole and dropped to one knee. He set the front sight post of the M-16 on the nearest target and squeezed the trigger. The assault rifle recoiled slightly as all three rounds found their mark. One struck the terrorist in the gut, the second in the chest. The third ripped away the better part of his neck and lower jaw. The impact spun him as he reflexively triggered a few rounds into the air from his machine pistol before dropping to the sidewalk.

By either the merciful act of some deity or just sheer luck, Roman managed to hit a second terrorist with two rounds from the .40-caliber Beretta. The terrorist was actually faced away, trying to retreat from the firestorm James was now pouring out, but he didn't get far. Both of Roman's slugs punched through the retreating terrorist's spine at a velocity of over three hundred meters per second. The terrorist pitched forward and skidded to a halt face-first.

James took the last two with his assault rifle. A 3-round burst lifted one terrorist off his feet and tossed him through a first-floor window. The second terrorist he ventilated with a pair of short bursts to the abdomen, the 5.56 mm rounds ripping the man's stomach and exposing his intestines. The terrorist screamed before succumbing to shock and then death, dropping to the sidewalk with a dull thump.

The Phoenix Force commando sprang to his feet and sprinted for the lobby doors as he yelled at Roman to get it in gear. His teammates were inside, and more than likely they needed his help. James had no idea what their condition was, but when a body crashed through a third-floor window as he reached the lobby, he figured it was pretty hot.

THE BLOW Rafael Encizo delivered with the butt of the MP-5 SD-6 smashed the terrorist's nose to jelly and sent him sailing through the window. Given the size of the room, there wasn't really much chance of firing his weapon without the risk of hitting one of his own. So when Encizo saw the terrorist charging him with a knife, its blade glinting under the bright lights, the Cuban swung the submachine gun at the terrorist's shins to trip him up, then followed up with a buttstroke to the skull.

Manning faired a bit better, rolling away from the autofire laid down by the remaining five terrorists, and came to one knee with the MP-5 SD-6 tracking. The report of the sound-suppressed weapon was undetectable over the cacophony of the terrorists's machine pistols, but the ratcheting of the extractor as it spit brass told the tale well enough. Manning took one of the terrorists with a head shot, blowing off the top of his exposed skull. Blood and brain matter splattered against the cheap wallpaper and the terrorist's body did an odd spin before dropping to the threadbare carpet.

Hawkins had gone to the left flanking position on entry, and dived to the floor to avoid the twin muzzles of submachine guns. He felt the heat on the back of his neck caused by the flame the weapons spit, a grim reminder that only his quick reflexes had saved him. Hawkins hit the ground and, as he rolled, he opened up full-auto with his subgun. The 9 mm rounds arced with his roll, forming a corkscrew pattern that was odd but still produced the desired results. One of the terrorist's took several of Hawkins's rounds in the face and his head exploded under the impact. The second sucked in a sudden, wheezing breath as one of the rounds drilled through his chest and collapsed a lung.

McCarter was probably the least surprised they had walked into a trap, but the sudden force and ferocity of the enemy's resistance surprised him. He'd expected a couple of armed men in the room, not half a dozen. The Briton hit the ground hard, banged his elbow and bit back the sharp pain that shot down the forearm and simultaneously up to his shoulder. He managed to turn on his side just as Manning blew away one of the terrorists. McCarter was aware of Hawkins's plight, but knew he couldn't do anything about it. In these close quarters, any of them would be lucky to walk away from a firefight.

Bullets chopped the floor in front of McCarter, raising dust, patches of carpet and wood splinters in front of his face. The material lifted by the intense autofire partially blinded McCarter. The Phoenix Force leader sprayed the area full-auto, cognizant to keep his arm fully extended to reduce the risk of hitting one of his team members. Initially he couldn't tell if he'd hit anything, but it was enough to keep heads down until he could clear the dust from his eyes and regroup so that his next shot might actually hit something.

The Briton decided to roll in the direction of the enemy's position, a totally unexpected maneuver, and then stood full height to find the remaining pair of terrorists, one on the right, the other on the left. He recognized one as part of the pair they were looking for, so he shot the other one first, putting a short, clean burst through the gunman's chest.

The delay gave McCarter's quarry enough time to aim his weapon at his adversary, but just as his finger began to tighten on the trigger, something whistled through the air and knocked the gun from the terrorist's grip. The Briton could only blink before his ears were filled with screaming. The man's hand was pinned to the wall on his right, a black throwing knife with holes in it vibrating where it had struck him. McCarter turned to see Encizo rushing forward. He'd always known Encizo was talented with a blade—he'd demonstrated as much time and again—but he was particularly glad of the fact at *this* moment. It had just saved his life.

Manning and Hawkins cleared the rest of the room as Encizo retrieved his knife, then began to tend to the terrorist's hand wound.

McCarter keyed the transceiver. "Red and gold teams are clear. Blue team, what's your status?"

James's voice came through a moment later. "Get your asses down here, man! We've got trouble!"

McCarter ordered Encizo to stay with the prisoner, then turned and gestured for Manning and Hawkins to follow. They took the rear stairs and could hear the sound of the firefight before reaching the second-floor landing. McCarter hadn't expected this kind of trouble, and he certainly hadn't expected such resistance. They hit the first floor without breaking stride and emerged in the lobby to find James and Roman taking cover behind the front desk while several terrorists fired controlled bursts at them from automatic rifles.

The Phoenix Force leader took a quick head count and determined there were at least five enemy gunners. He gestured for Manning and Hawkins to take a flanking position while he diverted the terrorists by heading for the desk where James and Roman were pinned down. At the count of three, McCarter leaped from the foyer of the rear stairwell and rushed toward the front desk. The terrorists opened up on full-auto, their weapons deafening even in the large lobby.

Manning and Hawkins went wide, moving along the side wall unnoticed until they were in position. Hawkins opened fire first, taking one terrorist with a double tap to the head. His second target turned toward the first as he fell under Hawkins's crack shooting, and the former Delta Force commando caught him with a 3-round burst to the chest.

The big Canadian rained a hail of lead on the remaining three terrorists, emptying an entire 30-round magazine. He caught the first terrorist across the midsection, blowing away a better part of the gun-man's stomach and both kidneys. The impact lifted the terrorist off his feet and he smashed through a glass coffee table that was positioned between the furniture the terror crew had been using for cover. The second terrorist managed to raise his weapon and fire a few rounds in the Canadian's direction before he was stopped by a round through the chest followed by one through the throat. Blood and pink frothy sputum erupted from the wound. The terrorist dropped his weapon in surprise and his hands went to his throat re-flexively even as his brain told him he was dead and he toppled forward onto one of the overstuffed chairs.

The last terrorist took several rounds to the chest; the first volley being that delivered by Manning, the other a 3-round burst from Hawkins. The terrorist stag-gered backward, tripped over a magazine rack and toppled to the ground, taking an expensive, antique lamp with him. The porcelain shade of the lamp ex-ploded on impact and showered the man's corpse with shards of ceramic.

The area went suddenly quiet as the echo of the weapons fire died. The fading sounds were followed by nearly thirty full seconds of silence as the mem-bers of Phoenix Force waited for more trouble. It didn't come. McCarter called for Hawkins and Man-ning to assist him. They rushed to the front desk and a quick once-over allayed their fears: Calvin James was alive and well. He hunkered over Roman and was carefully cutting the bloody clothing away from Roman's left arm.

"Is it bad?" Roman asked James.

"I've seen worse," James told him with a grin.

"In fact, he's *had* worse," Hawkins added with a chuckle.

McCarter threw the young Texan a sour "don't try to help" look, so Hawkins clammed up. It took James only a minute to confirm it was just a graze, and the Phoenix Force medic quickly used a field pack to dress the wound.

"You'll need to get to the hospital soon, but you'll live," James told him.

"I can't believe I allowed myself to get shot," Roman said. "Shit! I should have known better than to just walk in here like that."

"What happened, Cal?" McCarter asked James.

"I'm not exactly sure," James replied. "A bunch of them came out of nowhere and were headed for the lobby. I took them out, and then we figured you'd need our help so we made for the door. Roman reached the door first and went inside. I came in behind him just in time to see the guy we had on the door go down and Roman making like a bat out of hell for the front desk. That's when I figured I'd better get the lead out and join him."

"That was probably good thinking," Manning quipped.

"Where's Lopez?" James asked, using Encizo's cover name.

"He's upstairs with one of those blokes we've been looking for," McCarter replied.

"You managed to take one of them alive? Good work, guys!"

"Yeah," Manning replied.

"Well, that's good," James said, jerking his thumb in the direction of the dead terrorists strewed through the lobby, "because I think *one* of them we were looking for was in that bunch."

Hawkins and Manning groaned simultaneously.

McCarter shrugged. "At least we got one of them. Now, let's go see what this bugger has to say, shall we?"

PHOENIX FORCE MANAGED to clear the shambles of the hotel with their prisoner before the arrival of police reinforcements. Unfortunately that left Roman hanging behind to explain the situation while they patched him up, but it proved doubly effective in getting him to the hospital to have his arm wound treated. He promised to meet the team later to discuss what intelligence they had extracted from their prize.

McCarter could tell it would take some significant effort to glean information from their prisoner. The guy was dark-skinned and small, but muscular and strong, obviously the product of months of mental and physical conditioning. It was also immediately apparent that he was above average in intelligence. His responses to McCarter's questions were brief and pointed, and he used eloquent language when he talked to them. Most of all, he seemed unafraid of his captors and unwilling to trade information for leniency; he would have preferred dying over betraying his people, and he told them as much.

Which brought the Phoenix Force members to another conclusion: the guy was hardly a fanatic. Unlike many they had encountered in the past, he didn't give off any vibes that would have suggested the RDL was doing this for religious reasons, or even that they were performing terrorist acts for the sake of terror. No, there was more to it than that—much more—and the Stony Man soldiers quickly surmised that the activities and operations they had witnessed today were cold, calculated and designed to meet a number of specific objectives.

Within a half hour of their arrival back at Roman's observation post, McCarter received a phone call from Stony Man. It was Aaron Kurtzman, and the bubbly tone in his normally deep, bass voice seemed almost uncharacteristic.

"I have excellent news," Kurtzman reported. "Carmen's facial recognition software paid off. We identified one of the men that were observed traveling to Spain. We've got a name and some known connections. I think this is going to make things easier for you over there."

"Easier will depend on which one of them you identified, Bear," McCarter replied.

"What do you mean?"

McCarter sighed. "Well, the contact you gave us managed to find them, but we were only able to take one alive. The other bought it when our probe went bloody hard."

"I have a feeling that whatever happened, Barb and Hal aren't going to like it."

"Don't ask, don't tell, mate."

"I won't. Anyway, the one we identified was the shorter of the two."

"Well, that's good news, then, because I believe that's the one we've got," McCarter replied.

"Okay, here's the long-and-short of it. The guy's name is Poldi Vajda, a third-generation Hungarian Jew. His grandparents escaped the Holocaust with his father, fled to Switzerland. His father met a Swedish woman there who also happened to be Jewish, and they returned to Hungary by way of Poland about ten years after the war ended. Eventually they moved to Israel and settled in Jerusalem. This guy was actually born there, so he's considered an Israeli citizen."

"That's a touching story, Bear, but how does it help us?"

"I was just getting to that. It seems Vajda's parents were killed by a PLO attack in the late eighties, so he quit his job and decided to follow the growing Kach-Kahane Chai movement."

"I thought we'd ruled them out as a possibility," McCarter cut in.

"We have," Kurtzman said. "Or at least we had until we found out that the RDL is actually an offshoot. Reports from intelligence offices within the Israeli Defense Forces indicate that the RDL was actually started by an American."

"Who?"

"That's the part we don't know, but every one of Barb's contacts at the NSA with their finger on the pulse of the political environment in Israel says there may be some significant validity to the claim. Some time back, Striker worked a mission in support of a Mossad agent when the Kach-Kahane Chai tried to steal encryption computer chips from Fort Carson. We're trying to reach her now."

McCarter nodded at the mention of Mack Bolan and the insurgence of Kach-Kahane Chai. Bolan still filed after-action intelligence briefs that allowed Kurtzman and the team to keep Stony Man up to speed on his missions. While the Executioner called the shots on a mission, even when at Brognola's request, it was his practice to provide them with information so that if they needed a friend or two down the line and they couldn't reach him, they could move forward. It was just a fine example of the kind of leadership and professionalism demonstrated by Mack Bolan, and McCarter respected and admired the hell out of the big guy.

"All right, mate, we'll work the angles on this end. Have you heard anything else from Able Team?"

Kurtzman let out a grunt. "They hit someplace in Upstate New York and managed to capture a second member from the RDL's local recruits. They also neutralized a large part of the group during the hit, but we still believe there are a couple out there running around. We think they have plans to strike in another large city, but we don't know which one yet. I've got Carmen and Akira working on it now, but their plans called for cities all over the country."

"You'll figure it out," McCarter said. "We'll see what we can drag out of this bugger here. I know Calvin's got his bag of tricks with him, so I don't think it will take us long to get answers. We'll be in touch when we know more."

McCarter disconnected the call on the cellular linkup that sent coded digital voice signals directly to Stony Man via encrypted satellite transmissions. He returned to his team and found them now all focused, watching their prisoner with interest. The Briton got close enough to see James seated next to Vajda. A tourniquet encircled the terrorist's right arm.

"I think you'll find him much more cooperative now," James told McCarter.

The Briton nodded and said to Vajda, "All right, bloke. Let's start from the top."

CHAPTER TEN

Stony Man Farm, Virginia

The information Kissinger had transmitted to Stony Man was thus far staggering in its content and detail.

Harold Brognola had to admit that he was a bit surprised at how much the Stony Man group hadn't known about the Stormalite Systems weaponry before deciding to send Kissinger and Phoenix Force to the DSTO conference posing as a security detail. The Department of Defense, in cooperation with DARPA and the NSA, had managed to keep much of their activities with Stormalite classified, even from Stony Man's intelligence sources. That had Brognola a bit peeved at the Oval Office, but he knew there wasn't really much he could do about it. He understood that the President had to make calls of this nature, at times, and that was just the hard reality of the job.

Still, Brognola told the Man he didn't agree with it and it was now time to discuss the details. Often, the

Stony Man chief got his information through secure electronic communication channels or sent by courier, but in this case Brognola had decided to ask for a face-to-face meet. This time it was at Camp David.

"I'm sorry, sir," Brognola said in reply to what the President had just told him, "and I mean no disrespect. But I still cannot agree with your decision on this situation. Not entirely, anyway. My people should have been told about these weapons beforehand, so at least they knew what they were walking into."

"Hal, we didn't know what they were walking into," the Man replied. "I can understand if you're frustrated about not having more technical information. That was certainly someone's oversight, and you can be assured I'll deal with that. Frankly, I knew quite a bit about this program, but I'll admit I wasn't entirely aware of the implications of such weapons in the hands of a terrorist organization. In fact, that's usually what I ask you and the Stony Man program to keep up on, so I guess in a way this is my own failing."

"I understand, Mr. President," Brognola replied.

There was a long uncomfortable silence before the President said, "Give me a rundown on this situation to date."

Brognola sighed before replying. "Well, our weapons expert is working with Rear Admiral Remar down at the NAS Key West. He's informed me of some options we might have, but since we had no authorization from your office to contact Stormalite Systems on this, we've held back."

"You have it," the President said with a quick nod. "What else?"

"Able Team is headed back to the Farm as we speak," Brognola replied. "They hit a terrorist hideaway in Upstate New York, which as I'm sure you're already aware was the facility from which one of their teams struck in NYC."

"I believe they captured a couple of these terrorists," the President interjected. "Women, as I understand it?"

"Yes, sir," Brognola said. "One was cooperative, but the other's refusing to talk. Able Team's bringing all of the intelligence with them on their return and our cybernetics team will go to work on it immediately."

"So we don't know anything from this information yet?"

"It was fairly cryptic," Brognola said easily. "We did determine that the terrorists had planned similar strikes in Los Angeles, Salt Lake City, Chicago and Miami. Two of the leaders from this cell are confirmed as missing, status unknown. We believe they could be headed for one of these other cities to carry out whatever orders they may have. The alternative is they were the point crew, which, given additional intelligence, could mean that we might expect some more insurgents coming into our country before it's over."

"It sounds like what you're lacking most is intelligence," the President replied. "Unfortunately some of this may be my fault. I certainly haven't given you the support on this that you either need or deserve, Hal."

"It's not a problem, sir."

The President smiled, slightly, and said, "I appreciate that, but it *is* a problem, and one I intend to rectify immediately. What can I do to help?"

"Not much for the moment, I'm afraid, sir. However, I am confident we'll find out soon enough what's happening and which city these terrorists are headed for. Once we know that, then we may need the weight of the Oval Office to remain unmolested by local agencies. On the international front, the larger problem seems to be in Spain."

"Spain?"

Brognola nodded. "We tracked a couple of the terrorists involved in the theft of the prototypes to Madrid. We're not sure yet what they're doing there, but Phoenix Force managed to take one of them alive. The other was killed in a probe that went south."

"So Phoenix Force is active in Madrid right now?"

"Yes, sir, and I wanted to let you know sooner but—"

"But what, Hal?" he cut in. "I try to give you as much liberty as I possibly can, and in general I stay out of the details of your operations because you get results. I also give you some latitude when it comes to that lone wolf out there. But putting Phoenix Force into the middle of a city we all know is a hotbed of terrorism, and in a country with which the United States already has strained relations, is pushing the envelope just a bit, don't you think?"

Brognola cleared his throat before replying. "I'm sorry, sir, but I was acting in response to an emergency. After all, you *did* order me to find those prototypes and get them back. And with all due respect, I think it's incumbent on me to remind you that we almost lost one of our men in that attack. Terrorists with enough resolve to nearly bring down Phoenix Force are a force to be reckoned with. I knew our response had to be swift and direct."

"And you felt there was no other recourse?"

"I did, sir, and I still do, and I stand behind my decision."

"Fair enough," the President said, appearing to have calmed some. "I'm sorry. It's been a long week and I'm just touchy."

"I understand."

"Please continue."

"Yes, sir," Brognola said. "Well, as I was telling you, we've got a situation in Spain. My people are concerned that we could have a lot more trouble on our hands than we first suspected, particularly if the RDL plans to conduct operations on more than one front."

"What do you mean?"

From the sudden change in the Man's expression, Brognola was concerned that maybe he'd said too much too soon. They didn't have any evidence to suggest the RDL was a large organization, or that they planned to move in a large-scale way. Still, the weapons now in their possession could wreak wide-area havoc and destruction, and they had to be ready for that. It seemed that the RDL wanted to start civil unrest between the Jewish and Arabic population; hell, that much was obvious. But what they planned to do with the Stormalite weapons was still a mystery.

"I guess our biggest concern is not what we know,

but what we don't know. These weapons could be produced to become weapons of mass destruction. In the wrong hands, they could be devastating."

"Is the situation that serious?"

"I think so. John Kissinger and Rear Admiral Remar think so," Brognola replied. "And Phoenix Force and Able Team certainly think so."

The President sighed, stood, shoved his hands into his pockets and turned to look out the large window of his office onto the mountainous terrain surrounding Camp David. Finally, he turned and looked Brognola in the eye.

"Hal, I want you to stop this. I want you to do whatever it takes. Never mind that this Administration has already taken more heat than it could handle in the backlash of the last presidency, but what we don't need is a wide-scale war of ethnicity right here on American soil. And particularly not from two groups that already feel it's nothing more than a holy war. They consider the ends will justify the means."

"I totally agree, sir."

"Then I'd say you've got work to do."

Brognola rose. "Then if there's nothing else—"

The President stepped forward and offered his hand immediately. "Of course. You have work to do, and I should let you get to it."

"And we can count on your full cooperation and buy-in on this mission?"

The President nodded. "Whatever you need, Hal, you have my full support. Just put these maniacs down and do it quickly. They're still trying to suppress some riots and racial crimes in New York. We can ill afford any trouble of a similar nature in another large city."

Brognola nodded. "We'll find them and stop them, sir. Thank you, Mr. President."

Boca Chica, Florida Keys

JOHN KISSINGER DIDN'T know exactly what to expect when he squeezed the trigger of the SS-925 for the first time, but it certainly wasn't the easy recoil or the seemingly nonexistent report. The weapon was whisper-quiet, only because it did not have a gas-operated blowback. Instead, the gas was recycled in such a way that it was dispelled by ignition of the next charge in line, a charge that was electronically kicked off. When the report did finally sound, it was loud, but at that point it didn't matter since the paper target, reinforced by cardboard, resins and a sheet of particle board, had been all but decimated."

"God Almighty," Kissinger whispered as he removed his gun muffs.

"Impressive. Yes?" Remar asked.

"Yeah, I'll say. We got to see the heavier weapons, and I was impressed by those. We hadn't actually gotten to the handhelds when the terrorists struck. I'll be damned."

"Yes, that was pretty much our assessment, as well," Remar said. "At least, that's what our defense procurement people said when they saw a very similar demonstration."

Kissinger stared at the weapon in his hand with disbelief. "Lightweight, portable and able to discharge two-hundred, fifty thousand rounds per minute is what anyone would call the perfect weapon, at least in the pistol group."

"Autopistol group," Remar reminded him. "And its performance trials for SMG and AR were equally impressive. Those were demonstrated at a half-million rounds and one million rounds respectively."

Kissinger couldn't believe it. Even a weapons smith of his experience couldn't help being impressed. Having now fired this weapon alone, it told him that the situation would be precarious if Phoenix Force were to go against RDL terrorists—or any terrorists for that matter—carrying this kind of firepower. They'd be outmatched and outgunned without question. Even such skilled soldiers as they were, they would be up against insurmountable odds.

"If the terrorists are carrying these weapons during any encounter, our people wouldn't stand a snowball's chance in hell," Kissinger finally said.

"I would have to agree," Remar replied.

Kissinger set down the weapon and walked toward the range master's station. After a quick scan with a handheld device by the cadre, and declaring he had no brass and no ammo, they cleared him from the range. Paxton waited patiently in the staff vehicle. When they were securely inside, he drove them toward Kissinger's billets, which Remar had told him were on the other side of the station. Needless to say, the guest quarters weren't conveniently located.

"I would have found a way to get you closer,"

Remar said by way of apology, "if I'd been given a bit more notice about your arrival."

"It's okay, Admiral," Kissinger said, showing his host a congenial smile. "You've done more than enough. I don't know if my people have said it, but we certainly appreciate your cooperation in this."

"Oh, the pleasure's all mine. Like I said, Hal and I go way back. I'm ashamed to admit it, but I owe the guy a favor or two and he's never collected until now. Not that I don't see it as my duty, but I've had a lot of government guys throw their weight around in similar circumstances. Not Hal, though, that's just not his style. He's been a good guy about the whole thing, and a real gentleman."

"Thought maybe you'd skated on owing him that favor, huh?"

Remar returned Kissinger's jibe with a wink and said, "I was hoping. Truth be told, I'd forgotten all about it until Hal called me. Hadn't heard from the guy in ages, then all of a sudden, bang, he calls and I jump."

"I can understand that," Kissinger replied, unable to not be empathetic toward Remar's plight. Brognola was a hard man to say no to.

They rode the rest of the way in silence and Kissinger realized how tired he was. He caught himself nodding off twice and once even woke himself and realized he was dozing. He watched Remar for an expression, but the guy was looking out the window. He was probably tired himself. They'd had a full day and Kissinger still had a lot of information to review: three volumes of records, copies of procurement contracts and the like. He'd already sent copies of the information to Stony Man for analysis, so he was primarily focusing on the technical aspects of the weaponry.

When they arrived at the guest billets, Kissinger shook Remar's hand and then exited the vehicle. Before closing the door, he leaned and put his head inside. "Admiral, do you think there's any chance that perhaps our people could get their hands on some of those prototypes?"

Remar shrugged. "We couldn't give up the ones we have, because they're loaners."

That puzzled Kissinger. "Who loaned them to you?"

"Stormalite Systems," Remar replied matter-of-factly. "We don't own the things yet, Jones. The only part DARPA and the DOD have played in this is financing the additional research. Until we have a fully tested and workable product, there's no way we can expect to use these in any present military applications. Because of that, part of the agreement we had with Stormalite was that they held on to the patents until we agreed to purchase the products. Any profit from sales to other companies would go in their pockets."

"Minus the cut to our people, of course," Kissinger said, nodding his head.

"It's all perfectly legal," Remar said.

Kissinger nodded, although he didn't really care about that. The dealings between U.S. government agencies and foreign companies were of little concern to Stony Man unless it threatened U.S. security, or the President of the United States made it their concern.

Outside of that, Stony Man didn't get involved in such dealings, although it was probable that Aaron Kurtzman's truly remarkable database would have scraps of every bit of processed information regarding the transaction, less what had stayed out of any electronic storage medium. It sounded like that entailed quite a bit.

"Can we talk more about this tomorrow?" Kissinger said over a yawn.

"You bet. Get some rest, son."

Kissinger nodded, closed the door and turned toward his billet. He reached the door to the single-story, duplex quarters with its brick facade and shingled roof, which looked just like every other duplex with a brick facade and shingled roof on the block. Nope, still nothing extraordinary about the quarters. Paxton had arranged for getting Kissinger's bags inside earlier, so it was just a matter of unlocking the door.

Kissinger stepped inside, secured the door behind him with dead bolt and chain, dropped the keys on the table and went to the refrigerator. He opened the door to find only a pitcher of ice water and a few packets of Navy-issue coffee. Great. He was about to close the door when he heard a rattle—the sound of bottles clinking together—and turned to see six Lone Star beers on the door.

Grinning, he snatched one. Well, wasn't that just dandy? He'd have to remember to thank Paxton, or whoever the hell had arranged it, because he'd really had a taste for something to drink. Not a heavy drinker by any means, the Cowboy enjoyed a cold one or two, just like anyone else. He popped the cap, took a long pull, then smacked his lips with satisfaction. That was damn good—

Suddenly his throat was closed off and his lungs began to burn for sudden lack of oxygen. He stepped forward, trying to get two fingers inside whatever the attacker was using as a garrote. Kissinger knew he was dealing with a pro as soon as he realized there was no opening. His opponent had what felt like thick, heavy strands of twine twisted tightly so that the knot pinched the back of his neck. It wouldn't take long for Kissinger to lose consciousness at this rate.

The Stony Man weapons expert was hardly trained in the deadly art of hand-to-hand combat like his warrior friends. Still, he'd spent enough time with the DEA and CIA as an operational agent to know when it was a "kill or be killed" scenario, and this was sure as hell one of those.

He turned sideways enough to get within reach of a kitchen drawer. His opponent was trying to pull back on him, but the weapons smith realized almost immediately he outweighed his attacker and probably had him easily by two inches in height. He used that to his advantage, getting close enough to pull the kitchen drawer open as he reached back to splash beer in the enemy's face. The guy's grip loosened just enough for Kissinger to suck in a breath and then use that for one more extended burst of energy.

In a desperate move, Kissinger managed to dislodge one of the forks from the silverware drawer he'd opened to jab the sharp prongs into his attacker's thigh as he pushed backward suddenly and ran the would-be strangler toward the nearest wall. The man let out a grunt of pain. The maneuver distracted him enough to cause him to loosen his grip, and enough pain that he lost control of the garrote, but it wasn't enough to take him out of action. The next move was, though.

Kissinger pivoted left, driving an elbow strike to the man's ribs, then pivoted right and smashed his opponent's nose with the other elbow. The guy let out a yelp of shock, but it was cut off when the fork was driven into his throat. The man's hands went up to the vibrating fork and even in the dim light his surprised expression was obvious, which may have had something to do with his suddenly white pallor. Kissinger finished it with an uppercut that took the guy off the ground and landed him on his back five feet away.

Kissinger sucked air, panting, chest heaving, his head vibrating with the rattle in his throat. There was a sharp pain every time he inhaled, although he didn't feel any real obstruction. Kissinger headed to go for the phone, but quickly changed his mind and went prone instead at the sound of movement. He hit the ground, pressing himself flat as wood, debris, dust and fabric erupted above where he'd stood a moment before. He spotted his bag at the bedside and crawled toward it. He knew immediately the source of the destruction being unleashed on his quarters; he could hear the ratcheting of the subgun extractor and the low-toned popping sounds of the suppressor.

A tall, shadowy figure loomed suddenly near the foot of the bed, but Kissinger had managed to get in-

side his bag and wrap his fingers around the cold butt
of his SIG-Sauer P-226. He cleared the weapon, rolled
once away from the bed and came up squeezing the
trigger. The shadowy form jerked and twitched with
the impact of the rounds, the few shots he had managed to trigger going high and wide of Kissinger. After
four rounds in the chest, the body collapsed to the carpet with a thump.

And only then could Kissinger let out a sigh of relief.

CHAPTER ELEVEN

Stony Man Farm, Virginia

The men of Able Team could hardly believe their ears when Barbara Price described the action that had occurred in Florida and of Kissinger's near demise. They were gathered around a table in the War Room.

As soon as Lyons heard the news, he turned to Brognola and said, "We need to get down there now."

"That was my first thought, before common sense took hold of me," the big Fed stated. "We still don't know where your missing terrorists plan to hit, and you have to be ready to go at a moment's notice. I can't afford to have you running off to Florida. Murphy's Law says that as soon as I authorize it, the RDL will strike again."

Lyons eyed Brognola with a hard gaze. "We're talking about Cowboy here, Hal."

"I know that," Brognola said. "That why I'm going down there. I'll make sure there are no further incidents and that we get John back here in one piece."

"*You're* going?" Blancanales asked incredulously.

"Marvelous," Lyons added with a snort. "That's all we need, Hal, is you going down there and getting your ass shot off."

"I can still hold my own when I need to, Carl," Brognola admonished.

"That's enough, Carl," Price said. "Hal's made his decision and it's final."

Lyons sat back, folded his arms and remained silent. He didn't like this one bit. Kissinger was lying in some Navy infirmary under the guard of SPs who knew just enough about protection to be dangerous, and now Brognola was getting into it without any measure of security at all. Not to mention that Phoenix Force was in Spain, getting ready to walk into who the hell knew what. And where did that leave Able Team? Sitting on their sorry asses and waiting for the terrorists to make a move.

"Hal, I have to agree with Carl here," Blancanales said in his well-practiced way. "I don't see you going down there as a viable option. We're not suggesting you can't take care of yourself. We're just saying that we think it's best you reconsider letting us handle this."

"I appreciate the sentiment, but—"

"Excuse me, Hal, but I also agree with Ironman," Schwarz said. "First of all, you may be a seasoned field operative, but you're not a practiced one. Second, experience tells me where there's two terrorists, there are bound to be a hell of a lot more. Most important, you don't have the first clue what you're walking into. You can't honestly expect the Navy's people to be able to protect you."

"And who's going to watch your ass while you're watching Cowboy's?" Lyons said, no longer able to keep quiet. "This makes no sense, Hal. None. And I protest the entire line of reasoning here as dumb. Now send us down there and let us do our job."

Brognola searched each of their faces for a long moment.

Blancanales finally showed the Stony Man chief a cheesy smile and said, "Pretty please?"

Brognola sighed deeply. "All right, I give up. You win. I guess it didn't make much sense after all. I'm just concerned with this entire situation and the way it's panned out so far. It's not looking good. For the past forty-eight hours we've been in reactionary mode, and I don't ever like being there."

"None of us does, Hal," Price said quietly. She looked at each member of Able Team in turn as she continued. "There were two men who attacked Cowboy. One of them is dead and the other's at the NAS Medical Center at Key West in critical but stable condition. They think he may live, although he took two slugs to the chest. As soon as you're done here, get down there and find out what you can."

"Understood," Blancanales said as the other two nodded.

"All right, here's what we have to date on our intelligence. Cowboy was sent to Florida to gather as much information as possible on these weapons, and to see if he could arrange getting Phoenix Force some support in Madrid. We don't yet know what the RDL plans to do with the prototypes, but what we've learned about these weapons gives us cause for major concern."

"How so?" Gadgets asked.

"Well, this may make more sense to you than anyone here, Gadgets. The propellant for the ammunition in these weapons is ignited using solid-state electronics, which is why they have such a high cyclic rate of fire. Additionally, because of the electronics, any of these weapons can be remotely triggered by means of both wired and wireless networks."

Schwarz nodded. "Yeah, I had a little chat with Aaron about that when we first got in. He told me any series of carefully programmed networking protocols could set these things off, which not only puts users far from the action, but it also makes them unstable as hell."

"Why's that?" Lyons asked.

"Any weapon with an electronic trigger is subject to all of the same glitches as any other device of its kind. The chips used by Stormalite are your everyday, run-of-the-mill processors, just like you'd find in almost any personal computer. They're multithreaded, programmable, and contain upward of one-and-a-half gigabytes of memory. All the RDL's people would have to do is slap in a communications bridge, program the chip and, abracadabra, you have instant networking capability!"

Blancanales looked at Price and asked, "Did the prototypes have any of this inside them when they were stolen?"

"No, fortunately," she replied. "But from what I understand, it wouldn't take much."

"First-year electronics student could handle it," Schwarz said. "Of course, it would take someone a lot more skilled to program the things, but still not much more than child's play. Hell, there are thirteen-year-olds who can set up a wireless network in five minutes with the right equipment and some information from the Internet."

"Which brings us to the real issue," Aaron Kurtzman cut in.

All eyes turned to see the burly computer wizard roll into the room. He'd been working the angles for the past twenty-four hours, foregoing sleep as he supervised around-the-clock efforts of his cybernetics team. Kurtzman's team included Carmen Delahunt, a no-nonsense old-school FBI recruit, Akira Tokaido, a hacker extraordinaire, and Huntington Wethers, a former cybernetics professor.

"There's definitely no question about it," Kurtzman continued. "Not only can these weapons be remotely triggered, but they can do everything Stormalite claims they can, and then some."

"Has what you've discovered given you any clue as to the whereabouts of the terrorists or weapons?" Price asked.

"Oh, we definitely believe they were smuggled into Spain," Kurtzman replied. "In fact, Hunt's convinced that the RDL may have found local talent right there in Madrid to handle the prototypes."

"What do you mean 'handle'?" Lyons asked.

Kurtzman frowned. "Well, up until now we've been primarily concerned with the RDL using these weapons, without really considering the fact that what few they took would hardly be enough to conduct major operations."

"And yet, you've brought back a ton of evidence to suggest they were planning attacks all over the country," Price interjected. "The only way they could do that is by bringing the weapons right here into the States."

"Exactly," Kurtzman agreed.

"So is everyone of the opinion that a lot of the activity going on here could be just a ruse?" Blancanales asked.

"Not necessarily," Price said. "If they can create enough civil unrest, it would shift national attention to internal issues on a large enough scale that defense to outside insurgency would be diminished."

"It seems obvious to me that these weenies already have significant resources working internally. For instance, the cell leaders that escaped knew enough to probably figure we were coming for them. That means they somehow discovered that we took Babbit alive."

"Which can only mean that the terrorists probably smuggled the weapons into Spain and are planning to have engineers replicate them," Brognola concluded. "It makes perfect sense. You said it yourself, Gadgets, that a first-year electronics student could wire these things up for remote triggering. Let's accept the argument for a moment that the scale of any operation they could conduct at present with what little bit of weaponry they have would be minute. Now let's assume that whoever's leading the RDL discovers a way to mass produce the damned things. We could be in for a major disaster."

"Which is all the more reason *we* should get down to Florida and get Cowboy out of there," Lyons insisted.

Brognola nodded. "Get on it."

Madrid, Spain

PHOENIX FORCE HAD its information—thanks to the truth cocktail introduced by Calvin James—and now they planned to act on it. While James and McCarter got the details, Encizo, Hawkins and Manning cleaned the weapons, reloaded and stocked up on grenades. Simultaneously, the trio kept watch on the perimeter of the small house-turned-base-of-operations. They weren't taking any more chances. The RDL terrorists had caught them once with their pants down, and damn near a second time. There wouldn't be a third.

"You're sure you don't want to contact Hal before we go?" Encizo asked McCarter once they had left the house for their hotel. They still needed to pick up the rest of their equipment before leaving town.

"I'll get him from the hotel, mate," McCarter said. "There isn't much to report really. All we have is a name and location."

Yeah, it wasn't much, but it was something. Vajda had resisted the drugs well, but eventually his will was overcome.

As soon as they reached the hotel, McCarter called

Brognola while the others packed the equipment in Roman's van, which he agreed to loan them for the drive to Cartagena.

"Cartagena?" Brognola echoed. "Sounds like a strange place to hide the weapons."

"Not when you consider the intent. The ones they sent here to Madrid were just decoys, although the bloody weapons were supposed to be coming here."

"For what reason?"

"Apparently the engineers the RDL hired have their labs set up here. We were supposed to follow this pair from Aussie, guv, and we fell for it."

"This is one of the most clever groups it's ever been our sorry pleasure to come up against," Brognola replied. "It's a wonder they haven't killed us all."

McCarter sighed. "Well, I've considered the different ways I want to go down, and not one of them included biffing it here in Spain, so we'll just make sure that doesn't happen."

Brognola acknowledged the quip, then explained the situation with Able Team, Kissinger and the findings to that point by Kurtzman and his team.

"I'm sorry to hear about Cowboy, but I'm sure Carl and the boys can take care of business just fine. They'll get it straightened out, Hal. And you were right to let them go in your place."

"I know," Brognola agreed.

"It sounds like Bear was spot-on in what he told me. Not much has changed since I spoke with him last."

"So your plan is to drive to Cartagena?"

"Eventually," McCarter replied. "First, we have a

little remaining business to accomplish here in Madrid. We're planning to follow up on a lead extracted from Vajda. They've got the engineers under heavy guard at some abandoned factory on the outskirts of the city, and as soon as we've dealt with them, we'll head for Cartagena."

"Wouldn't it be faster to let Jack take you there?" Brognola asked.

"I considered the possibility, but he'd have to file a new flight plan, and that would just create more delays. We got it from our CIA contact here that certain of the officials in the higher offices are quick to turn a blind eye to terrorist activities, but they'll jump a bloody mile to put down legitimate operations."

"That's probably fairly sound advice," Brognola replied. "Spain's government, and her people, joined in many of the protest campaigns that ensued when we invaded Iraq. You could probably view it as a form of rebellion."

"I view it as a form of bloody stupidity."

Brognola sighed and said, "Well, either way, you've got full support now. Do whatever you think is necessary, and try to keep casualties to a minimum. And try to remember that many of these guys are going to be scientists, not fighters, and some of them may possess quite a bit of useful information."

"I'll keep it mind," McCarter promised. "We need one other bit of information, though. Is Bear handy?"

"I'm on, David," Kurtzman's voice replied. "Been listening in the entire time."

"Your tip on the American was a good one," Mc-

Carter said. "We asked this Vajda about him and he told us that there leader was a 'former American' who had defected to Israel and renounced his citizenship. He said the man's name was Wallace Davidia. Can you check that name against your files and see what you can tell us about him?"

"We'll do that," Kurtzman replied. "Give me fifteen minutes, then engage your portable system and we'll upload the information from DBSat four, link tunnel seven, with the ID and pass code of the day."

McCarter nodded and replied in the affirmative that he understood. "You guys give our best to Cowboy."

When the Phoenix Force leader disconnected the call, he closed his eyes and laid his head back, wishing he'd been able to sleep better on the flight from Adelaide. There hadn't been a lot of time for any of them to rest up, reviewing intelligence reports and trying to glean every scrap of information they could on the advanced weapons. Up until now, they'd been acting in sort of a hurry-up-and-wait mode, almost as if operating in a vacuum. The capture of Vajda had turned the tables, although it had almost proved too late for Kissinger.

McCarter tried to push from his mind the thought that Cowboy had almost bought the farm. The loss of Yakov Katzenelenbogen still wore on the Briton. He'd spent too many years watching good men fall. Sure, he understood the realities of this cold and brutal business, and he'd learned to accept them right along with his fellow mates. But these were also his friends and brothers in blood, and just because he accepted something didn't bloody well mean he ever had to get used to it.

No, he'd never get used to it.

The sound of T. J. Hawkins's voice intruded on his thoughts. "So what's the plan here, boss?"

"Well, with the information Vajda provided, I think it's safe to say these buggers are through," McCarter said.

"Uh-oh," Encizo interjected. "Sounds like we got a cocky Cockney on our hands."

"You know it, mate," McCarter said. "I'm bloody well tired of sitting on my arse while we wait for the RDL to make their move. It's time for some action."

"You call what happened in Almagro sitting on our asses?" James asked. "Sheee-it, I'd hate to see what you think real action is."

"I think our British friend is just getting too old for this," Hawkins cracked.

"Up all of your bloody arses," McCarter said tiredly.

Everyone in the group broke out in laughter, but the moment soon passed and they got down to the business. The warehouse where Vajda said they were waiting for the weapons was in the factory district of Azuqueca, which was on the northeast side of the city. Vajda hadn't known the exact numbers, but he'd indicated resistance would be high. Phoenix Force was counting on that. The more of the terrorists they could bring down in remote locations like Azuqueca, the better off they were, since it would reduce the chances of civilian casualties to bare minimums. Brognola had been quite clear about that, if nothing else. He didn't want a huge body count that the President or U.S. ambassador to Spain would have to explain to the local government, and McCarter couldn't blame him. The Stony Man chief had enough problems on his hands with someone almost offing Kissinger without having to worry about Phoenix Force causing an international incident.

"It will have to be a quick hit, mates," McCarter told them. "We'll do a fast recon of the area when we arrive, and then decide the best way inside from there. We hit them quick and fast, we'll evacuate the engineers and any other innocents we might find, and then we're gone again."

"What are your plans for Cartagena?" Manning asked as he turned off the highway onto a road that would take them into Azuqueca.

"Haven't actually decided that yet," McCarter replied.

"News is sure to travel fast about our activities here to those waiting in Cartagena," Encizo reminded him. "For all we know, they might already have skipped out."

"That part did occur to me," McCarter said. "I'm counting on good fortune here and little else. We can't spend a lot more time on this before we're going to have to produce results. Hal told me the Man's behind us totally now, and he's advised Stony Man to do whatever's necessary to put these RDL blokes down for good."

Nobody said another word for the remainder of the

fifteen minutes it took to reach Azuqueca. McCarter checked his watch and realized it was still a few hours to dawn. There was no time for planning and strategy. Besides, the chances the terrorists were expecting them were slim, unless someone had managed to get word to them about the fight in Almagro. McCarter sincerely doubted it. The only one who had walked away alive from that was Vajda, and he was safely hidden away in custody of the CIA. Eventually they'd transport him to the United States, and he'd be tried for his crimes against the American people.

As they arrived at the road that Roman's people had told them led to the factory, McCarter produced what Carmen Delahunt had named "Labrador" from the breast pocket of his fatigues. Their newest toy—its namesake a reference to the way it "retrieved" information—was the equivalent of a small, handheld device with a liquid crystal display and an ASCII-based keypad. The unit was capable of receiving encrypted text or numerical data through a satellite linkup, but security was a problem because of the open-ended communication channels. Stony Man's cybernetics team was able to provide some security by using a programming algorithm to scramble the text-based ASCII files, convert them to UTF-16 encoding form and then transmit via a secure shell—SSH—protocol. However, the communication channel was only one-way, so they couldn't send information back through the device except when they plugged it into a wired network.

McCarter unlocked the keypad and then entered

the encryption codes that would link him to Database Satellite 4. Once the communication path was established along the open SSH tunnel via link tunnel seven, McCarter entered his user name and pass code, and a minute later he was receiving the information. The file didn't take long, even for a wireless connection, because it was being transmitted in Unicode 16-bit form, which provided an equal balance of transmission speed with storage concerns. In less than a minute McCarter severed the connection. The blue-white light of the display was almost bothersome to his tired eyes as he began to read about the man they knew only as Wallace Davidia.

CHAPTER TWELVE

Cartagena

Boaz Rasham strode through the massive warehouse with a purposeful stride. His mission: find Wallace Davidia as quickly as possible.

He'd told his friend before they had ever begun the mission that he had a bad feeling about these plans, and now the true horror was coming to fruition. Nearly twenty of their people were dead, which was almost half the total force in Madrid, a force that was vital to the success of their operations. Only a dozen were here to guard the convoy to Madrid, including Wallace and himself. The rest of their forces were awaiting instructions in Chicago and the West Bank village of Arabeh, just east of the city of Jenin. The vast majority of their efforts would take place in these areas, provided there were no further incidents.

In some ways, Rasham couldn't help his feelings of sadness and disgust. He didn't want to begrudge his friend and brother of accomplishing his goals, but not every goal was worth this kind of sacrifice. How Wallace had ever hoped to keep things together was beyond Rasham's comprehension. At first, he'd trusted Davidia's judgment, but now it seemed his friend and colleague was getting sloppy. How could they maintain their vigil? And how much longer could their men and women hold out against these unknown forces?

Rasham finally found Davidia standing near a truck, smoking a cigarette and supervising as the last of the weapons were loaded into the back of the old panel truck. In fact, it was so old that the thing creaked and rocked under the weight of the men as they loaded the last weapon. They had decided to leave the cargo packed inside the ATVs. There wasn't much chance they would be stopped by Spanish authorities, but Davidia wasn't willing to take the chance, and Rasham had happily agreed.

"What is it, Boaz?" Davidia said. The stress was evident in his voice. "Are you ill?"

"I'm afraid I have bad news, Wallace."

Davidia stood fully erect and shook his shoulders ever so perceptibly. "What is it?"

"An unknown force attacked our people in Madrid that you placed there to assure that anyone who followed the trail of our decoys was eliminated. Your plan failed."

"Have they discovered the warehouse?"

Rasham shook his head.

"Then the plan didn't fail," Davidia replied, letting out a deep sigh. Obviously he seemed unaffected—even relieved—at Rasham's news.

Rasham was seething now. "The plan didn't fail? How can you say that? Sixteen of our people are dead, and one of them is missing. I understand from what I've been told that the missing person is Poldi Vajda. If they've taken him into custody, he will eventually break."

"Bullshit! Both of our decoys were well trained in resisting almost any interrogation technique, and it's a violation of Spanish law for officials to utilize chemicals in questioning suspects. Not that they would question him anyway. Why do you think I chose this country to conduct our preparatory operations in? This government seems very willing to look the other way when it comes to men of our persuasions."

"What makes you believe that it's the police who will question Poldi?"

"You don't even know if it is Poldi Vajda, and even if it were, he would never betray our cause." Davidia shook his head and continued, "He wouldn't betray us in a million years."

"Not consciously, no," Rasham agreed. "But we have no way of knowing into whose hands he's fallen and what might become of him."

"What's your point, Boaz?"

"I've repeatedly warned you that this kind of thing might happen, and now it has. We're up against a much more clever enemy than either of us had originally thought about, and that means we're vulnerable now. You should cancel this mission and wait until the odds are better."

"I will not do that."

"You will cost us dearly if you don't reconsider this," Rasham insisted.

"I have considered it, and I have listened to your incessant protests, and I have decided we shall continue on mission. Don't you see it, my friend? Whoever's behind this attack is hoping that we'll give up, that we'll retreat like rats and come out fighting another day when the risks aren't so many and the stakes so high. And now you want to play right into their hands? They'd like nothing better! They want us to give up!"

"Who are 'they,' Wallace? Just who is it that you're fighting here?"

"I'm fighting them all," Davidia replied, beating his chest with his fists for emphasis. "I'm fighting every one of these rat bastards who represent part of the element that places a foul stench on the entirety of the human race. These Arabs have never amounted to anything, and I don't think they ever will. From the moment that their first ancestors were put on this planet, God's been telling us to wipe them out. And up until this point we have failed in that mission. Well, I'm not going to fail! Do you hear me? I'm not going to fail God, and neither are you!"

Davidia took the cup of coffee that someone had just handed to him and tossed it away. The foam cup struck the wall, splattering coffee everywhere. Steam immediately rolled from the hot liquid as it ran down the wall. "The Arabs are like the steam off dog shit, Boaz. It is a naturally occurring process, but it's offensive all the same. When I was a cop in America, we used to write citations for people who let their dogs shit on the sidewalk and didn't bother to clean it up.

And do you know why we did that? Was it because we didn't have anything better to do?"

Rasham shook his head and shrugged, even though he'd heard this lesson a thousand times. When Davidia was in this kind of mood, it was just better to placate him. It wasn't that he didn't respect his friend's wisdom. Davidia was a leader, scholar and brother of the Resurrected Defense League, and he always would be. But like many brilliant leaders, he had an edge of insanity. It was one of those edges that would cause someone within their own organization to assassinate Davidia. Of course, he wouldn't do it, but someone would. And while everyone would mourn the passing, Rasham knew that many—him included—would breathe a sigh of relief, as well.

"We would write these people up because what they were allowing was for animals to perform acts that would take away from the beauty of their own neighborhoods. And that's what we've allowed to occur all over the world. That's our true crime. That's when I get down on my knees every night and pray for forgiveness, Boaz. I don't want to be found guilty on the day of the White Throne Judgment. I want God Almighty to know that we have done what He set us here to do and that we will not fail Him again. So no, Boaz, we will *not* give in and we will not surrender, no matter what. Do you understand?"

"No, I've never understood this," Rasham pressed. "I've just about had enough. You talk of God and accomplishing His mission, but you do it with the blood of your own people. Or maybe they're not your people. Maybe you're just using them to settle your own vendettas!"

The warehouse suddenly resounded with the echo of the slap, but it came so fast that it didn't even seem to Rasham that Davidia had moved. He was suddenly infuriated when he realized that Davidia had struck him, and he couldn't really feel any pain from the slap because his face was heated by all of the blood suddenly rushing to it. Rasham let out a howl of rage and charged Davidia.

The ex-cop was no stranger to sudden attack, not to mention the fact that he had ten years and the better of fifty pounds on Rasham. But Rasham was a former member of an Israeli Special Forces guerrilla warfare unit at Elyakim army base, well trained in the Israeli fighting art of Krav Maga, and he could hold his own against most. He meant to insure that Davidia took a good beating for what he'd done.

Davidia sidestepped the charge and tried a simple trip, but Rasham leaped over Davidia's extended foot and then crouched and delivered a leg sweep. The blow sent Davidia off balance and Rasham was on him the moment he hit the ground. The Israeli tried for a solid punch to the forehead, but his knuckles cracked on the concrete floor instead as Davidia twisted and moved his head to avoid the punch. Rasham ignored the pain, just as he'd been taught, and tried to deliver a low shot to the sternum. If done with a certain intent, it would kill a man, but Rasham only desired to knock the wind out of Davidia.

It didn't work. The American was ready for the trick and immediately deflected the punch. Suddenly the tables were turned. Davidia threw his hips forward, bucking Rasham away like a rodeo horse would toss a rider. Rasham wasn't completely taken off guard, but he was thrown forward enough to give his opponent the edge he needed. Davidia landed an elbow strike on Rasham's chest, forcing the air from his lungs, very similarly to what Rasham had just tried to do to him. Rasham's lungs burned with the sudden exertion and he couldn't regain his breath because a vise-like hand was suddenly clamped over his mouth.

Davidia twisted Rasham's face away and drove a rock-hard punch to the Israeli's neck. The blow sent a shooting pain down Rasham's shoulder and he began to see stars as his lungs starved for oxygen. The pain was almost too intense, but he pushed it from his mind. He couldn't let Davidia overwhelm him. Not in the view of all of his colleagues. He would lose his self-respect and the respect of his men.

Rasham went for the extreme measure, delivering a sudden and sharp blow to Davidia's groin. The man let out a grunt followed by a surprised yelp, and his grip loosened on Rasham's face. The former Israeli commando knew an opening when saw one. He twisted from Davidia's grip and rolled away. He came to one knee, gasping for breath as Davidia groaned, holding his testicles with one hand while he climbed slowly and agonizingly to his feet.

Panting and keeping his eyes on Davidia, Rasham stood, as well. The two men faced off with each other. Rasham's arm was limp and he was nursing his shoulder, trying to rub some feeling back into the extremity, which had been neutralized quite effectively by the shot Davidia had given to the nerve in his neck.

Simultaneously, Davidia was panting and protecting his groin, staring daggers back at Rasham. It was the first time the two had ever come to blows outside of training, but Rasham didn't care. Davidia might have been the elected leader of the group, but the men and women of the RDL still secretly looked to Rasham for day-to-day leadership. While Davidia had spent much of his time learning philosophy under Rabbi Meir Kahane's distant relatives and most devote followers, Rasham had been preparing his people for this day. They respected him and they believed in him, and that was something he wouldn't let anyone take away from him—not even Wallace Davidia.

"This…is…" Rasham said between deep breaths, "…no longer about…your self-proclaimed mission… from God. This is about…honor and integrity and loyalty. We owe this to the people we lead, Wallace."

Davidia studied Rasham with his dark brown eyes and for just a moment there was a flicker of anger. But then that flicker faded and it was replaced by an expression of dark and mixed emotions. Rasham could tell there was a conflict within his friend, and he'd done all he could to make Davidia realize that this wasn't just about turning the weapons against innocent villagers and promoting bloodshed between two factions who had waged war with each other for millennia. It had become about honor and loyalty to those who were sacrificing themselves for the cause.

"Okay, Boaz," Davidia finally said, still groaning with the trauma to his groin. "You win. We will find out who has done this and we will destroy them. I will go

Get FREE BOOKS and a FREE GIFT when you play the...

LAS VEGAS
GAME

Just scratch off the gold box with a coin. Then check below to see the gifts you get!

YES! I have scratched off the gold box. Please send me my **2 FREE BOOKS** and **gift for which I qualify.** I understand that I am under no obligation to purchase any books as explained on the back of this card.

366 ADL D749

166 ADL D747
(MB-05R)

FIRST NAME	LAST NAME

ADDRESS

APT.#	CITY

STATE/PROV.	ZIP/POSTAL CODE

7	7	7	Worth TWO FREE BOOKS plus a BONUS Mystery Gift!
🍒	🍒	🍒	Worth TWO FREE BOOKS!
🔔	🔔	♣	TRY AGAIN!

Offer limited to one per household and not valid to current Gold Eagle® subscribers. All orders subject to approval.

to Madrid personally and hunt every last one of them down."

Rasham nodded, then came forward and threw his arms around Davidia. The two men embraced each other.

When they parted, a bit awkwardly, Rasham said, "I hope that I did not do permanent damage to your manhood."

"No, my friend," Davidia replied. "It was just the wakeup call I needed."

Madrid

THE WAREHOUSE LOOKED dark and abandoned, which didn't mean that it was. There was a part of McCarter that considered the fact that Phoenix Force might be walking into an elaborate trap, but he dismissed the idea after careful thought. That would have meant not only that Vajda had lied under drug-induced interrogation, but that Roman and his people were in on the game, as well. McCarter couldn't buy that; it was a too farfetched.

McCarter waited patiently for the rest of his fellow warriors to return. He'd sent them in pairs—Manning and Hawkins, James and Encizo—to conduct soft probes of the warehouse and to see if they could find a quiet way inside. They'd had ten minutes and less than two remained. The teams returned right on time and delivered their reports.

Manning and Hawkins had found what sounded like the best way into the warehouse undetected. There were two wide windows, about eight feet apart, on the north side of the warehouse. They were open just slightly but enough to get inside without having to move them. This news surprised McCarter.

"Looks like Gary and T.J. win the prize," James said.

"I don't like it," McCarter replied. "It seems too easy. If these RDL blokes were so paranoid about keeping their weapons engineers under lock and key, they wouldn't have provided such an easy way in."

"That's only the half of it," Manning said.

"How so?" Encizo asked.

"Well, experience tells me that even if it wasn't a trap, we might be better off just hitting this place in blitz mode. We try to go through quietly, and they're waiting for us, it's possible they routed us right where they wanted to."

Hawkins nodded his agreement and added, "Not to mention that we're now all stacked up on each other. It'd be like shooting monkeys in a barrel for the terrorists."

McCarter was silent for a moment, then studied each expectant face in turn before saying, "Would have, should have, could have…we could discuss this all bloody day and it wouldn't make a damn bit of difference. Let's take the opportunity and hope for the best. Good luck, mates."

They nodded at McCarter and then moved into position. They planned to approach one at a time, Hawkins on point, while the rest covered. A pair of wire snips from Manning's belt made short work of the tall, chain-link fence. When they had a large enough egress, Hawkins went through the fence and sprinted as quietly as possible to the window. He kept his back to the wall below it and waited. There were no shouts, no reports of gunfire—nothing. It was damned dead, and McCarter still couldn't shake his suspicions. He just couldn't believe it would be this easy, but so far they hadn't met any resistance. The RDL terrorists were probably in the warehouse, just waiting to nail the coffin shut.

Encizo was next, followed by McCarter and James, with Manning on rear guard. Phoenix Force reached the wall unscathed and apparently undetected. McCarter counted out three on his fingers and then gestured to window. Hawkins raised the window with the butt of his MP-5 just enough to allow entry, then got to his feet and dived through the opening without even touching the frame.

They continued through the window in the same order as they had approached it. Manning had just finished his entry and they were about to fan out when bright lights suddenly flooded the room. Every member of Phoenix Force froze. McCarter realized they were in some kind of weapons laboratory. It was a vast room with large rectangular workstations throughout it; there were tools and other gunsmith equipment on the tables and benches against the outer walls.

Fortunately, Phoenix Force had avoided immediate detection because the workstations hid them. It was possible they could still utilize the element of surprise if those who had entered the room just now weren't afforded an opportunity to sound an alarm or to shout a warning. McCarter looked at Encizo as the sound of voices echoed in the room. He pointed to his own eyes and then in the direction of the talkers. He then slashed his finger across his throat in a cutting motion, and followed that with a stop signal by displaying the palm of his hand.

Encizo nodded. The instructions were clear: establish position but don't take the enemy just yet. The Cuban's skills with a variety of knives made him the perfect takedown man when Phoenix Force needed somebody neutralized quickly and quietly.

The Cuban moved forward on hands and knees until he reached a vantage point with which he was comfortable. McCarter could tell that the voices weren't getting any closer, but they weren't going away, either. The entire team watched Encizo quietly, but the apprehension was obvious in everyone's expressions. The Cuban began to communicate using hand signals, reporting: four terrorists, two male, two female, well armed. He then pinched his nose and scowled, and McCarter knew exactly what that meant: they had stepped into the room to smoke.

But why in here, where there were likely all kinds of flammable elements? Okay, so they couldn't go outside because they would give away the fact that the warehouse wasn't abandoned if anyone just happened by at this hour of the morning. And for some reason, wherever they had been, they couldn't smoke. So they'd come in here, where there was probably bullet wax and gunpowder and other propellants and accelerants, and lit up.

They were idiots. Who cared? Either way, Mc-

Carter didn't see any reason to take them out, so he signaled Encizo to hold off and watch only. Five minutes passed, then ten, and the foursome just continued to talk and to laugh through a second round of smokes.

Finally the lights winked out and the sound of a door slamming shut signified that Phoenix Force was alone once again. Every member visibly relaxed. McCarter even heard Hawkins produce a faint sigh.

Encizo crawled quietly back to their position. Keeping his voice low, he said, "Damn, that was close."

"It could have been worse," Manning reminded him.

"Yeah, they could have come in and shot holes in us," James whispered.

"Ditto," Hawkins replied.

"Never mind that," McCarter replied with irritation. "You said there were four, Rafe?"

Encizo nodded. "First females I've seen, though. That was a little surprising."

"Were they cute?" Hawkins asked.

"Pervert," James replied.

"Knock it off," McCarter said, hushing them with a wave. He couldn't blame them, though. They were all tired and a little punchy, but he couldn't let that affect their mission. "Pick some other bloody time to cut up. This isn't it."

"What do you want to do here?" Manning asked, more to probably change the subject than for any other reason.

McCarter scratched his chin. "I find it hard to believe these blokes have only left four behind to guard this group of weapons engineers."

"Did anyone at the Farm have a clue if these engineers were volunteers or prisoners?" James asked.

"Not a frigging clue," McCarter said. "That's why Hal wanted us to be discretionary whichever way we choose to go here."

"Well, I'd have to say assume that they're hostiles until we know otherwise," Encizo said.

"Agreed."

"You know, this looks like the gun lab where they're planning to reproduce the prototypes," Hawkins said.

"That was my assessment, as well," Manning agreed. "You're thinking we could just set some demolitions right here and neutralize the operation without firing a shot."

"That would definitely stop the terrorists from using this place," Hawkins said, casting a hopeful glance in McCarter's direction.

The Briton shook his head. "Sorry, mates, but no dice. We have to make sure that we know the status of those under guard, up or down, before we start blowing shit up."

Manning winked at McCarter and said, "But that doesn't mean it can't be part of the plan."

"Do what you have to," McCarter said with a nod. "We'll take care of the human factor."

With the plan in place, Manning turned to the satchel of tricks he had slung around his shoulder as the rest of Phoenix Force moved single-file toward the door. They reached it without incident. McCarter looked at each of them in turn and said, "As soon as we're through, fan out. We don't know what we can expect on the other side, and I don't want us clustered together if it goes bad. Understood?"

When they had all affirmed his instructions, he said, "Let's do it."

CHAPTER THIRTEEN

Boca Chica, Florida Keys

Lieutenant Commander Paxton greeted the men of Able Team at Runway 07 and immediately offered to drive them to the hospital. After Paxton had shaken hands with each of them in turn, Lyons doing the introductions, he said, "I'm certain Mr. Jones will be glad to see you gentlemen."

"We'd like to see the corpses of the two men who attacked him first, if you don't mind," Lyons replied.

Paxton furrowed his eyebrows and said, "Excuse me?"

"Well, is John going somewhere soon?"

"Well, uh, no, sir, but I just figured—"

"Don't mind him," Blancanales said, stepping in immediately to be the voice of reason. "He's always grumpy when he doesn't get his morning coffee."

"Of course, sir," Paxton said.

As Paxton turned and headed for the staff car with

Able Team in tow, Blancanales threw Lyons a look. The Able Team leader shrugged with a "what did I do?" expression, but Blancanales didn't dignify the situation further.

Lyons was being a jerk, and he knew it. He truly was worried about Kissinger, but he didn't want the guys with the Naval Criminal Investigative Service getting to the forensics people before Able Team had a chance to conduct their own investigation and get a look at any material evidence. They weren't investigators, sure, but their number-one business was terrorism and they knew their business better than the boys at NCIS.

Once they were in the staff vehicle and headed toward the infirmary, Lyons told Paxton, "Sorry about that back there. I'm just a little apprehensive about this situation. My boss doesn't want the Navy fucking up the investigation or forensics screwing up the evidence, and frankly we don't, either."

"That's perfectly understandable, sir," Paxton said. "But I don't think you'll have to worry about it."

"How's that?" Schwarz asked.

"Well, the admiral has quite a bit of pull down here in Key West. More than you might think, as a matter of fact."

"You're talking about Remar?" Lyons said.

Paxton nodded. "Yes, sir. I guess he's a personal friend of your boss, and that means you guys must have some serious pull, because normally the admiral doesn't play the Washington politics."

"Neither do we, son," Blancanales said pointedly. "What can you tell us about this attack?"

"Really not much, sir," Paxton replied, shrugging. "We had just dropped off—that is the admiral and I— had just dropped off Mr. Jones at his quarters and then we headed for the officers' housing. Admiral Remar and I only live a few doors down from each other, so I planned on dropping him off just as usual. Next thing I know, he's calling me to say that someone shot up the place and Jones was bound for the hospital in an ambulance."

"Have you had a look at the attackers?" Lyons asked.

"No, sir, and I can't say as I want to," Paxton replied. "I leave these kinds of things to those best qualified to handle them. I'm not a cop or a medic, and I aim to keep it that way. I saw enough growing up in central Cleveland to last me a lifetime."

"Remind you of somebody we know?" Lyons spared his friends in the back seat a wink and a grin. They nodded their assent and then Lyons asked, "What's the story with the weapons used?"

"Yeah, did you notice anything special about them?" Schwarz added.

"No, sir. Actually, I didn't see them, but you could ask the admiral. He actually went to the billets and took a look before the SPs taped the entire place off."

"And nobody's been in there except him?"

"As far as I know," Paxton replied. "The medics said they found Jones outside, sitting on the porch with a gun in his hand. I guess it took them some time to talk him into surrendering his weapon to the SPs so they could take care of him without the fear of getting their asses shot off."

"And John would have done it, too," Lyons replied.

They arrived at the medical center and Paxton led them to the third floor. Two SPs guarded the door to Kissinger's room and they carefully scrutinized Paxton's identification as well as the Able Team's forged credentials before admitting them. Kissinger was seated upright in bed, a soft brace wrapped around his neck. A short, odd-looking man sat in a chair near his bed, and a quick study of the insignia on his uniform told Lyons it was probably Remar. Kissinger greeted his trio of friends with a mock salute and a contented grin. The expression on his face said it all: he was damn glad to see them.

"Gentlemen, welcome to Key West," the short man said, standing. "My name is Kendall Remar. I've been host to Mr. Jones here the past couple of days, although I don't seem to be doing a very good job."

"Don't sweat it," Lyons replied. "The name's Irons, and these gentlemen are Deputy Marshals Black and Sanchez."

Remar nodded at them, then addressed Lyons directly. "I talked to Brognola a few hours ago. He called ahead and told us to expect you."

"Did he say what—?" Lyons began.

"He didn't say what or why," Remar cut in. "And he told me not to ask a lot of questions, so you don't have to worry about the third degree. Like I told Jones here, I'm sure you're not using your real names, and chances are I wouldn't want to know what they were. Hell, you're probably not even U.S. marshals, but I can pretend with the best of them. I'll probably stay alive longer that way. I'm no hero, men. I'm just an old salt and a patriot, so you don't have to worry about me getting in your way."

"Yeah, Paxton here told us you did a stand-up thing keeping the hounds off this for a little while longer until we could find out the story," Schwarz said. "We appreciate it."

"Nothing I wouldn't do ten times over," Remar said. "These bastards violated my home and damaged someone under my protection. This incident has just pissed me off and steeled my resolve. Whatever you guys need, consider it done. You'll have my cooperation and full cooperation of the United States Navy."

"That's good of you," Lyons said. "But right now what we could use, Admiral, is a little privacy with Jones here. You mind?"

"Not at all," Remar replied, turning and heading for the door. "We'll be in the cafeteria getting some coffee. Let's go, Paxton."

"Aye, sir."

And then they were gone.

Blancanales stepped forward and shook Kissinger's hand, clamping a warm hand on his shoulder. "It's sure good to see you alive, Cowboy."

"Thanks, uh, Deputy."

The men chuckled and then Blancanales headed for the door. "I'll tell our two pals outside to take a break."

Lyons nodded and waited until Blancanales had secured the door tightly behind him, then he pulled the chair Remar had occupied closer to the bed and sat. "You doing okay, Cowboy?"

"I'll be doing better when I can get the hell out of this bed."

Lyons grinned. "We'll have you out of here before the day's through. Hal wants you back in Wonderland ASAP."

"No deal," Kissinger replied, shaking his head.

Schwarz had only been half listening, really, having taken a standing position behind Lyons and looking out the window. Kissinger's retort got his attention and he fixed the Stony Man weapons master with a hard stare. "What do you mean, no deal?"

"Sorry, but there's still a lot of important work to do." Kissinger's voice was beginning to sound froglike, cracking here and there, and occasionally he wheezed between sentences. "Remar's going to get some more of those prototypes from Stormalite Systems, and I'm going to Spain to help train Phoenix Force in using them."

Lyons shook his head emphatically. "No way. Hal will never go for that, Cowboy, I'm telling you straight."

"We could barely get him to let us come down here in his place," Schwarz added.

"I don't really care, guys," Kissinger said. "These weapons aren't anything to be messing around with. Especially if you don't know what the hell you're doing. I've fired the pistol, and I can tell you the thing can deliver a serious shitstorm of firepower. Any of you guys tries to learn using those things on your own and you're asking for trouble."

"We've already got that," Schwarz replied.

"Yeah, and we've been there before," Lyons said. "We can send anybody to help out Phoenix Force."

"They aren't going to need just anybody," Kissinger said, not without a tinge of hostility. "They're going to need *me,* and Hal's just going to have to deal with that."

"Why is this so important?" Lyons asked. "I mean, we got the rundown from the information you sent Bear, and it doesn't sound like this stuff is that difficult to use. I know we've all fired much more powerful weapons and operated high-tech equipment before. Why is this so different?"

"Because it's not just about using these weapons. You also have to know how to defend yourselves against them. That's what I've been trying to tell you." Kissinger let out a dry, wheezy cough and then continued. "There's no way to protect yourselves unless you know what you're up against."

"Well, just what are we up against?" Schwarz asked.

"Hell itself," Kissinger replied.

WHEN ABLE TEAM had finished at the hospital, Paxton took them to the motor pool and signed them out a car under Remar's authorization. The team wanted to visit the NCIS crime lab's armory where the weapons used by the terrorists had been secured. Following that, they planned to talk to the medical examiner. Paxton had indicated no identification was found on either body, which didn't surprise Able Team in the least. Remar had told them that the base was on lockdown and full alert, and that SPs and a detachment of Marine Corps MPs were to be on the lookout for any suspicious vehicles.

"The situation isn't good, Hal," Lyons announced into one of Kurtzman's special phones.

"I think we've already agreed on that point," Brognola replied.

"No, it's much worse than we thought," Lyons said. "Cowboy's okay. Suffered a minor fracture to the larynx, but the doctor said he'd heal up fine if he's not exposed to any more trauma and keeps his mouth shut for a while."

"Fair enough," Brognola replied.

"Only trouble is, he's not planning on doing that," Lyons continued.

"What's that supposed to mean?" Price interjected.

Lyons hadn't known she was listening in on the conversation. "Well, it seems that he's been doing his homework on these weapons. Remar told us less than an hour ago that he planned to talk Stormalite Systems into delivering some additional prototypes to Phoenix Force, all apparently at Kissinger's behest. But Cowboy also told us that he plans on going to Spain to acquaint them with this new firepower."

"Ridiculous," Price said.

"As well as being out of the question," Brognola added.

"That's just about what we told him you'd say, but his mind's made up," Lyons replied. "Frankly, after what he told us today, I'm actually on his side. He told us he was sent here to find out everything he could about these weapons, and as Stony Man's chief technical expert on firearms, he's the most logical choice."

"The only problem is that if the RDL terrorists are on to Kissinger, and he goes back to Spain, they'll be on to Phoenix Force," Price said.

"We may have to take that chance, because David and the crew are about to walk into some major shit," Lyons countered. "We're going to see what we can find out about Cowboy's attackers."

"It might provide us some additional clues," Brognola said.

"Yeah, except that my money's on the fact these are our missing leaders from that cell we hit in New York. I mean, Cowboy did what he had to do, but if these guys were the only remaining link to whatever the RDL has planned here in the States, then they took their secret with them."

"That's it, Carl," Brognola grumbled. "Look on the bright side of things."

"I'm being practical, Hal." There was a long silence before Lyons spoke again. "We'll do our best to see if we can find out what's—"

Lyons never got to finish his statement because glass and heat suddenly rained on him. He ducked in the seat, cursing and dropping the phone so he could retrieve his pistol. He looked up to see Blancanales bleeding from the face. The vehicle was shimmying and vibrating like mad and Lyons could tell that Blancanales was doing everything he could to keep the vehicle under control. It just wasn't enough and he could feel a sense of vertigo as the vehicle slowly tipped onto two wheels and more glass from the driver's-side window filled the interior.

Lyons tucked his chin to his chest and threw his forearm over his head in a measure to protect himself from the flying glass and from cracking his skull on something. Above the noise, he heard Schwarz emit a yelp of pain, and then the noise and racket of metal grinding on pavement took over. Lyons was now close enough—his head in Blancanales's lap practically—to see that Blancanales's knuckles were white. He'd maintained his grip on the steering wheel even though the vehicle was now skidding on its side.

A natural reaction, and Lyons wasn't about to blame the guy.

Miraculously the vehicle scraped and screeched its way to a stop in short order, and it didn't tip completely upside down. It took only a moment for all three of the Able Team warriors to realize that while the vehicle wasn't in motion, it was probably a good idea they get it in gear. There was no mistaking the plinking of bullets against the rear of the vehicle.

"Bail!" Lyons shouted.

They didn't have to hear it twice. Lyons managed to get his head out of Blancanales's thigh in record time, using the A-post on the passenger side to pull himself upright. The door and frame on his side were crumpled, preventing him from opening the door, and although he could have gone through the window, Lyons figured it was better to exit through the windshield the old-fashioned way: forcibly. It took several tries before he'd managed to kick enough of the safety glass out that he could peel it back.

Lyons heard the rounds continue striking their car even as he squeezed through the windshield frame. He reached inside and assisted Blancanales while simultaneously calling Schwarz's name over the din of the weapons reports. When Blancanales was free, the two men hunkered behind the cover of the vehicle, pistols drawn, and looked for any sign of their attackers. Schwarz appeared from practically nowhere and crouched between them.

"What's—?" Lyons began, but his teammate didn't give him the chance.

"I'll tell you later," he said.

"What do you want to do?" Blancanales asked.

"I think they've only seen me," Schwarz said. "Seems like the best plan would be to do a mad dash for better cover and draw their fire."

"Are you smoking dope or something?" Lyons asked through gritted teeth as the bullets ricocheted off the pavement and car or just zinged by over their heads. "You won't get ten feet and they'll cut you down like so much liver."

Schwarz inclined his head. "I could head for those buildings right there. If I make a run for it, there's a good chance they'll think I'm alone and outnumbered."

"Um, hate to break this to you, Gadgets," Blancanales interjected, "but we *are* outnumbered."

"There's nothing saying you've got to wait for me to get there before you two do your thing, boys."

Lyons looked at Blancanales, who just shrugged. The Able Team leader chewed his lower lip a moment and then replied, "All right. I'm doing it against my better judgment, so don't get your ass shot off. We've got enough troubles right now without losing you, too."

Schwarz grinned shyly and said, "Gosh, Carl, I didn't know you cared."

"Move out," Lyons grumbled.

Schwarz double checked the load on his Beretta 93-R, turned the selector to 3-round bursts, and then lurched from the relative safety of the sedan. The chatter of weapons fire, which had dwindled to mostly small bursts or single shots, increased thunderously as soon as Schwarz became visible to the attackers. Blancanales slapped Lyons on the shoulder and the two men left the cover of the vehicle, heading in the other direction.

There were six terrorists in all, lined up in front of a large customized van and holding M-16 assault rifles. One terrorist had discarded a rocket launcher at his feet, and Lyons knew in an instant he was the one who had taken out the car. It was a miracle Blancanales had managed to keep control of the sedan as long as he had. Both Able Team warriors opened up simultaneously with their pistols.

The big .357 Magnum Colt Python Elite bucked and with fury as Lyons took action. They had managed to take Able Team off guard, and Lyons wasn't happy about that at all. The warrior's first two 230-grain rounds took one of the terrorist's in the chest and left plum-size exit wounds. The man staggered against the impact, and only the van stopped him from being knocked immediately to the pavement. His eyes rolled into his head as he slid to the ground and left a gory streak on the shiny silver van.

Blancanales snap-aimed his Glock 19 and squeezed the trigger twice, which delivered a pair of 9 mm skull-busters into a second terrorist. The guy's head exploded as his weapon fell from numbed fingers, and he dropped to his knees slowly before slumping forward. His head, or what was left of it, smacked wetly on the pavement.

Lyons got to one knee and took out two more terrorists. He grazed the arm of the first one, but the distraction was enough that when the terrorist turned to address his wounded arm, the big ex-cop got him through the neck. The man's head tilted oddly on the axis of his spine and then he collapsed right where he stood. The other terrorist was taken out of play when the man's M-16 jammed. Lyons shot him twice in the stomach, shredding the man's intestines, which then pushed visibly through the abdominal wounds. The man let out a shout of agony before he dropped to the pavement.

As Lyons ducked behind the vehicle and drew a speed-loader, Blancanales continued firing at the terrorists.

Schwarz reached the cover of a nearby building and lined up the sights of his Beretta 93-R on the nearest target. The 120-grain full-metal-jacket rounds punched through a terrorist's thigh and hip, shattering bone and dropping him to the pavement.

Schwarz followed up with two more bursts, one directed at the remaining terrorist and the other at movement he detected behind the wheel. Only one of the rounds he shot at terrorists trying to kill Blancanales and Lyons connected, but the driver took all three in the chest and head, spattering the walls and windows with bloody flesh.

Blancanales and Lyons took the last terrorist simultaneously with a sustained dose of heavy fire. The gunner spun, doing a grotesque dance as the two commandos hammered him mercilessly.

An eerie silence ensued in the aftermath of the heated gun battle. The Able Team warriors held their positions for a couple more minutes, willing to wait out any further wave, but after some time Lyons knew they had taken out any remaining opposition. He gave the all-clear signal to Schwarz, then he and Blancanales approached the van and the pile of bodies while Schwarz covered them from a safer distance. Less than a minute passed before they heard distant sirens begin wailing.

Lyons studied the carnage for a moment and then shook his head. Quietly he said, "So much for taking prisoners. These guys aren't pissing around. Do or Die seems to be their motto, and they're going to make damn sure we don't forget it."

Lyons went to the front passenger door and opened it. A few flies had already begun congregating on the nasty, bloody mess left by Schwarz's handiwork.

As he began to search the body, Blancanales grabbed his attention. "Hey, Ironman, you'd better come take a look at this."

Lyons walked to where his partner was standing and looked into the open door of the van. One corner was stacked floorboard-to-ceiling with crates that looked to contain a ton of military supplies, including firearms and grenades. Additionally, there were three long, silver cases and two smaller ones. Blancanales pointed to the cases, and Lyons quickly saw the reason for his teammate's concern. Each of them bore the a label the monogram SSL, and an emblem that looked all too familiar.

"Holy shit," Lyons whispered. "Stormalite Systems, Limited."

"These weapons belong to them. These are prototypes, Ironman."

"But how did they—?" Lyons didn't finish his statement, instead turning to look at the disarray of bodies spread across the pavement. "Wait a minute. These guys were carrying M-16s." He turned back to the van and pointed at the crates. "And those are stamped with U.S. Marine Corps routing instructions and DOD security warnings."

"Which means this is legitimate equipment that was probably either lifted from a Marine armory or heisted right out from under their noses," Blancanales concluded with a sharp nod.

"Yeah, and I'm not buying the latter story. That means someone let these dudes onto this installation and got them this equipment," Lyons replied. "These terrorists are getting support from our own people."

CHAPTER FOURTEEN

Madrid, Spain

Phoenix Force went through the open doorway and immediately fanned out, ready to meet whatever resistance might await them.

The terrorists who had been in the room less than a minute earlier were still visible. They had nearly reached the end of the hall that separated the two halves of the warehouse, and they were going through the entrance when the noise of Phoenix Force's entry caught their attention. The lighting was dim, but it was bright enough that the terrorists could tell these weren't the friends they were expecting from Cartagena.

Rafael Encizo and T. J. Hawkins had gone low, so they were in a better position in the narrow hallway to take the offensive. Encizo's sound-suppressed subgun coughed in response to the terrorist posturing, and a 3-round burst of 9 mm rounds punched through the abdomen of one of the females. The impact spun her into the wall, before she slid to the cheap, cracked linoleum.

Hawkins got one of the males with a single head shot.

McCarter and James pressed themselves against the walls opposite of each other and took the other two out quickly. The Briton's 3-round burst punched through the surviving female's chest, stitching an ugly, bloody pattern across the front of her fatigues. The deadly bullets slammed her against the wall before her body pitched forward to the floor.

James's first shot was a bit wild and caught his target in the knee. The terrorist's weapon clattered to the floor, but as he bent to grab hold of the bloody wound and opened his mouth to scream, James put a second round in the top of his skull. The bullet crushed the brain, traversed the spine and exited from the lower right portion of the guy's back.

McCarter and James held their positions, weapons trained on the door, while Encizo and Hawkins acted on their team leader's signal to advance. When the pair reached the end of the hallway, the little Cuban covered the door while Hawkins frisked the bodies. He gave a quick shake of his head in McCarter's direction upon clearing the terrorists, and then their attention was redirected as the door at the other end of the hallway suddenly opened. McCarter and James turned simultaneously in the direction of the noise, and the Briton cursed himself for not instructing James to cover their back.

The figure that emerged hardly looked like terrorist material. She was short and slender with dark hair, and dressed in black pants, black boots and a black shirt. In fact, she was dressed in black from head to toe. Her mannerism—the way she carried herself—didn't seem like that of a hardened terrorist or combat professional; at least, not until she spotted the men of Phoenix Force.

The woman went for the floor as she reached behind her. McCarter almost shouted a warning but then choked it back. They were trying to keep this quiet. James didn't think about that, his earlier training in SWAT taking over.

"Drop it!" James roared.

That bloody well did it. The woman produced a pistol and triggered a round. Except that it wasn't a round—it was more like ten rounds. McCarter was in awe, because it appeared that the weapon only fired once yet he could hear the ricochet off the floor and walls of the hallway as multiple projectiles bombarded their position. McCarter and James hit the floor simultaneously and opened up with their MP-5 SD-6s. Their initial shots missed the woman, but as she rose and turned to go for the door, she staggered and let out a shout of pain. She got through the doorway and closed it behind her, the clang of the heavy metal reverberating down the cavernous hallway.

James cursed loudly. "What in the hell did she fire at us?"

The sound of a door opening behind them redirected their attention before McCarter could reply.

They turned to see that Encizo still had the door covered, and as a new pair of terrorists emerged, the Cuban made short work of them. He leveled his submachine gun and triggered a trio of 3-round bursts at virtually point-blank range. The quite visible expressions of surprise the terrorists displayed at seeing Encizo lying on the ground near the bodies of their comrades were replaced by shock as 9 mm rounds punched through their flesh.

The first terrorist took Encizo's rounds in the gut. He stumbled forward and came to rest on the body of one of the females. The second terrorist was also gut shot, but the shocked expression disappeared when first his throat and then his skull were bombarded by the rising corkscrew burst Encizo had delivered. The guy tipped backward and disappeared behind the half-open door.

McCarter and James got to their feet simultaneously and rushed toward their comrades. Hawkins was just rising and said, "Did you guys see that?"

"Got a firsthand view," James said.

"Our secret's out, chaps," McCarter said. "We'd better—"

The hallway suddenly rang loudly with the reports of automatic weapons fire. The walls and door near Phoenix Force exploded around them, showering them with bits of wood, drywall and sharp metal while clouding the air with choking dust and drywall residue. The warriors got beyond the door and into the room and closed the heavy metal door behind them. They immediately noted that the room had no windows or doors. It was poorly lit, cluttered with cots, and a table in the center of the room was covered with radio equipment surrounded by cardboard boxes of expended military rations and bottled water.

"Great," James said, upon quickly taking in their surroundings. "We're trapped."

MANNING WOULD HAVE preferred to be helping his teammates, but he had a demolition job to do, and do it he would. Stony Man's connections had managed to provide him with more than enough demolitions to do the trick. Manning had also noted that there was plenty of accelerant to help him do the job. Several cases lined the shelves containing bulk quantities of nitro solvent and gun oil. There were also reloading machines mounted to the various workstation desks, and where there was reloading equipment there was bound to be gunpowder. It didn't take Manning long to find bundled packages in cabinets beneath the workstations, along with powder measures, scales, dies and a slew of other reloading equipment.

But it was the powder that interested the demolitions expert the most. Manning had never seen this brand name before, and a quick check of the label confirmed it had been manufactured in Australia. While Manning didn't recognize the name of the city, he was betting Port Noarlunga wasn't too far from Adelaide, and that this gunpowder had been specifically crafted for Stormalite Systems and their special breed of firearms. Manning was even more convinced when he withdrew his knife, poked a small hole in the side of the bundle and watched in fascination as a highly crystalline white powder began to spill into a pile on the floor.

Manning smelled the end of his knife, then wet his pinky and ran it quickly through the spilling stream of powder. He touched his finger to his tongue and immediately experienced a burning, metallic taste. Okay, so it definitely wasn't cocaine, which meant it was just as advertised on the label—some kind of gunpowder. Manning began to ponder how the terrorists might have gotten the stuff into the country undetected, but that moment passed when he suddenly felt another presence behind him.

The alarm bells went off in the big Canadian's gut and only by turning just slightly to his right did he avoid having his throat cut wide open by a wire garrote. Manning got his forearm up near his head, a reactionary movement that came from years of training. The piano-wire garrote was a simple device, yet lethal in the hands of an experienced user. Manning's particular attacker seemed to be anything but that. Manning was sideways to his attacker now, and on his knees, and his well-calculated and well-timed movements had given him the advantage.

Manning reached down, grabbed the back of the attacker's boot and yanked forward while simultaneously rising from his position. The maneuver threw the attacker off balance and onto the floor. The movement caused a release of tension on the wire intended for the soft flesh of Manning's throat, and the sudden absence of that pressure catapulted the garrote across the room. Manning was so fixated on neutralizing his opponent that he never heard it hit the ground. He was on his opponent in seconds, and the moment of shock he experienced when realizing he was about to punch a woman, cost him a kick to the face that nearly broke his jaw.

Manning's ears rang with the blow, but he couldn't let himself be distracted. It had almost cost him dearly. The woman was on her feet as quickly as he was, and there was no mistaking the glint of the outside streetlights on the knife blade. She charged Manning with a hiss and the veracity of a wounded animal. The Canadian sidestepped the attack and delivered a sharp karate chop to her wrist while simultaneously hitting the side of her head with a palm strike. The sounds of wrist bones cracking were audible in the high-ceiling room and the blow to her head redirected her strong forward movement. The terrorist screamed in pain as she dropped the knife and Manning's blow to the head sent her crashing into a stack of bar-stool-like chairs.

Manning cursed at the noise, but only a moment elapsed before it didn't matter. The hallway was suddenly filled with a cacophony of automatic gunfire—it looked as though his comrades had lost their edge. Manning stepped forward to check the pulse of the terrorist but recoiled quickly when he realized she was still conscious. Her tenacity and strength surprised the Phoenix Force warrior. He'd seen that maneuver take down men much bigger and stronger than this small, lone female who was now reaching for a pistol in shoulder leather.

Manning whipped his SIG-Sauer P-239 pistol from its holster, snap-aiming at the woman as she finally cleared her own pistol from leather and squeezing the trigger twice. The first .357 Magnum slug hit the terrorist in the right chest, punching through a lung. Blood erupted from her mouth in a foaming spray even as the second round struck her in the chin, traveling onward to rip away the lower part of her jaw. The woman's pistol clattered from her splayed fingers. Manning stepped forward and put a mercy round through her head.

The big Canadian stood over her a moment as he caught his breath. These RDL terrorists were hardcore; at least, more hardcore than he and his teammates had originally been led to believe. Not only did they have members from either gender, without any seeming discrimination, but they seemed almost fanatical about not being taken alive at whatever cost. And that kind of loyalty and dedication only made worse the fact that they were now in possession of cutting-edge technical weaponry.

The shooting in the hallway had stopped and Manning resisted the urge to investigate. His teammates could take care of themselves. The first order of business would be to get this place rigged to go sky-high, and he wasn't going to accomplish that standing around. Manning holstered his pistol, after realizing he was still pointing it at the obviously dead woman, and turned to the work at hand.

It was time to finish what he'd begun.

"OKAY," MCCARTER SAID. "So we have a situation here. What does everyone think we should do?"

"Would it be too early to consider prayer?" Encizo muttered.

"I can't believe we allowed ourselves to get pinned down," McCarter replied. "I bloody well should have thought about putting a guard on our backsides."

"Don't beat yourself up, David," James told him. "It could have happened to any of us."

"Yeah, but it didn't happen to *any* of us, it happened to me," McCarter snapped. "I almost got us all killed."

"Are we still alive, David?" Encizo asked.

McCarter looked in the Cuban's eyes and then after a moment he nodded slowly.

"All right, then, so you've learned something and lived to discuss it later. Let's not relive it."

"Agreed, mate. Thanks."

Encizo grinned and nodded.

"If we're all done with the therapy session," Hawkins said, "I'd like to discuss how we're going to get out of here."

"Grenades," McCarter replied.

"My thought, as well," James added. "They're surely headed this way, and we don't stand a chance against those weapons."

"What I can't figure out is how those weapons got here," Encizo said. "All of our intelligence pointed to those weapons being in Cartagena."

"No, the prototypes are in Cartagena," McCarter said. "And we were in too much of a frigging hurry to get here that we didn't ask Vajda about there being any more of these weapons elsewhere."

"But if they had these weapons, then why steal the prototypes?" Hawkins asked.

"Let's figure that out later," McCarter said. "I'm sure we'll find the answers when we get to Cartagena. Right now, let's just get ready to get out of here."

The men nodded in unison, checked the actions on their weapons, and then each man palmed a grenade. McCarter counted to three and opened the door. There was an immediate response, with rounds slapping the door frame and ricocheting off the metal door. James and Hawkins tossed their grenades first, one an M-67 fragmentation and the other an AN-M83 HC smoker. Thick clouds of white smoke immediately blanketed the hallway, drifting slowly and lazily upward toward the vast open ceiling above. The warehouse was actually sectioned by thin drywall covered with cheap wood laminate, but the area above was still completely open. Still, it obscured the hallway well enough to keep the terrorists from clearly seeing their enemies.

The frag exploded a moment later and the Phoenix Force warriors could hear at least one scream. It appeared they were having an effect. McCarter and Hawkins tossed two more M-67s into the hallway and the thickening smoke hid many of the flashes but did nothing to contain the ground-shaking blasts or the smell of expended explosive and ammunition. The sounds of the special Stormalite weaponry dissipated enough that McCarter and his team felt it safe to engage. The warriors stormed the hallway, keeping low as they moved, their weapons directed straight ahead.

Encizo felt a series of rounds buzz past his head, but he knew it was conventional weapons fire, so he kept moving. It was possible they had taken out all of the Stormalite weapons with the grenades, or at least their users, and that would be enough to seize the advantage. The Phoenix Force warriors were quite accustomed to fighting against terrorists that weren't holding weapons superior to their own.

Hawkins estimated he was about one-third of the way down the hallway when he sensed he'd advanced too far ahead of his teammates. It was still smoky in the hall, and they were walking as blindly as the terrorists were. For all he knew, he could walk right into one of them. A moment after the thought crossed his mind, he did. The terrorist was as surprised as Hawkins, but not nearly as quick to react. The ex-Delta Force soldier's reflexes took over and he swung the stock of his MP-5 SD-6 in an underhand maneuver. The metal frame struck the terrorist somewhere on the face and the man grunted with the impact. Hawkins then dropped to his knees, fired another butt stroke to groin area and watched with satisfaction as the terrorist collapsed.

Hawkins was now in a position below the smoke where he could see clearly see the enemy numbers: there were still quite a few, also on the move, although they were retreating. Hawkins also counted several dead or wounded, the victims of the heavy grenade action. He shouted for his teammates to go low, and as they obeyed, Hawkins opened up with his MP-5 SD-6. McCarter, Encizo and James followed suit a moment later, and they sprayed the area with lead. The terrorists began to drop like flies, some silently and others with cries of pain that were clearly audible even above the synchronous ratcheting of four rolling-bolt systems.

Two of the terrorists managed to escape the on-slaught by ducking into the room where Phoenix Force had made its initial entry. McCarter immediately moved forward, signaling for Encizo to follow while instructing Hawkins and James to cover them. The pair reached the door unscathed, but before they could get inside a trio of terrorists appeared at the end of the hallway with automatic rifles that were not familiar-looking.

"Oh, bloody hell," McCarter muttered as they hit the ground.

The sound coming from the weapons was thunder-ous, almost mechanical, and the air above their heads was suddenly alive with hot lead. A thick cloud of black smoke curled around the threesome firing on Phoenix Force's position; it was a very precarious po-sition at that.

McCarter and Encizo raised their SMGs and began firing simultaneously, but the Briton's weapon jammed on the first 3-round burst. He cursed roundly and rather than waste time clearing the jam, he drew a 9 mm Browning Hi-Power from his hip holster and began capping off rounds at a rapid but controlled rate. The terrorists quickly realized the error of their ways, having obviously expended all of their ammunition in a few hurried seconds.

Hawkins got the first one with a sustained burst that stitched the terrorist from crotch to head like a sewing machine needle going through a thin piece of cloth. The terrorist dropped his weapon and danced backward under the assault. His back finally reached the wall and he jerked a few more times as Hawkins added another short burst for good measure. The terrorist was little more than a chunk of bloody, mangled flesh by the time he hit the floor.

Encizo and McCarter got the second terrorist, this one a female, simultaneously, while James dropped the last terrorist with a double tap to the chest that left gaping exit wounds and a third round that severed a carotid artery. The echo of the firefight died and the corridor became deathly still for only a moment. And then the reports of weapons fire resumed behind the door to the reloading room.

GARY MANNING DIDN'T WAIT for the pair of terrorists to announce themselves.

As soon as they came through the door, the explosives expert rolled away from where he was placing the last igniter into the block of C-4 plastique. The air around where he'd been a moment before was suddenly filled with a hail of bullets. The big Canadian completed his roll and settled in a kneeling position, MP-5 SD-6 held at the ready with the selector on 3-burst mode.

Manning triggered the first trio of rounds, shooting

the weapon from the closer terrorist's grip with the first two rounds and catching him in the ribs with the third. Manning immediately followed up with a second volley, but he couldn't see its effect because the sudden sound of breaking bottles and the eruption of heat and flame washed over his head and forced him flat to the floor. The remaining terrorist had obviously fired stray rounds into one of the cases of nitro solvent lining the shelves. Sparks and heat had done the rest.

Manning lifted his head at the sound of screaming and immediately noticed that the remaining gunner was awash in flames. The human torch wailed and cried out, dropping his weapon and begging for mercy. Manning started to raise his weapon and deliver a mercy kill when his comrades came through the door and swept the area with their weapons. Manning lowered his weapon when he noticed McCarter having to sidestep to avoid the flaming figure that was staggering backward. The Briton watched the terrorist stagger past with a surprised expression, and it was finally Encizo that raised his MP-5 SD-6 to his cheek and delivered a single shot to the man's skull. The terrorist dropped to the floor with a dull thud.

Manning rushed forward and began to push his friends away from the growing flames. "Get out of here now!"

When they were in the hallway, Hawkins said, "We need to search this place for these engineers."

"You guys get out now," Manning replied. "I'll do a quick sweep."

"It would be faster if we all do it," Encizo suggested.

"No time, mates," McCarter said, shaking his head. "Then we've got all five of us dead if this place goes instead of one."

"Listen, David, I know this stuff better than anyone, which means I'm the most logical choice for the job," Manning insisted. He handed him a simple-looking black box and said, "Here's the detonator. You four get out while the getting is good, and if I'm not out in five minutes then you blow this place to hell and back. Got it?"

The others looked at McCarter, each one with their own expression of protest, but the Briton's expression told Manning he was right. He realized that if any of them stood a chance of getting out alive, what they couldn't do was stand around arguing about it. And Manning was the most qualified, given his expertise in demolitions. He knew better than any of them how much time he had, and he also knew how the stuff would blow and where the safest spots would be when it did.

"All right, you heard the bloke!" McCarter finally snapped. "Move your bloody arses!"

They all headed in the direction of where they knew they would find the front exit while Manning went off to search for survivors. It didn't take him long. He found the engineers at the opposite end of the hallway, about ten in all, with gaping wounds in their backs. The terrorists had lined them up and shot them without cause or provocation rather than let them fall into the hands of the enemy. Manning was sickened by the thought but he didn't wait for an engraved invitation to join his comrades in making a quick exit.

It looked as though Phoenix Force had reached another impasse, and Manning was beginning to wonder when it would end.

CHAPTER FIFTEEN

Boca Chica, Florida Keys

John "Cowboy" Kissinger could hardly believe it when he heard Carl Lyons voice his theory.

"What did you just say?" Kissinger asked. He shook his head and added, "I'd believe just about anything you told me, Ironman, but I won't believe that Remar's involved with this."

"Think about it, Cowboy, even for just a minute. These terrorists attacked you and Phoenix Force in Adelaide. Those guys went their way and you went yours. So how else could they have known you were here?"

"I was with Remar a very large part of the time," Kissinger countered as he climbed out of the hospital bed.

"And just where do you think you're going?" Schwarz asked.

"I'm leaving with you guys," Kissinger said.

"What makes you think we're going anywhere?" Lyons said.

Kissinger didn't answer as he pulled the wire leads of the cardiac monitor from his chest. He then began to concentrate on the intravenous catheter inserted in his arm that pumped saline and vital antiinflammatory medication into his body.

"Ironman's talking to you, Cowboy," Blancanales said gingerly.

Kissinger stopped peeling the tape from around the IV site. He studied the members of Able Team with a cool gaze. "Come on, boys, you think I just came off the banana boat yesterday?" He coughed twice, grimacing with the pain and then said in a hoarse voice, "If you've found evidence linking these terrorists to someone in the military, then surely you found something that told you where they're going to hit next."

Schwarz smugly looked at the other two in satisfaction. "I told you he'd say that."

Blancanales pinned Kissinger with a studious gaze. "Well, the fact of the matter is that we didn't get any closer to finding out where this whole thing is headed, Cowboy. But that's hardly the point. I mean, you can't honestly be up to just walking out of here. Your throat's fractured."

"I'll live," Kissinger replied quietly.

The Stony Man weapons expert twitched as he gingerly finished removed the tape around the IV catheter and then yanked the small, white plastic shaft from his arm. The site near the wound began to bleed rather profusely. Lyons searched rapidly for a towel, but Kissinger beat him to the punch by tearing some tissues from a nearby box and stuffing them in the crook of his arm.

"Well, just so you know," Lyons said, "Hal wants you to get your butt back to the Farm. He said your going to Spain was out of the question."

"Fine," Kissinger replied. "I've never disobeyed Hal's orders before, and I'm not going to start now."

"That's probably a very good idea, Cowboy," Blancanales replied. "If you go rogue on us and Hal orders your retrieval, we won't have any choice but to come after you. You know that."

"Yeah, I know it," Kissinger grumbled. "But I'm not staying in this morgue any longer. I hate hospitals."

"Getting you out of here shouldn't be a problem," Gadgets said. "You don't answer to the Navy."

The door suddenly swung open and a nurse entered followed by two orderlies and one of the SPs assigned to guard the door. The nurse took one look at the scene and then stepped aside, deciding to let the orderlies act the part of heavies.

"You need to get back in bed, Mr. Jones," the nurse said. "Right now."

"Sorry, ma'am," Kissinger replied in his usually congenial voice. Kissinger loved the ladies almost as much as he did the Stony Man armory, and he could never be anything but polite. "But I'm afraid I'm going to have to get up and out of here."

"I'm sorry, sir, but you're—" one of the orderlies began, stepping forward.

Lyons inserted himself between the orderly and

Kissinger. "Under the protection of the U.S. Marshals there, chief. So why don't you step off?"

The orderly was a big, beefy black guy with massive arms and he made the mistake of putting a hand on Lyons's chest.

It took the Able Team warrior less than a second to respond. In a blinding moment to the rest of the observers, Lyons got a pressure point in the soft spot between the orderly's thumb and index finger, twisted outward on his hand while simultaneously grabbing him by the throat and slamming him against a nearby wall. The second orderly stepped in to assist his friend, but Schwarz nonchalantly stuck out his foot and tripped him, sending the poor fellow crashing into the unyielding metal bed frame.

Schwarz and Blancanales then settled palms on the butts of their pistols as the SP started to reach for his extendable, metal baton. They didn't say a word, instead favoring him with a warning smile. The SP obviously determined with quick foresight that discretion was the better approach against these men and slowly moved his hands out to his sides so they were in plain view.

Lyons applied some additional pressure to the orderly's throat and quietly said, "A word of advice, chum. Before you start putting your hands on people, it might be wise to know who you're dealing with."

As Lyons released the orderly, Blancanales said, "Now listen carefully, people. Mr. Jones here is under the protection of the U.S. Marshals Service, and he's decided to refuse any further care. You can't force it on him, so you're better off just letting him go with us, and we'll be on our merry way and out of your hair."

"And maybe we'll just forget that you assaulted a U.S. Marshal," Lyons added, sparing the orderly a glance. The orderly returned Lyons's stare with a sour look of his own, but he remained silent, preferring instead to rub gingerly at his tender throat.

As the men of Able Team stepped aside to permit the group to leave, the nurse said to Kissinger, "If you wish to go with these men, that's fine, sir. However, you will have to sign an AMA form, indicating your wish to refuse treatment and acknowledging you've been advised of the risks." The nurse looked at the men of Able Team in turn and added, "That's the law."

Kissinger nodded with a smile and then the crew filed out. The weapons expert had just finished dressing when the door opened again and Admiral Remar entered. One look at the group and he could tell that something bad had gone down.

"What's going on?" he asked Lyons.

"We're leaving," Lyons replied. "And we're taking Mr. Jones here with us."

"But he—"

"Look, sir," Lyons cut in. "No disrespect intended, but we already had your goons try to stop us. I'd prefer if you didn't get in on the act, as well."

Remar's eyes widened. He was obviously surprised to hear Lyons talk to him that way and he wasn't sure what he'd done to deserve it. He looked pleadingly in Kissinger's direction, obviously hoping for a measure of support, but Kissinger didn't meet his gaze. It took the officer only a second to realize what was going on. He studied each of the men of Able Team and Lyons noted that there were as accusatory expressions in the eyes of his comrades as there were probably in his own.

"Oh, I see," Remar said. "You guys think I had something to do with the attack on you earlier today."

"Can you blame us?" Schwarz asked.

"Actually, I can't," Remar replied.

That took them all off guard, and even Kissinger was looking at Remar now with a mixture of suspicion and surprise. "You mean, you actually understand how we might think you're involved?"

Remar chuckled. "I'm not just some obtuse old man who joined the Navy yesterday. If I know anything, it's that you federal boys are as suspicious as they come, and particularly when someone just tried to blow your heads off. But I can tell you that I had nothing to do with it."

"So how do you explain the weapons these guys had, Admiral?" Lyons asked. "And I suppose you have some answer for how they drove around this installation as free as birds, and not a single person decided to report their equipment as missing."

"That's because the equipment wasn't missing," Remar replied. He held up a manila folder he'd carried in with him. "I just got the report back from our database. The lot numbers from that ammunition and the serial number on the weapons the terrorists were carrying came from the J3 armory installation at Truman Annex. Specifically, while the equipment was marked as property of the Marine Corps, it actually belongs to the JIATF-East."

"The who?" Lyons asked.

"Joint Interagency Task Force, Eastern Command," Blancanales said. "I read something recently about them. They're quite an unusual and diverse agency, formed by the DOD and the President to monitor the air and maritime operations near U.S. coastal waters. They're comprised of at least a half dozen federal agencies, including DEA, FBI and NSA."

"Not to mention the NCIS, customs officers attached to a Coast Guard unit, and a U.S. Army Special Forces detachment that works for the DIA," Remar said. "They also have relations with the governments in Britain, the Netherlands and France to assist with the deterrence and interdiction of drug trafficking or smuggling along legitimate shipping lanes and international trade routes."

"None of this explains away the fact that you're the only one who had significant knowledge about the Stormalite weapons," Lyons said.

"I don't think this has anything to do with Stormalite Systems," Remar replied. "Unless you know something I don't, which is entirely possible. I think you might like to know that these weapons were released from JIATF-East and were supposed to be on their way to Illinois."

"Well, someone had to authorize the release of that armament to those terrorists, and you're one of the few on this installation that has that kind of pull. So I don't see how this proves your innocence at all."

"Maybe it does," Blancanales said slowly.

Lyons looked at his long-time friend and ally incredulously. "What?"

"I think we ought to contact Hal as soon as possible and let him know what's up. Not only will he need a full report about the attack on us here, but I think he's going to be pretty interested to hear where exactly these weapons came from, and subsequently where they were headed. Admiral, do you mind if we take that report with us?"

"Not at all," Remar said. "That's why I brought it. But before you leave, I *do* think you should know something. It may not mean anything yet, and it's certainly my problem to deal with, but I figure after what you guys have been through that I at least owe you the truth."

"And what's that?" Kissinger said.

"While you were distracted by this morning's little welcoming party, the Stormalite weapons were taken from the armory."

"Great," Kissinger said. "That's just dandy."

"That's not the worst of it," Remar said. "You should also know that because of the lockdown, no one is permitted on or off this base. And since I cannot find Paxton, as of 1300 today, I officially reported him as AWOL."

"Are you saying you think he's behind all of this?" Pol asked.

"I'm also positive of it. All law-enforcement personnel have orders to take him into custody if he's found."

"And what if he doesn't want to go quietly?" Lyons asked.

Remar's look was as hard as cold steel as he replied evenly, "Then they shoot to kill."

Stony Man Farm, Virginia

BARBARA PRICE ENTERED the Computer Room and found Brognola standing over Kurtzman's shoulder. The two men were staring intently at a computer screen. As usual, neither one of them had slept more than a few hours at a time since the attack in Australia.

"You guys need to rest," she told them.

Brognola pulled the soggy, half-chewed cigar from his mouth and replied, "Good morning to you, too."

"Coffee?"

"Perish the thought," Brognola replied, dismissing the very idea. He replaced the cigar with a few antacids. "My stomach's gone on strike."

"Bear?"

"Uh-huh," he said, holding out his coffee cup, although never taking his eyes off the screen.

Price shook her head with disgust, and then snatched the cup and went to the pot to pour him a fresh cup.

"Here." Price handed the coffee cup back to Kurtzman, who nodded and accepted the steaming brew with a grateful expression.

"You said it was important I get in here in a hurry," Price told Brognola. "What's going on?"

"Able Team ran into some trouble in Florida," Brognola said, sitting at a small table. "They were ambushed by a group of terrorists much like Cowboy was, although by a significantly larger force."

"Right on the installation?" Price asked. "How could that happen?"

"I don't know, and I don't know that we ever will.

What *is* interesting to me is that they were driving around in a customized van and carrying a cache of U.S.-made weapons and ammunition."

"As it turns out," Kurtzman interjected, finally turning his attention from the computer, "these weapons were from the Truman Annex, which isn't too far from the main installation."

Price's eyebrows rose. "Well, that's interesting."

"Not nearly as interesting as the point from which these weapons originated," Brognola said. "They were actually shipped in to the U.S. by Cargolux, a carrier stationed in Luxembourg. The weapons were received at Key West and held in the special unit armory for transport to their final destination."

"And guess where that was?" Brognola said. "Great Lakes Naval Base."

"Chicago?" Price cocked her head. "I don't understand."

"Neither did we, until I had Aaron start digging into the background of Remar's aide, Delmar Paxton. Bear, you want to do the honors?"

Kurtzman nodded and then pointed to a large screen. He punched a key on the computer and displayed the face of a young black man, about twenty years of age, wearing Navy dress whites. "Paxton was a first-class cadet in OCS. Hell, look at him. He could be a poster boy for Navy recruitment everywhere. But he's got a background that suggests he wasn't always such a nice guy. Paxton claimed on his entry paperwork that he didn't know who his father was. In fact, he told Navy recruiters that he believed his father was dead. He grew up in a pretty tough neighborhood, but everyone the NCIS talked to said he was generally a good kid."

"And since we didn't know anything about his lineage, it didn't seem like he had any connection with what's happened here," Brognola added helpfully.

"So I'm guessing," Price said, looking at Kurtzman, "that you found something to contradict Paxton's story."

"Did I," Kurtzman said with a grin. "Paxton's father was, in fact *is*, alive and well. Seems he's retired Navy himself. He's living in Chicago and working as a civilian on the base. His specialty is network administration and he operates at the GLNB out of the Networks Information Interchange Center. And here's the mother of it—the guy's Jewish."

"Paxton's a black Jew?"

"Yes. Jewish lineage always runs through the mother in the Hebrew society. She's black and of Jewish descent, but Paxton's father also happens to be Jewish," Brognola stated.

"Here's the last known picture of him, taken about four years ago when his identification card was renewed." Kurtzman tapped a button and the face of an ordinary-looking man in his sixties appeared on the screen. "His name is Guy Hauser. Paxton took his mother's name."

"Paxton's father was part of the baby boomer generation that came out of Vietnam," Brognola said. "He and some of his comrades conducted operations for the Navy. He was part of an SOG on loan to the CIA, and he specialized in configuring detonation of explosives by radio frequency transmitters along the Mekong Delta."

"They'd rig the shorelines with heavy explosives in key areas where Vietcong operatives were reported to be leaving weapons caches smuggled up the river from Cambodia for guerilla forces," Kurtzman explained.

"Anyway," Brognola continued, "one of the men he served with was named Davidia."

"Wallace Davidia?" Price asked. "He's the one Mc-Carter asked me to check into."

"No. This was James, his father. It seems that James Davidia and Hauser stayed in touch after the war. Davidia got involved with the Jewish Defense League, Anti-Defamation League, and any other special-interest group whose primary objective was the promulgation of Jewish rights. He got Hauser involved later, and the two apparently swore that no matter what happened they would instill the same sense of obligation in their children."

"And obviously the same sense of moral turpitude," Price said with a sigh. "So you believe the RDL cooked up this scheme when Paxton came on as Remar's aide and told Wallace Davidia about the weapons."

"Why not?" Brognola asked. "It makes perfect sense if you think about it. And we already know that the RDL had planned similar operations to the one conducted in New York City. We just didn't know where."

"And now we think we do know," Kurtzman said.

"Chicago," Price replied.

Brognola nodded. "Exactly."

"So what do you want to do?"

"Well, I've instructed Able Team to get back here as quick as they can with Cowboy, and then they're to go on to Chicago."

"What are you planning to have them do there?" Price asked the big Fed. "I mean, if they managed to stop the terrorists from getting the weapons out of Florida, do you think there's still a threat?"

Brognola nodded and said, "There is when you consider that while the terrorists kept Able Team busy, Paxton managed to get away with the Stormalite prototypes on loan to Remar and then disappear."

"So he's probably headed to Chicago," Price concluded.

"To meet up with his father, who now just happens to be a certified IT contractor on a military installation *and* a networking expert."

"So there's a pretty good chance they're going to trigger the weapons remotely," Price stated. "But for what reason?"

"It doesn't really matter at this point," Brognola said. "It seems obvious they have the resources to do it, and unless we hear something soon from Phoenix Force, we're going to have to assume that Chicago's the real target, and whatever's going on in Spain is a ruse."

"It certainly doesn't sound like a ruse to me," Price said. "And it definitely didn't seem that way to David."

Brognola sighed, sat back and rubbed his eyes. "Either way, the greater threat would still be here on the homefront. We'll support Phoenix Force in every way possible, but we have to consider any attack on U.S. soil as the priority."

"Agreed," Price said. "You say the word, we can pull them out and get them and Jack back here in no time. We may need them to assist Able Team."

"Fine," Brognola said. "But for now, let them pursue whatever leads they got from Vajda. I'd hate to think that while we were looking one way, the RDL pulled the wool over our eyes again. They're damned resourceful, and we can't afford another miscalculation."

Price agreed with the big Fed chief one hundred percent. It was no longer a matter of waiting and wondering. They were now going to have to go from a responsive mode to a reactionary one. Up to this point, they had been at the mercy of the Resurrection Defense League and the missing pieces of the puzzle that had made it seem as if they were operating in some sort of vacuum. Now the facts were out, and the mission seemed clear. The President was ready to back their play, and Price meant to insure that she didn't let him or Brognola down.

There were two things that absolutely couldn't happen from a mission standpoint: Paxton and Hauser couldn't be allowed to get a remote-access triggering system set up on the weapons, and the RDL terrorists in Spain couldn't be allowed to leave the country intact. Both objectives were a tall order, but Price was confident of one thing. The men of Able Team and Phoenix Force would see them through it.

CHAPTER SIXTEEN

Cartagena, Spain

"Mr. Brown, it is a pleasure to meet you," Captain Luis Ballestero said.

"Likewise," McCarter said, taking the hand Ballestero offered.

"We, um, weren't told anyone was expecting us," Calvin James said.

Ballestero smiled although there wasn't really much warmth in it. "And I was not told to expect five of you, Mr.—?"

"Black," James replied with a grin.

"Yes, of course…Mr. Black," Ballestero replied.

Encizo cleared his throat and said, "It would appear that we're both suffering from a deplorable lack of information, Captain."

Encizo could tell immediately that neither Luis Ballestero's mock sincerity nor his sarcastic tone was lost on his teammates. The guy had been waiting for them in the outer office of Edwin Laplander, a deputy representative in Cartagena who reported to the Counselor of Local Security at the U.S. Embassy in Madrid. Manning and Hawkins had opted to stay in the vehicle when they'd arrived in Cartagena, while the rest of them went inside to talk to Laplander. Price had told them that Laplander wouldn't even be told of Phoenix Force's arrival until about an hour before they actually arrived, so Laplander had obviously called Ballestero immediately after being notified. The deputy counselor introduced Ballestero as head of the Cartagena police's antiterrorist unit. Because of Cartagena's visibility as a port city, the diplomats in high office had always felt it better to allow local authorities to manage their own affairs, both in the interest of economic trade and the peace and security of the country. Cartagena was no exception.

"I've spoke at some length with Mr. Laplander, and I can assure you that you have no reason to be worried," Ballestero continued with a forced smile. "We do not tolerate the operation of terrorists within our country, despite any so-called official reports you might have read in the documents of your State Department. If such an activity were taking place, we would know about it and deal with ourselves."

"Tell that to the ten innocent people just massacred in Madrid," Hawkins snapped.

"Put a lid on it, mate," McCarter warned him.

Hawkins clammed up.

Laplander had obviously noted that the conversation was taking a turn for the worse and decided to intervene in the interest of keeping the peace. "Gentlemen, please, let us not walk so stiff-legged around one another. Now obviously, Captain Ballestero, we don't at all doubt your sincerity about the security of Cartagena. After all, we know that you assembled your unit almost single-handedly, and no one doubts their abilities, least of all the government of the United States."

Laplander turned to McCarter and said, "Isn't that right, Mr. Brown?"

"Whatever you say, Deputy Counselor," McCarter replied. He returned his attention to Ballestero and eyed him frostily.

"But if you don't mind, we'd like to take a look at some warehouses down on the port side of the city," Encizo said, keeping his voice even, so as not to come off threatening to Ballestero. "Could that be arranged, Captain?"

"Quite easily, sir," Ballestero said, finally deciding to step back a few inches from the inimitable presence of the fox-faced Briton looming over him.

The captain put his hands behind his back, turned a perfunctory 180, and walked to the large bow window that overlooked Cartagena's port. "I can arrange just about anything that you would need or desire. But I have already been notified of the events in Madrid, and that it is most probable you are the men behind those activities. And I can assure you, gentlemen, that the Spanish government will not tolerate such activities from a group of mercenaries."

McCarter opened his mouth to reply, but it was Laplander who actually came to their defense. "Captain, that these men aren't just some hired guns. They come recommended by the highest authority in our government."

"So they purport to be antiterrorists?"

"We've been around the block a time or two, guv," McCarter announced.

"We shall see."

"Um, Captain Ballestero, about that tour…" Encizo began.

Ballestero snapped his heels together. "Yes, of course. If you'll come with me, we'll be on our way."

"Actually, we've got our own ride outside," McCarter said. "We'd prefer to follow you if you don't mind."

"Not at all," Ballestero said, and headed for the door.

James followed behind him, then Encizo, with McCarter bringing up the rear. As they reached the door, Laplander put a hand on the Briton's shoulder. The Phoenix Force leader turned and found Laplander had leaned forward.

"Luis is a pretty good guy," Laplander said quietly. "Don't give him any trouble. I understand you're here to do a job, but things have been just fine and I don't need an incident on my hands. Is that clear?"

"Crystal," McCarter said. And as he went to close the door behind him he added, "Although you might want to tell that to the frigging terrorists."

MANNING AND HAWKINS watched the trio emerge from the building. Hawkins immediately noticed the shorter,

Spanish police officer walking with them, and turned to Manning with a look of surprise.

"How did the cops know we were here?"

"Don't have a clue," Manning said, shaking his head. "I'm sure David will tell us soon enough."

But it was soon evident that would have to wait, because as their friends reached the bottom steps, the immediate area was awash with the sounds of gunfire. And it didn't take long in observing the stone chips and dust rising from the steps that Phoenix Force was the intended target. The Spanish officer went one way while McCarter, Encizo and James went the other. Encizo was closest to cover, a large stone statue attached to a pillar, but McCarter and James weren't quite as close.

Manning and Hawkins went EVA as soon as the shooting started, pistols drawn, while remaining behind the doors of the minivan for what flimsy cover they would provide. Pandemonium had erupted on the busy street. It was the end of a work shift, so most of the denizens of Cartagena's downtown area were on their way home. Women and children began to scream, running in every direction, some of them right into traffic. Tires screeched, horns honked and people shouted in the chaos, which made it more difficult to pin down the location of their attackers. Manning and Hawkins studied their surroundings, looking for the source of the shooting. Hawkins soon spotted the winking of muzzle-flashes from a darkened window in an abandoned building across the street, and alerted the rest of his teammates to the origin.

Manning, Hawkins and Encizo began laying down a heavy dose of covering fire to give James and McCarter time to grab cover of their own. Despite the Spanish cop's short and somewhat rotund appearance, Manning noted that the little man who had emerged with his teammates was moving quite fast enough on his own.

The majority of innocents were out of the way. Manning pointed at one guy who was sitting inside his vehicle and staring stonily at the Canadian. He waved the guy out of the way with his pistol, and the dude blew out of there by tromping on the accelerator, not even bothering to make sure the road ahead of him was clear. Fortunately he didn't run anyone down in his haste to get clear of the situation.

Manning caught a glint of light on metal at the window, sighted carefully down the slide of his P-239, and then squeezed the trigger. While nowhere near the marksman David McCarter was, Manning was a fair shot with a pistol, and this round was apparently on target. The window cracked, glass shattered and there was a shout and visible spray of blood.

Only a moment passed before the front door of the abandoned building opened wide and four terrorists emerged. They traversed the front of the building, moving away from Phoenix Force, then ducked into an alleyway that separated the abandoned building from another that housed a string of shops. Manning and Hawkins immediately took off in pursuit. The big Canadian could hear the shouts of his companions, but he tuned them out. He'd witnessed firsthand the ability of these terrorists to slaughter innocent people on a whim, and he couldn't risk letting them out of sight. If he did, someone else would surely die. And he was much more ready to live with the consequences of disobeying orders than he was at watching anyone else die today.

If he had his way, the only ones to die from here out would be terrorists.

"GO FOR THE CAR, mates!" McCarter ordered Encizo and James.

The Briton jumped behind the wheel with Encizo taking shotgun and James in the rear.

James was about to close the door to the minivan when Ballestero suddenly leaped inside and pushed his way past them. James felt like tossing the guy out on his ear, but the engine revving to life told him there wasn't time. He'd barely had a chance to get the door closed and take his seat when McCarter whipped the wheel to left and jammed on the accelerator while downshifting to second gear. He avoided the backed-up traffic and crossed the center lane and into the path of oncoming traffic. Everyone grabbed hold of something simultaneously, but another quick maneuver had them up on the narrow sidewalk. McCarter scraped the side of the building with the minivan but quickly turned the corner and accelerated up the alley.

"What, are you part of the wrecking crew now?" Encizo asked as echoes of grinding and scraping on the wall died inside of the minivan.

"Actually, I thought I'd remodel, mate," McCarter replied, flashing the Cuban a wicked grin.

"This is exactly what I asked you *not* to do!" Ballestero beat McCarter's seat with his fists.

Encizo spared him a hard look and asked, "What exactly would you like us to do? They attacked us. And I noticed your people were nowhere to be found."

"That's not the point. You should still be letting us handle this! Your people guaranteed mine that—"

"Who's 'us,' Captain?" James asked him with an incredulous expression. "If you've got some way to lend us some support, or some people to spare, I'd suggest you get them on the horn. You have a way to do *that?*"

"As a matter of fact, I do!" Ballestero announced, displaying his radio triumphantly. He flipped a switch and began talking so rapidly in Spanish that even James, who was fluent in the language, could barely understand him.

The chase continued up the alleyway and it only took McCarter a few seconds to catch up with Manning and Hawkins who were still in dogged foot pursuit. The terrorists had a significant lead on them, but McCarter planned to close that gap in short order. He slowed the vehicle long enough for James to open the door and coax Manning and Hawkins into the van, and as soon as he'd given the all-clear signal, the Briton lurched into fourth gear and sped up just as the terrorists turned the corner on the next major street.

McCarter reached the street a moment later, downshifted to slow the engine, then disengaged the clutch as he yanked on the emergency brake and jerked the wheel. The minivan went into a power slide and stopped in the dead center of the street, engine still running. McCarter dropped the emergency brake, popped the gearshift into second and then gunned the engine as he smoothly depressed the accelerator. The powerful little van powered up the street. The crowds here weren't as bad—particularly on the sidewalk—but the terrorists were nowhere to be found.

"Dammit!" Manning cursed. "We lost them!"

"Maybe not," James replied. He pointed at a street vendor who, at that moment, was shouting and waving his arms.

There was the unmistakable sound of pistol fire and then the man was tumbling forward and clutching his stomach. McCarter swore under his breath and jammed on the brakes to avoid rear-ending a small two-seater that had suddenly stopped to rubberneck the scene on the sidewalk. Encizo bailed and the three Phoenix Force warriors in back followed suit a moment later. Ballestero started to jump out, but McCarter grabbed his coat sleeve and restrained him.

"Best to let us handle this one, mate." He favored Ballestero with a warning smile and added, "Trust me."

Hawkins was the youngest and fastest, so he was soon leading the charge up the street and parallel to the sidewalk, his comrades on his heels. The four warriors reached an intersection where some of the crowd had cleared and they could see the terrorists splitting up, two taking the side street while the other two continued up the lane. Hawkins gestured toward the pair that had diverted, alerting his teammates that someone needed to stay on them, and he continued his pursuit of the two on the straightaway path. He risked a quick glance to see that James was still with him, then he poured on the speed. Of their group, James was probably second fastest, his lanky form able to keep stride with Hawkins's smaller, lighter weight frame.

Hawkins saw an opportunity approaching and decided to take advantage of it. He was pacing his quarry at a breakneck pace and he was sure they were getting tired. After all, they had been running all of this time, and at least Hawkins and Manning had been given a slight break.

There was a garbage can coming up quickly, the metal meshwork kind, and Hawkins knew it would be his one chance to put an end to this chase. Otherwise, they stood a pretty good chance of losing the terrorists for good. Hawkins pumped the last bit of speed he had from his burning legs and soon gained a lead. As he ran past the garbage can, he lashed out with a jumping side kick. The metal can was heavy, but its cylindrical shape allowed it to roll, which it did very nicely under the impact of Hawkins's kick—right into the path of the terrorists. The two men tripped over the can and landed on their faces.

Hawkins doubled back and grabbed the nearest terrorist by the shirt lapels. He started to haul the man to his feet, but the flash of light on metal caught his attention. The second terrorist had recovered quickly from the fall and produced a knife. Hawkins watched the blade start to descend, knowing that to defend himself meant to release his quarry. He couldn't let that happen, so he pivoted with his body weight and used the terrorist he was holding as a shield. The knife wielder couldn't stop himself, and he ended up stabbing his own partner. The terrorist screamed with the agony of having a five-inch steel blade buried in his back.

The terrorist didn't have time to recover from the shock of stabbing his partner, because his jaw was suddenly dislocated by a well-placed punch from Calvin James. The terrorist's hand dropped from the knife, the blade quivering as his head snapped sideways. James followed with a kick to the knee that dislocated the patella and dropped the terrorist to the pavement.

Hawkins spared only a moment to look into the eyes of the terrorist he'd been holding by the lapels, the shock and fear evident in the deep brown eyes, and then they started to glaze over. The knife had obviously struck something vital because the next moment passed and the terrorist slumped in his grip. Hawkins let him fall to the ground in a heap. He then turned and fixed the remaining terrorist with a hard stare.

"We've got some questions for you, partner," Hawkins told him.

MANNING SUDDENLY SLOWED enough to draw his SIG-Sauer. Encizo had hoped to take the terrorists alive, but it seemed clear they weren't going to halt on their own accord, and it was even more obvious that Manning didn't see any chance of catching their younger, faster quarry. The Canadian started to aim on the run, but then hesitated, and Encizo figured the realization had struck his friend that there were just too many bystanders to risk a wild shot delivered on the fly. If it had been just them and the terrorists, the story would be different, but this many people heightened the risks. They had enough blood on their hands, and Encizo was happy with Manning's judicious actions. They didn't need to add any more innocents to the count.

The chase continued up the sidewalk and then the terrorists suddenly slowed.

"Down!" Encizo roared.

Manning obeyed, and the air above their heads was suddenly filled with multiple rounds. Seconds later, the windows of three shops showered glass on the Phoenix Force duo. Manning's elbows were sliced by the razorlike shards and Encizo's pants were torn at the knees as he ducked just in time to avoid having his head blown off by the deadly firestorm. Two newcomers were leaning out the back of plain gray panel truck, gripping the handholds on either side of the frame as they triggered a pair of Stormalite System assault rifles.

Encizo had noted the truck passing by a few seconds earlier, then noticed that it slowed suddenly when there was no traffic in front of it. The markings didn't indicate it was a delivery vehicle, and for the vehicle to suddenly halt like that had been a bit too strange to ignore. It was when the rear door had rolled up that Encizo shouted the warning. It was the Cuban's quick identification of the truck as a potential threat that had saved his and Gary Manning's lives.

The truck slowed a bit more, giving the terrorists an opportunity to reload. A third figure appeared at the back and called to the two terrorists that had been running from Manning and Encizo. The first one managed to make it up into the back of the truck with the assistance of his friends, but when the second tried to hop in, Encizo seized the advantage by clearing his S&W 4506 from shoulder leather, snap-aiming at the terrorists and triggering a round in one singular motion. The sleek pistol bucked in his grasp and a 230-grain .45-caliber ACP round struck a spot square between the terrorist's shoulder blades. The man's body arched as he released his grip on his comrade's hand and fell to the pavement.

Encizo sought the cover of a parked car as the terrorists opened up with another volley from the Stormalite assault rifles. He could hear Manning cursing and turned to see the Canadian's back pressed against the thick, concrete base of a streetlight. Traffic had ground to a halt and people on the sidewalks were quickly heading for the nearest shelter as a flurry of metal struck the walls and ripped up concrete chips from the sidewalks all around them. One civilian was unlucky, several of the rounds perforating his belly, chest and skull simultaneously and tossing him through a front display window.

Encizo watched the destruction helplessly, citing a brief prayer for the innocent victim and any family he might have. He then turned in Manning's direction and shouted for the Canadian's attention.

When he had it, Encizo said, "We've got to disengage. There are just too many people to get in the way!"

Manning nodded, but the sudden wail of sirens down the street demanded attention before he could conjure a reply. Two compact police cars roared in their direction, heading straight for the truck, which couldn't make a quick escape because of the logjam of vehicles left in the wake of the destruction and ensuing panic. Encizo began to scream at them, leaving his cover and running in their direction, but they didn't see him. Their focus was entirely directed at the men holding the weapons in the back of the truck.

And by that fact, the police had now become the focus of the terrorists. Encizo looked back and watched helplessly as the terrorists reloaded and leveled the weapons at the approaching squad cars. He and Manning obviously realized the terrorist's intent simultaneously because they both risked breaking cover to move into the street, firing their pistols repeatedly at the enemy. One of the terrorists lost a piece of his ear when a round grazed his head, but not before he and his cohort delivered a cloud of firepower that rivaled a swarm of hornets.

The windshields of the two police cars literally disintegrated under the barrage of the Stormalite assault rifles. One of the vehicles swerved immediately, catching the back panel of the other before crashing into a parked van. The second police vehicle spun out of control, and with two corpses as passengers, it continued uncontrollably on that course until bouncing onto the sidewalk and ramming into a storefront.

Brick, glass, metal and plaster exploded in every direction as the awning of the store collapsed onto the decimated squad.

Encizo dropped the empty magazine of his pistol, slammed a fresh one home and released the slide. He heard the screeching of rubber on pavement and turned to meet whatever threat awaited, but he couldn't describe the relief at seeing the minivan. McCarter emerged from the driver's side with an FN Minimi machine gun in each fist.

The Briton leveled the weapons and triggered simultaneously. The truck had started moving again in herky-jerky motions, but not before McCarter soaked it with a heavy dose of destructive lead. He swept the muzzles of the machine guns side to side, raising and lowering with unerring accuracy as he pounded the back of the truck. The one terrorist who had made it into the truck alive died in the onslaught and one of the holders of the special assault rifles tumbled from the back of the truck.

Another terrorist was pitched onto his back when his arm suddenly detached from the rest of his body. The one remaining gunner who had managed to escape McCarter's deadly assault reached up and started to pull the truck door downward, but he took a hail of slugs in the thighs. He pitched forward, holding on to the strap of the door, even as both legs dangled from what was left of the bone, sinew and muscle that had once held them intact. The vehicle suddenly lurched away from the scene and he could no longer maintain his hold on the strap. The door of the truck reached the floor before the terrorist who had closed it reached the pavement.

And Phoenix Force watched helplessly as the truck disappeared down the street.

CHAPTER SEVENTEEN

"Mr. Brown, I protest this madness!"

McCarter looked at Ballestero as smoke poured from the muzzles of the machine guns now pointing skyward and replied, "Sure you do."

Manning and Encizo approached. They had retrieved the Stormalite assault rifle one of the terrorists had dropped. It was an odd-looking weapon, nothing McCarter had ever seen before. It had a strange shape and profile, something like a cross between a French FA-MAS G-2 and German G-11. Encizo noticed McCarter studying the weapon and handed it to him. The Briton took it gingerly, looked it over a brief moment and then passed it back to Encizo.

"There's still a chance to catch them," Manning told him.

"Sorry, mate," McCarter replied, shaking his head, "but not until we know the status of the others."

"They're still MIA?" Encizo asked with concern.

"They'll turn up soon enough," McCarter said with

a frown, signaling that he wasn't really sure if he believed it or not.

As if on cue, a loud whistle resounded. All eyes turned to where they could see Calvin James waving at them from the intersection. McCarter issued instructions for everyone to get in the minivan. The Briton whipped the vehicle into a J-turn and sped to their waiting comrades. Wedged between the two warriors was one of the terrorists that had fired on them. James detached the man from their support and roughly shoved him toward Ballestero. The weary pair then climbed into the minivan.

"Would he talk to you?" Manning asked.

James shook his head. "No, he's the strong and silent type."

Hawkins immediately noticed Ballestero's eyes dart to the terrorist's injured knee. He had put one of the terrorist's arms around his thick neck and had his other around the man's waist. There was a small, dark spot on the inside of the terrorist's leg, an indication that he probably had an open fracture. Ballestero looked at James, who was essentially ignoring the terrorist, and then looked pleadingly in Hawkins's direction.

"This man needs medical attention," Ballestero protested.

"Then you'd better get him some," Hawkins replied.

"And you might want to see about your men, too," Enciso said, jerking his thumb in the direction of the wrecked squads.

All Ballestero could do was render a helpless expression.

McCarter leaned over the steering wheel and past Encizo who was in the front seat. He studied Ballestero for a long moment, then said, "We're going to the warehouse district. I would suggest if you plan to show up with your men that you let us know."

"The next time I see you, it will be when I'm zipping your bodies into rubber bags."

"We'll see," James snapped.

Then the door closed and McCarter set off for the warehouse district.

WALLACE DAVIDIA WATCHED as the truck tore into the broken, unkempt parking lot and ground to a noisy halt. He stood at the door to the warehouse and waited for Rasham to climb down from the cab. The expression on his friend's face made it abundantly clear what had happened. The attack on the Americans had failed, and just as Davidia had expected might happen, rushing to avenge their brothers and sisters in Madrid had simply cost them more aggravation and embarrassment, and the unnecessary deaths of their rapidly dwindling numbers.

Rasham's behavior was submissive, his look defeated. He stopped in front of Davidia, hung his head and said quietly, "We failed, Wallace."

Davidia didn't take the least bit of satisfaction in the fact that he'd been right. The fight between him and Rasham had been little more than a minor squabble between brothers and allies who were as united in their objectives as they were divided in their political views. He couldn't take solace in righteous indignation or viewing himself as intellectually superior to others. His father had taught him that; the death of his wife had taught him that; the Kach-Kahane Chai had taught him that. All through his life Davidia had been forced to learn humility. To admit mistakes was strength, but to cover them up was weakness. He'd taught this to his lieutenants, and Rasham had learned a lesson about hit the hard way today.

The driver appeared with a survivor. He had the stump of the man's arm tied off with a tourniquet just below the shoulder area. The wounded man's skin was pale and he looked as though he might pass out at any moment. Davidia looked down and noticed that the guy was carrying what was left of his arm in his other hand. Pretty unlikely that they would be able to save it, but there was always a possibility.

"He's going into shock," Davidia told the driver. "Get him to Dr. Stein before he bleeds to death."

The driver nodded and assisted the man into the warehouse. Davidia turned and gave his disheartened friend a warm smile. He threw his arms around the man, embraced him and kissed him on the cheek to let him know he was glad to see Rasham alive. Then he fixed him with a practiced gaze.

"Boaz, look me in the eye." When he had Rasham's attention he said, "I know this is going to be hard for you to believe, but I don't derive any happiness in your defeat. In fact, I'm filled with remorse. Tell me what happened."

Rasham explained it all to him: the attack on the American commandos at the satellite embassy offices; the foot-chase through the streets; finally, he described the brutal firefight that had ensued on one of Cartagena's side streets. Davidia listened carefully, nodding and mumbling assent as Rasham gave him the important details. Finally a small but distinct smile came to his lips.

"Did you get a good look at any of these men?" he asked.

Rasham shrugged. "Perhaps one or two of them."

"Were they of various ethnic backgrounds?"

"The two that I saw were very much different. One looked Hispanic, possibly Central American, and the other was taller and more European-looking. Perhaps he was even a French mix. I don't know, it was hard to tell."

"But you say there were more than just these two men."

Rasham nodded. "At least two more, and I'm sure one of the ones I saw was a local policeman."

"Probably a liaison," Davidia said absently.

"What?"

Davidia shook his head and replied, "I've heard of a very similar force before. You see, my friend, you hear things when you're in the law-enforcement community. Things that make you believe that my former government isn't quite as innocent as it would like the rest of the world to think it is. They're involved in special operations, just like any government would be. They have men to do the same kind of dirty work today that they had twenty years ago. The kind of special work that my father did in Vietnam, and the kind we're about to do. It's actually a historical moment, my friend. Because we're about to do to them what they have done to others so many times, and we're going to be the heralds for our people as we call them to arms against the Arab scourge."

"Please, Wallace, don't start your ranting again. I don't think I can stomach it now."

Davidia might have been angry with Rasham in another time, but within two days they would have won their final victory and the world would be at war with the Arab people.

"We can talk more about this later," Davidia said. "For now, we have more pressing matters. I received some information while you were gone. There's been a change in plans. Paxton had to steal the prototypes from the armory at Key West and deliver them to his father in Chicago personally."

"You're right," Rasham said with a nod. "That is certainly a deviation from our original plans."

"Given that we no longer have the facility in Madrid, it certainly accelerates our timetable," Davidia replied.

"What do you mean?"

"Martha telephoned a while ago. She told me that these same foreigners you described launched a raid against our warehouse in Azuqueca and blew up all of our equipment. She said they were forced to kill our engineers so they wouldn't talk to them."

"I don't believe we should accelerate our plans now," Rasham replied. "I think we should suspend any further activities for the time being. This will give us a chance to plan and recuperate our losses."

Davidia shook his head. "I'm sorry, but I have to disagree with you. I think the entire problem is in the fact we've waited too long. Stopping now would be exactly what they want. If we quit, we won't have another chance and they'll hunt us to the ends of the Earth. I want you to take the weapons to Israel tonight via our freighter."

Rasham's expression was one of surprise. "You're not coming."

"I have the business in America awaiting me."

"So you still plan to go to Chicago?"

"I don't see as I have much choice," Davidia replied. "We can no longer move within the original schedule. Every delay will prove more costly, both in the time we have to accomplish our objectives and in lives. I surmise that whoever these men are they will not rest until they've eradicated every last one of us, and we can't afford to wait any longer."

The sound of a vehicle approaching claimed Davidia's attention. This part of the wharves was deserted and the entire area in the part of the warehouse district abandoned. Not even the police came here except on a very occasional and routine patrol. Frankly, they didn't want to know what went on down here. Many of these warehouses with their broken windows and condemned buildings were homes to vagrants and petty criminals. There was no telling what went on in some of the other buildings.

Davidia had paid quite a number of officials to insure that they could work here unmolested until they departed for Madrid, which meant that if there was now a vehicle approaching that it could only be the enemy. Davidia looked at Rasham with a bitter feeling in his stomach.

"Did you allow yourself to be followed?"

"No!" Rasham said. "I swear it! I made sure that there was no one."

"Is it possible you were deceived?"

"I would have known if we were followed, Wallace."

Davidia nodded. "Okay, get inside and ready our people. We've got visitors, and I'm sure they're hostiles."

Rasham nodded and, with his driver in tow, they headed into the warehouse. Davidia followed immediately behind them, shaking his head. It *was* possible that this was just an innocent tourist who had gotten lost, or perhaps some kind of real-estate developer. Either way, they would see the truck because there wasn't time to hide it, and if it happened to be the police they would probably check it out. There was nothing he could do about that now. They would deal with whoever came to challenge them.

And they would deal with them swiftly.

"THERE'S THE TRUCK," Encizo said, pointing toward the vehicle that was visible through the side window.

McCarter braked smoothly and then traversed the fence at a slower pace until they reached an opening that led into the parking area. He stopped there, and all of them studied the place in turn. It was quiet, and the Briton wasn't sure what they could expect. If there were any more weapons like the ones that had been used against them on the street, there was a pretty good chance their minivan could become Swiss cheese before they'd gotten five feet inside the fence line.

McCarter said, "For once, mates, we might have to accept the possibility that we're adequately outgunned."

"Yeah," Encizo said. He brought the rifle into view and said, "And even if we knew how to use this damned thing, it wouldn't do us any good. We don't have any of the ammunition."

"Well, the RDL terrorists are getting it somewhere," Calvin James remarked.

"I saw a lot of the powder they used as an accelerant for the ammunition," Manning told them. "As I said, it's made in Australia."

"Which means that the RDL probably has an inside connection with Stormalite Systems," Hawkins said.

"Possible," Manning admitted.

"Either way, we don't have time to debate the bloody thing," McCarter said.

The ex-SAS team member reached into the back of the minivan and began to distribute weapons. They had reloaded their pistols on the ride over and their heavier weapons were already primed for action. McCarter and Encizo took MP-5s, choosing to forego their sound-suppressed cousins for the assault. James opted for an M-16/M-203 combo and Manning was toting the granddaddy of all automatic rifles, a Belgium-made FN FAL.

Hawkins primed and readied one of the newer weapons to the Stony Man arsenal, and one Hawkins had grown quite fond of in its past few trials on Kissinger's fire-and-maneuver courses. The Sturmgewehr Model 551, manufactured by the SIG company of Switzerland, was an early development effort commissioned by the Swiss army. Like its military version, the Stgw 90 assault carbine, the SIG 551 chambered standard 5.56 mm NATO ammunition, and was particularly effective when loaded with SS109 hardball rounds, which just happened to be Hawkins's preference for the rifle. It was tough and durable, with 30-round detachable box magazines that could be clipped together for easy change-outs. Because of the craft worthiness of the design and its light weight, it made the perfect antiterrorist rifle, capable of delivering up to ninety rounds of death at a rate of seven hundred rounds per minute and a muzzle velocity of 3000 fps.

Hawkins traded positions with McCarter, taking the wheel. He would make the initial entry and position the vehicle so as to make most effective use of the two FN Minimi machine guns in back, which still had plenty of life left in them. The Phoenix Force warriors donned their digital VOX headsets, checked one another's gear, then, once all confirmed they were ready, McCarter called for their attention.

"We'll have less than a minute to make entry, mates," he told his team. "T.J., you'll have the best cover when we split off. The windows in that warehouse are high, which means they'll have the initial advantage. See if you can get those machine guns on top of the roof of that truck. It will give you a better chance of giving us some useful cover fire. Like I said, less than a minute. Any longer than that and we'll be sitting ducks to however many of those bloody rifles they still have. "

"And don't forget that they also have one of the Stormalite grenade launchers," Manning said.

"Thanks for reminding us," James quipped.

"What are you blokes worried about?" McCarter asked them. "None of us is good-looking enough to live forever."

Just as McCarter feared, the shooting began as soon as they were inside the fence line surrounding the parking lot. It was going to get nasty. Even inside the relative dampening effects of their modern minivan, there was no mistaking the sound of rounds ricocheting off the pavement. A few managed to chip the rear side window and one even penetrated the windshield and narrowly missed Hawkins's head.

"Steady as she goes, T.J.," McCarter said.

Hawkins didn't reply, obviously choosing to keep his mind on what he was doing. Through some miracle, he got them to an area behind the parked truck and the men of Phoenix Force bailed. They pressed their backs to the relative safety of the truck as James peered around the corner and studied the door.

He looked at his teammates with a grin, pulled back on the shell of the M-203 to validate that the weapon was in battery, then peered around the corner and, with a quick adjustment of his muzzle, squeezed the trigger. The chug of the weapon was followed a moment later by a massive explosion as the 40 mm HE grenade struck the door and immediately blew a massive hole in it.

James loaded a second HE grenade on a path just slightly parallel to the first and Manning passed him two AN-M83 HC smokers, which he rolled toward the door. They immediately popped and hissed, the thick, white smoke obediently and quickly clouding the area. Fortunately for Phoenix Force, there were no winds coming in off the Mediterranean. The shooting wasn't the steady buzz it had been when they first drove toward them. The terrorists were firing from the high windows of the warehouse, just as McCarter predicted, but they weren't using specialized weapons.

"Those are conventional small arms," Encizo said.

"Don't get comfy," McCarter warned him. "Let's move!"

The Phoenix Force warriors filed out, heading toward the door in a low run while watching for any opposition. McCarter couldn't shake his uneasiness. The terrorists had been given the opportunity to strike out with the new weapons, but they had instead chosen to attack with standard fare. The only way that made sense was if they weren't planning to put up much of a fight, which didn't make much sense, either. But it didn't matter, because if he had his way this would be the final confrontation with the Resurrected Defense League.

James went through the ragged, smoking hole that was the only remaining testament to what had once been set of large double doors. Encizo followed behind him and then McCarter, with Manning on rear guard. They spread out as soon as they were inside and the enemy didn't hesitate to engage them immediately. The perimeter of the warehouse was lined by a catwalk, but the center area was clear. They'd walked into a bad situation. Aside from a few wooden shipping crates and couple of trucks, they didn't have much in the way of cover.

McCarter felt two rounds sizzle past his ear and he turned in the general direction of the fire and sighted for a target. He didn't get the opportunity to act on it, though. The air outside was suddenly filled the familiar chatter of the FN Minimi machine gun and McCarter's would-be assassin was Hawkins's first target of the day. The window next to the terrorist exploded and the man's body began to twitch. He staggered forward, his machine pistol falling from his hands, and then teetered precariously a moment at the railing of the catwalk before going over the side. McCarter didn't wait to see his body hit the ground.

The machine gun continued to be a solid undertone to the cacophony of weapons reports inside the warehouse.

Encizo and Manning split away from each other, firing their weapons on the run. The Cuban managed to grab a lucky shot, catching one of the other terrorists lining the catwalk in the ribs. The man twisted, surprised that he'd been hit, and Encizo put two more rounds in his back that slammed him face-first into the wall.

Manning rolled away from a terrorist, coming to his feet and charging toward a crate for cover in a zigzag pattern. He made it to the crate unscathed, then aligned the sights of his battle rifle on the terrorist who was trying to reposition for a better shot. Manning triggered one round, two, then paused. The Canadian was a crack marksman with a rifle, and both rounds landed on target. The 7.62 mm round shattered the stock of gunner's Uzi, and the second took off the top of his skull. The Uzi fell from the catwalk, the terrorist following a moment later.

Calvin James eventually reached cover, but not without sacrifice. A bullet tore a furrow in his thigh and nearly dropped the man. The Phoenix Force warrior got his back to the front of another crate. He quickly inspected the wound and saw that it was bleeding profusely. He hadn't really felt it, probably more because of the adrenaline pumping through his veins than anything else, but it wasn't more than a bite and certainly nothing debilitating.

You don't get off that easy, he told himself.

James loaded a 40 mm version of the TH3 grenade filled with thermite chemical. Based on the ever-popular white phosphorous, the thermite grenade burned hotter and longer than a Willie Pete, in addition to containing a special chemical that doubled as both an antipersonnel weapon and an incendiary. James jacked the slide on the launcher into place, located the pair who had fired on him and, with the pull of the trigger, proved that human hair and flesh didn't have a terribly high ignition point. The thermite grenade hit the wall above the terrorists and exploded, raining white-hot molten iron onto them. They screamed, their clothing igniting as the iron burned into the skin at a temperature exceeding 4,000 degrees Fahrenheit.

McCarter saw Calvin James's plight and immediately noted the blood running from his thigh. He slapped the VOX device and over the din of the auto-fire he demanded the man's status. James looked in his direction and tossed a thumbs-up.

The Briton wasn't sure he believed it, but he had bigger troubles of his own at the moment, as he noticed two terrorists coming down the stairs of the catwalk and trying to flank his position. McCarter raised the MP-5 to his shoulder, sighted on the terrorists, and squeezed the trigger. The weapon was set to 3-round bursts, and the Briton's marksmanship was superb. The first trio of rounds slammed into one of the terrorist's chest and sent him sprawling into a stack of empty cardboard boxes, much to the surprise of his female comrade. The woman terrorist tried to draw a bead on McCarter, but he had her dead to rights and she was entirely too late. His second 3-round burst punched through her skull, leaving her corpse effectively headless as it teetered forward and smacked the concrete floor.

Encizo noticed immediately that a number of the terrorists were beginning to pull back from their positions, even though they still had the upper hand and the advantage of overhead cover.

He keyed his radio. "Targets are retreating."

"Watch for a sucker play," McCarter replied.

James, who had been pinned down, wasn't even taking fire. Only Manning seemed occupied, and even he appeared to be the aggressor rather than the defender. McCarter watched as the Canadian took two terrorists that were running in opposite directions, both of them with head shots.

"There may be an explanation for that, boys," Hawkins's voice broke through. "I've got bogies making out of here. They're on those damned ATVs again."

It dawned on McCarter why they hadn't been using the weapons against them. They needed to get them out of the country! With their warehouse in Madrid destroyed, they didn't have any choice but to protect what remained of the investment. They had escaped with perhaps a dozen weapons, maybe less, and they got them out of the country quickly and quietly. McCarter remembered what Halsford had told him in Australia about export sales of the ATVs, and it suddenly became clear how they'd managed to get them out of Australia and into Spain so easily. They were smuggling the components in the ATVs.

"Stop them!" McCarter said as he lurched from his position and signaled for the rest to follow.

They emerged outside in time to see Hawkins trying to stop the small fleet of ATVs that were heading for the opening in the fence line, but he was taking some additional fire from inside and it was making it difficult. McCarter ordered his teammates to spread out and provide some covering fire, but he knew even as they did that they stood little chance of stopping them. Once more, the RDL had eluded them and with the weapons still in their possession.

And McCarter didn't have the first bloody idea where they were headed!

CHAPTER EIGHTEEN

Stony Man Farm, Virginia

John "Cowboy" Kissinger sat in the Computer Room at the Farm, being debriefed.

"What useful information did you glean from Remar about the Stormalite weapons?" Brognola asked him.

"Well, you already have some idea of the specifications from the information we sent you out of Australia, plus the additional schematics I brought back. Was any of that helpful to you, Bear?"

Kurtzman nodded. "We know a lot more than we did when we started this little adventure, although I'm not sure we could entirely decipher those schematics."

"That's true," Price replied. "What we looked at seemed fairly complicated."

"Well, in many respects it is," Kissinger said.

The Stony Man gunsmith grabbed a Dry Erase marker off the table and went to a nearby board mounted to a wall. The white board not only served as a instructional aide, but it had electronic sensors built into the corners. Using special kinds of markers, the board was capable of capturing and displaying images digitally. The sensors were connected to a feed that could then transmit whatever was projected or drawn on the board across vast distances via a network download or special telecommunications software created by Akira Tokaido. Many times, Price and Kurtzman would use this to point out map coordinates to the teams in the field or to designate specific drop areas.

"I know you've all fired a gun before, and through the training I've conducted in the past I know you all possess a good understanding of the way conventional firearms work. In review, a triggering mechanism releases a hammer, which strikes a primer that ignites the powder in the shell case of a bullet. The subsequent pressure then propels the round down the barrel, which is rifled with grooves that give the bullet its particular rate of turn, or spin. Simultaneously the opposing gases caused by ignition of the powder pushes the weapon's bolt to the rear and an extractor grabs the spent cartridge and expels it through the ejection port. The next round is then moved into position by a spring-loaded magazine and the bolt comes forward and pushes the waiting round into the chamber. Additionally, let's not forget that when the slide comes back with the bolt, a catch usually draws the hammer back into position or, in some cases, the firing pin, and readies the hammer or firing pin for the next squeeze of the trigger."

"It's basic training all over again," Kurtzman quipped.

"Not quite," Kissinger replied, beginning to draw a rough diagram of the pistol he'd first seen in Australia. "Not when you think about these weapons created by Stormalite Systems. This drawing, while crude, gives you some representation of the ingenuity of this technology. This is a rendering of a pistol I test-fired while I was there. It's the SS-925. It chambers 9 mm ammunition, and with four barrels attached, it's capable of expending approximately two hundred fifty thousand rounds per minute, based on about sixty-thousand rounds per minute per barrel."

"Say what?" Huntington Wethers cut in, looking at Kurtzman with a disbelieving expression.

Kurtzman simply smiled and they all returned the floor to Kissinger.

"Now, I told you about how a conventional weapon fires a bullet, and you already know that the system is triggered by solid-state electronics, thereby requiring no moving parts. However, firing electronically rules out ammunition with a primer or rim fire cartridges, and of course caseless bullets are out of the question. So Stormalite's engineers, and here's the most brilliant part I think, came up with the idea of providing special ammunition that expands and locks in place based on nothing more than the pressure coming from the load in front of it."

Brognola clucked his tongue and said, "So you're telling me that these rounds are stacked inside the weapon, and the only thing that keeps them in position until fired is the explosive force of the propellant charge that ejected the bullet in front of it?"

"That's exactly what I'm saying, Hal," Kissinger said.

"Fascinating," Carmen Delahunt said quietly.

"It is pretty amazing," Tokaido said in agreement.

"But it's so simplistic when you really think about it," Kissinger continued. "And the most amazing thing is that because no metal parts are required except the ammunition and barrel, the weapon is able to be compact and lightweight."

"What about accuracy?" Kurtzman asked.

Brognola grunted and said, "When you can fire that many rounds per minute, who cares about accuracy?"

"Touché."

"Actually, these weapons are deadly accurate," Kissinger said. "Because one shot takes only about one-five-hundredths of a second, you burn the capacity before feeling the recoil. That means better control, of which accuracy is the natural byproduct."

The room fell silent with the awe-inspiring points Kissinger was making.

"However, there are a few flaws in this technology, more logistical than technical. But I believe we could use those to save the lives of every man in the field."

"And what exactly are these flaws?" Brognola asked.

"Outside of Australia, nobody possesses the technical expertise required to use these weapons with any reasonable longevity. The ammunition is comprised of a special alloy, and no one vendor possesses all of the formula. Unless it's manufactured to exact specifications, the weapon is worthless. If specific concentrates in the alloys are deficient, the ammunition will slag under the heat and pressure. Conversely, if there's too much of other specific concentrates, the ammunition is too heavy and it reduces the range and velocity to proportions that make the weapon about as effective as a BB gun."

"Cowboy, are you saying that the RDL risked everything to steal these weapons, but yet they have no way of manufacturing the ammunition for them?" Brognola asked.

"Not exactly," Kissinger said. "The fact of the matter is, Remar thinks that someone inside Stormalite is actually working for the RDL."

"That is a possibility," Brognola said. "Have you pursued those angles, Barb?"

Price nodded. "We've crawled up the back end of every employee and contractor working for Stormalite, as well as defense contractors here in the United States. We even checked out Remar's background."

"You should have asked," Brognola replied. "I could have saved you the trouble."

"Maybe so, but the only one who comes up dirty is Paxton."

Brognola sighed. "There *has* to be someone else working with the terrorists on this. I can't believe that Davidia and his people would risk all of this unless it was a sure thing."

"Who exactly is this Davidia, anyway?" Kissinger asked.

Price took a few minutes to bring him up to speed, including the connection between Davidia and Paxton. Kissinger felt himself wince involuntarily at the mention of Paxton. He'd seemed like a pretty good kid, and then it turns out he's a traitor to his country and a dangerous liability. What bothered Kissinger most was that he'd been monumentally naive enough to think the kid was a straight shooter and an asset to the U.S. Navy.

"Wow, guess I've missed a lot in the last forty-eight hours," Kissinger said, shaking his head. "And I thought you were keeping me busy down there."

"So if I understand this now, there is a possibility that these weapons will become ineffectual if we focus on finding out who's providing the RDL with the accessories and take them out of the picture."

Kissinger nodded. "Right. And something I forgot to mention is that the propellants used in these weapons are a special concoction manufactured exclusively for Stormalite by a very reputable chemical company in Port Noarlunga, Australia. Remar assures me that all of the companies involved with the process did so under a very strict contractual agreement due to the widespread impacts this would have on global defense initiatives for every country in the world."

"So even if the terrorists were to figure out the formula to the alloy," Price concluded, "there would still be the issue of the powder."

"Or vice versa," Kissinger concluded.

"So what's your suggestion?" Brognola replied.

"There's a project and programs director at SSL's key administrative offices in Brisbane. Remar knows this guy pretty well, from what I understand. His name is Anthony Scheffler, and Remar swears up and down the guy's clean. In fact, Scheffler is apparently risking his job to help us."

"How so?" Price asked.

"Well, his company has ordered him to stay away from any strong personal ties with anyone they work with."

"Then it would seem that Stormalite has something to hide," Kurtzman said. "I think we should ask the Australian Ministry of Justice to go in and lock them down until we can decide what to do."

"No, that probably wouldn't be the best idea," Brognola said.

"Agreed," Price told him. "We start sniffing around a company under the protection of the Crown, and it turns out we're wrong, we might as well kiss any future cooperation goodbye."

"Well, we're going to have to come to a decision and we're going to have to do it quickly," Kissinger said. "And since you won't let me go to Spain, then maybe you can arrange to get Scheffler and some of the additional prototypes to Phoenix Force."

"I'd be curious to know why Scheffler's doing this," Kurtzman said with a suspicious tone. "I mean, what does he stand to gain?"

"You'd have to do some more significant digging into his background, Aaron, but there isn't time for that," Brognola replied. "We need to contact Phoenix Force and find out where they're at."

A hooting signal began sounding overhead in a very specific series of tones. "Speak of the devils," Kurtzman said, reaching over to engage the speaker phone.

"That's Phoenix Force calling," Kurtzman said.

"At last," Brognola said. "Let's hope it's good news."

Chicago, Illinois

DELMAR PAXTON TRIED to contain his excitement as they merged off Interstate 80 and onto the northbound Kennedy Expressway.

Paxton hadn't seen his father for more than a year now, and he was anxious to reunite with the man. Most people wouldn't have considered Guy Hauser anybody special, but Paxton didn't care what they thought. He knew what the true story was, and how the government had betrayed his father and so many other Vietnam veterans. Some of his father's friends hadn't agreed with his viewpoint at all, and some of the bonds he'd formed with his fellow soldiers had deteriorated as the years passed by. But there was one bond that hadn't broken, one forged from blood and hardened by the suffering of the Jewish people. And that bond held firm between his father and a man named James Davidia.

It was strange that these two men, who had come from entirely different backgrounds, would have ended up friends. But friends they were, and Paxton suspected that James Davidia's involvement with Jewish rights advocates provided more of an outlet and separation from the trauma he experienced in Vietnam. Or maybe it had given him a new war to fight, and one that perhaps he could win. At first, Guy Hauser couldn't dedicate himself to the cause with the same passion as his friend. He didn't find much cause to be proud of

Judaism, particularly given his race. But Davidia eventually convinced Hauser of the importance of Jewish rights, especially *because* of the prejudices Hauser had experienced.

Eventually, Paxton's father had given in and begun to work with Davidia. They lived in separate cities, but they didn't miss any opportunity to meet for an annual hunting trip, and Paxton could remember they would take "secret" trips to each other's homes now and again for holidays. In many ways, Paxton and Wallace were like cousins, sharing their own memories and secrets. Like Paxton's father, Wallace Davidia didn't accept his father's almost fanatical dedication to the Jewish heritage. Until the fateful day that Davidia's wife died at the hands of a violent crime, a crime that just happened to be perpetrated by an Arab in the country illegally. The death of his father to a stroke came very shortly thereafter, pushing Wallace Davidia over the edge, and it was then that Paxton saw his childhood friend changed forever. Paxton believed something died that day, and Davidia left the country to go on his own self-proclaimed crusade. A year later, Paxton joined the military.

Growing up as a black in an underprivileged neighborhood of central Cleveland was tough enough, but to be Jewish was practically unbearable. Not only had Paxton had to repress his heritage, one that his father had always preached he should be proud of, but his mother and father mandated he practice in secret. He hadn't been allowed to wear traditional clothing, neither had he been permitted to speak of his graduation to manhood through the traditional bar mitzvah ceremony. He had to lie to friends, what few he had, and on the advice of his mother, he falsified his paperwork when applying to become a naval officer.

The fact was that Paxton had been lying most of his life, and he was tiring of it. Soon he knew he wouldn't have to run any more and he could live in peace with his father. By now, Paxton knew the military would be on high alert. He was probably listed as AWOL, and the number-one suspect behind the theft of the Stormalite weapons. They were right, of course, but that wasn't really the point. Paxton hadn't lied to the man calling himself Jones when he said he liked the Navy. In fact, it had always been Wallace's plan that Paxton's name stay above reproach.

The arrival of the very intense men from Washington had changed all of that. It seemed quite clear after Wallace's men blew the assassination attempt on Jones and his friends that they were going to find out about Paxton's involvement soon enough. It wouldn't take a genius to figure out that Paxton was the only one who knew where the men were going and what they were driving. When he heard that the attack failed and the men from Washington had single-handedly defeated eight well-trained and well-armed men, Paxton knew they wouldn't be too forgiving.

U.S. Marshals my ass, he thought.

Paxton pushed the three men from his mind and decided to focus on the job at hand. They didn't know where he was and there was nothing he could think of that would tie him to Chicago. Their plans for this city were still a secret, and by the time the government figured it out it would be too late. Things would be better once Paxton was reunited with his father and Wallace arrived to take charge of the situation.

For the sake of the operation, Paxton had agreed to meet his father in a location where his escort team could keep an eye on things. In the very back of the van he was riding in, Paxton had stashed aluminum cases disguised as ordinary fabric suitcases that contained two SS-925 pistols, eight SS-7100 assault rifles, and a nine-tube grenade launcher. They would be able to provide initial support while also insuring they weren't being observed. Paxton had shotgun in their nondescript van, with one of Davidia's most trusted lieutenants behind the wheel and two more of the RDL terrorists in back.

Paxton was uncomfortable with the idea that he was working with Israeli terrorists. The antiterrorism mentality in America had overwhelmed the American psyche, and Paxton knew that in the eyes of the government, the men accompanying him *were* terrorists. Davidia had always tried to pass the men and women of his organization off as freedom fighters, but Paxton wasn't buying it. He knew what kind of operations they conducted, and he also knew they had slaughtered innocent people in New York City as well as other remote locations.

But Paxton was able to swallow these things when he thought about his father. Guy Hauser had served with distinction in Vietnam, and had to do things in the name of the American people that were best not ever discussed openly. But instead of a hero's welcome, civilians at the airport greeted him with a barrage of bags filled with dog shit. And instead of giving him a job and allowing him a living, Guy Hauser had had to struggle most of his life. His job as a networking engineer had been the first decent position he'd held since returning from the war. Paxton's father had struggled most of his life, spending every dime he made to support his family. Even after his parents were divorced, Guy Hauser didn't hedge on his responsibilities to his son, despite the fact that Paxton's mother wanted him to disown his "deadbeat father." It was just another lie, but this was one that Paxton refused to tell. His deception of the U.S. military had been in the interest of his father's cause, and because a small part of him feared Wallace Davidia.

Paxton met his father in a large shopping mall in the downtown Chicago. The place was busy, even in the middle of the day. It was lunchtime, so finding a quiet corner table at a decent restaurant wasn't easy. Still, they managed and the reunion between father and son was consummated with a strong embrace.

"It's good to see you again, Delmar," Hauser said. "It's been a long time."

"Too long, Dad," Paxton replied.

"I'm just sorry it had to be under these circumstances," Hauser said, looking around. Nobody seemed interested in their conversation, but they decided to keep the subject as generalized as possible. "I heard those incompetents that Wallace hired blew it for you."

"It's water under the bridge now," Paxton said.

"I noticed you're not wearing your uniform. Are you on a less-than-official leave?"

"You could say that," Paxton replied. The waiter brought them coffee and Paxton waited a sufficient time after he left before continuing. "I have to tell you that I'm not entirely comfortable with Wallace's plan here."

"Which part?" Hauser asked.

"All of it. It seems too risky to me."

"Life's full of risks." As Hauser studied his son over the rim of his coffee cup, he added, "I hope that's one of the lessons I taught you well."

"Do you think what we're doing is right, Dad?"

Hauser didn't look surprised by the question. "I used to. These days, I don't know anymore. I sometimes wonder what it was my country did to me that was so bad that I would betray her. I begin to doubt this cause. After all, we have freedom of religion in this country. And we also have the right to go about our lives without worrying that we're going to get tossed in prison for our political views or personal code of morals and ethics. So yes, I wonder now and again.

"But then I get around Wallace and he starts talking about honor and dignity, and filling my head with that idealism. He can be quite persuasive when he wants to be, and he's more like Jim than he might admit to you. But then, I'm telling you something you already know. You practically grew up with the guy. You two were like brothers once."

"I know, but it seems we've drifted apart some and I'm not sure why."

"That sounds almost nostalgic."

"It's the truth." Paxton looked around them again to make sure they weren't being observed. He knew he was probably being paranoid. There was no way the Navy could know where he was. "I brought the equipment with me."

Hauser looked up from the menu and there was something like panic mixed with anger in his expression. "*You* brought those things here? Why?"

"Because Wallace's people couldn't handle it themselves and I knew you were the only one who could program them properly. I was out of time and out of options there. If we'd waited any longer, those men from Washington would have been on to our plans."

"What men?" Hauser asked.

"They were friends of Jones's, the guy I told you about before. They claimed to be U.S. Marshals, but I think they were actually part of some kind of black ops group."

"Does Wallace know about this?"

"He will when he gets here. Which reminds me, when—?"

"I don't know yet," Paxton said. "But let's not talk about it now. Let's just enjoy our food and then we can head to my lab. It's all ready to go."

Paxton wanted to argue with his father, but he bit back any such urge; to do so would have been disrespectful. For now, he could be satisfied with a nice quiet lunch and some good conversation. He knew he'd feel better once they were safely in Hauser's lab. All of this would work itself out in due course, and then he could be at peace, finally at peace. And he would no longer have to worry about the three men he'd escaped from—especially the blond one with the cold blue eyes. That look was burned into his psyche.

And it would haunt his dreams for a long time to come.

CHAPTER NINETEEN

International Airspace, Mediterranean

David McCarter lay down on the cot with a contented sigh and closed his eyes.

He felt the vibration of the plane beneath him, but he wasn't going to let it bother him. A decent rest—even a few hours—would do wonders to improve his disposition. It would also improve the health of the rest of his team. Since touching down outside of Madrid less than forty-eight hours earlier, they had participated in three major encounters with the RDL terrorists and they still didn't have a clue as to the group's plans.

But McCarter wasn't going to worry about it. Since taking leadership of Phoenix Force for the late Yakov Katzenelenbogen, McCarter had matured in a number of ways. Before he'd been content to push the envelope, usurp authority and generally be the black sheep of the crowd. Taking ownership of keeping himself and the rest of his comrades-in-arms alive had seemed to suit his restless nature. In some ways, McCarter had originally been suspicious and doubtful of his appointment as team leader, but it didn't take long before he settled into the new role. McCarter was the kind who always grabbed the bull by the horns, and he'd decided he wasn't about to let a little responsibility scare him off.

The Briton was just in that drifting place, about to surrender to blessed sleep, when the overhead console buzzed for attention and the interior of the craft was bathed in reddish light. It was the signal that priority communication was incoming. McCarter groaned, opening one eye as his cheek was resting on the pillow, and watched as the rest of Phoenix Force remained motionless.

Sometimes it sucked being the guy in charge. When McCarter sat up and reached over to flip on the LCD communications screen, he knew the man whose face filled the picture could somewhat appreciate the point. Harold Brognola pulled the cigar from his mouth and flashed McCarter a wry grin.

"I trust this is important?" McCarter queried, rubbing his eyes.

"I take it you can't sleep," Brognola said.

"I can when you're not waking me up," McCarter replied.

"Sorry, but this is urgent. Are you awake enough to hear it?"

McCarter looked at the rest of his crew and then replied, "I'm the only one, but I can pass on the message."

"The others are out?"

"Like a blooming light," McCarter said. "I'll let them sleep. They've earned it and they need it."

"Okay, I'll keep it brief then. We think we know where the weapons are headed. One of our agents managed to talk with a dock worker in Cartagena who spotted a freighter being loaded with our missing ATVs. The freighter was actually going back empty and advising that she didn't have any cargo to declare. Her final port of destination is listed as Tel Aviv."

"Seems like a strange place to be going with these weapons," McCarter said.

"We think so, especially since we've also got intelligence reports that Wallace Davidia is headed for the States."

Brognola then explained the situation in Chicago and recapped the information Kissinger had given them on the weapons. He also told McCarter about Able Team's plans to locate Paxton's father, their suspicion that Paxton had the prototypes loaned to Remar and of Stony Man's suspicions that Davidia planned to use Hauser to equip the weapons for remote firing.

"So this Davidia's going to Chicago, but you think the weapons are heading for Israel."

"Yes."

"That doesn't make a whole lot of sense to me, Hal," McCarter admitted. "First, they steal the weapons under the noses of queen and country, and then they move them to Spain where, supposedly, they plan to mass produce them."

"Right, and they picked Spain because it seems the most lax and least experienced when it comes to anti-terrorism tactics. But I think you guys threw a monkey wrench in the works when you managed to capture Vajda alive. I don't think that Davidia had planned on that. And I also don't think that he believed we'd figure out there was a tie between Paxton and Hauser."

"So where does that leave us?" McCarter asked.

Brognola cleared his throat and replied, "I think they're planning something in Israel. I think it would have to be something big and spectacular enough to turn the rest of the world on its ear. I also think they want to tie up the hands of the American people long enough, and they only way they see of doing that is by igniting a war between the Jewish and Arab populations in our own country."

"It's ingenious," McCarter admitted. "Sick and twisted, but bloody ingenious."

"Let's suppose they were successful in pulling it off," Brognola said. "We already know it doesn't take much to push the buttons on either side. It would be quite easy to set off two warring factions who are already poised for conflict."

"They've been that bloody way for centuries, Hal."

"True, but a large part of the fighting has always been confined to the Middle East and its immediate territories. If you think about it, not a single superpower has ever chosen to become involved in the Middle East conflict until the United States stepped in to overthrow the Hussein regime. It's too large, too difficult and too much of a political quagmire."

"Not to mention the amount of money it takes to maintain any kind of serious military presence there," McCarter said.

"Okay, but let's consider also for a moment that this isn't about money," Brognola countered. "And let's also assume this isn't about making nothing more than a political statement. The RDL could have done any number of things to do that. Hell, they could blow up a Palestinian embassy somewhere if they just wanted to make waves and get noticed. Instead they risk everything to steal these weapons and then transport them to Israel. That can only mean one thing—they plan to stir up trouble on the West Bank."

"You think they're planning on hitting one of the Arab-controlled villages with these weapons?"

"Worse," Brognola replied. "I think they plan to hit one of their own villages, or at least one controlled by Israelis, and blame the Arabs for it. If they get enough people stirred up on both sides in the United States, the world's self-imposed policeman, and then light a powder keg in Israel, a U.S. ally and the scapegoat for all that's wrong with the Arab-Israeli conflict, imagine the global implications. We'll have rioting on the streets of America and in Jerusalem and Palestine."

"And then World War III starts between Jews and Arabs all over the world," McCarter concluded.

"Exactly, and it makes perfect sense if you understand Davidia's background. The guy's an American who renounced his citizenship eight years ago to join the Kach-Kahane Chai movement. He was a decorated policeman in New York City. His father and mother are devout Jews. His wife's killed by a Palestinian, who subsequently gets off on a technicality, and now he's pissed off and wants revenge."

"Sounds like Davidia has his own special plans for ethnic cleansing," McCarter said. "And he becomes a hero to the Israelis because he's fighting against Arabs everywhere in a war *he* helped to start. Bloody brilliant."

"So that's the gist, and we think our theory here is pretty solid," Brognola said. "Here's your mission— find out where the weapons are headed and put a stop to them. Cowboy has arranged for a guy to meet you in Jerusalem. He's flying in from Brisbane, Australia. He's the chief development project leader for Stormalite, and he's bringing some special equipment with him."

"What kind of equipment?"

"The kind you're going to need if you plan to fight the RDL on equal terms. Kissinger briefed us earlier today on the capabilities of these weapons. They have some weaknesses we think you can exploit, but we don't want to take any chances. Your contact's name is Anthony Scheffler. I'm sending the rest of what we have to you via encoded channel. Study the information you get carefully, and whatever you do, don't take any chances. You need to put them down at any costs. Is that clear?"

"Clear as mud, but we'll carry on," McCarter said.

"Good enough. Now get some sleep. And good luck."

The image of Brognola's face winked out and McCarter set the communication system in standby mode to receive the electronic data Stony Man was transmitting. He would have liked to sleep, but his mind was racing with the possibilities. Israel was a big place, and if all went according to the way Brognola had propositioned it, something would break in the next twenty-four hours. And it was Phoenix Force's job to make sure that didn't happen.

The biggest problem was that despite the fact they could get the cooperation of the Israeli government, they were walking into a situation where neither side could be considered friendly. Such operations didn't fall into purview of regular police officials, even those specialized in antiterrorist techniques. The only additional cooperation they could have expected to enlist was that of the IDF special forces. There were a hundred villages along the West Bank and any one of them could have been a key target.

The best they could do at this point was rely on intelligence and hope the terrorists made a mistake and revealed their position before it was too late. McCarter was certain that Brognola would have their CIA and contracted operatives be watchful for the freighter. Maybe some useful information would fall out of that. For now, he wouldn't worry himself too much. The important thing was to get some sleep.

He picked up a phone near his bunk that provided an internal wire connection directly to the cockpit.

Jack Grimaldi immediately answered. "Flight deck."

"You heard all of that, mate?" McCarter asked, even though he already knew the answer.

"You betcha. Next stop, Tel Aviv."

McCarter thanked the pilot and then hung up the phone. As he laid his head on the pillow and wondered how he would ever fall asleep, he drifted off to dreamland.

Chicago, Illinois

AS SOON AS Able Team's plane touched down at Meigs Field, they took their waiting rental straight to the Chicago Police Department headquarters. Price had advised them that their arrival was previously disclosed to the offices of the mayor and police commissioner. They were ushered into a conference room and joined a few minutes later by a man introducing himself as Thomas Grebe, deputy police commissioner.

"You gentlemen must have some pull back there in Washington, D.C.," Grebe told them.

"Why's that?" Gadgets asked.

"Because I don't know too many people who can get away with pulling the mayor and police commissioner of this city out of their respective meetings and into an ad hoc conference call on little more than a request."

Schwarz smiled and replied, "I would have to guess that the Oval Office, particularly the Office of Homeland Security, has a few special privileges where the mayor and commissioner are concerned."

Grebe's eyes went wide. "I see. Well, I wasn't told—"

"Don't sweat it, Deputy Commissioner," Blancanales said with a casual wave. "We're all on the same side and we just want this to go down without too much trouble."

"Understood, but what exactly do you mean when you say 'this'?" Grebe asked.

It was Carl Lyons who answered him by holding up a photograph of Paxton. "This man's name is Lieutenant Commander Delmar Paxton. He's a Navy officer who has stolen government property and aided and abetted terrorists. And now he's hiding somewhere in this city with his father, Guy Hauser. Your job is to help us find them."

"It might also help to get word out to your field detectives, members of your community policing neighborhoods, and CIs," Gadgets suggested.

"And under no circumstances are you to attempt to arrest these men," Blancanales added. "Just issue the APB and we'll give you a way to contact us directly if they're spotted."

Grebe took the photograph of Paxton, and also one of Hauser, and studied them a moment. He then placed a call on the conference phone and less than a minute later a woman in a business suit entered. He passed the photographs to her, along with descriptions that Kurtzman had printed for Lyons to give.

"Put out a BOLO to units right now on these two, and also prep APBs for each station house and the oncoming shifts. Don't leave anyone out. Is that clear?"

"Yes, sir," the woman said, and then she was gone.

That done, Grebe returned his gaze to Able Team and looked at each one of them in turn before finally staring Lyons in the eye. "Now I don't suppose you're at liberty to tell me just what these two men have done, exactly."

Lyons shrugged. "Not in so many words. Some of the information is restricted. But I know what kind of red tape this might cause for you, and since the men and women in this agency are at risk, I can tell you a few things."

"You must swear this information to confidentiality, Deputy Commissioner," Blancanales reminded him, "at least where that information wouldn't pose an immediate risk of life and limb to your people."

"And even then you might have to keep your mouth shut," Lyons interjected.

Grebe was quiet again for some time before saying, "I have a feeling I'm going to regret this when I've grown old and tired, but you have a deal. Talk to me."

ONCE ABLE TEAM had finished with Grebe, the three men drove to the Networks Information Interchange Center at the Great Lakes Naval Base. Kurtzman had searched payroll records and personnel files inside their system. Not even the country's best military and technical minds could keep out the computer expert. It took Kurtzman a few clicks of the mouse, a couple dozen lines of programming code, and an old tunneling trick using Telnet and the SSH protocol to crack the computer system at the NIIC. Within minutes, he knew just about everything there was to know about Hauser, including the name of the guy's boss.

"Step into my office," Dr. Vernon Zuki said, directing Able Team to chairs spread throughout his cluttered office.

Zuki was a small Polynesian man with thick glasses and an unassuming disposition. In fact, the most prepossessing thing about him was his mode of dress. According to the intelligence brief Kurtzman had transmitted to Able Team during its flight to Chicago, the man had dual master's degrees in Information Systems and Information Technology, and a Doctorate of Sciences in Artificial Intelligence. He'd obtained one of his degrees from MIT, spent a small time in the country on a 2B work visa, and then eventually applied for citizenship and was accepted. Yet here he sat in a blue jeans and a fashionable shirt and sweater vest.

"So I understand you're here to inquire about Guy," Zuki said. It wasn't a question.

"Yeah," Lyons replied. "How long have you worked with him?"

Zuki didn't hesitate. "It will be four years exactly on the twentieth of this month."

Lyons exchanged looks with Schwarz and Blancanales, before saying, "That's very precise."

"Precision is the name of the game in my line of work," Zuki said.

Schwarz smiled. "Ours, too."

Lyons handed Zuki a picture of Paxton. "Have you ever seen this man before?"

Zuki looked at the picture for a few moments before smiling. He handed it back to Lyons and said, "Many times. There's an identical picture sitting on Guy's desk. It's his son."

"Correct," Blancanales said.

"Dr. Zuki," Blancanales went on, "since you've worked with Hauser for some time now, I'm sure you have a pretty good assessment of skills."

"Of course," he said. He leaned forward on his desk and said, "In fact, I have his annual performance review somewhere, if you'd like to see it."

"No, that will be fine. But thanks for the offer."

"You don't wish to see it?" Zuki asked, flashing a surprised expression. He sat back in his chair, crossed his legs and pushed his glasses on his nose. "Guy is up for promotion. I had assumed when I got the call from the director that you were here about that. I now surmise my assumption was wrong."

"It was," Lyons said with a frosty smile.

"Doctor, how well do you know Guy Hauser?" Blancanales asked. "I mean, outside of his technical skills. Have you ever had dinner with him, or been to his house? Have you ever met his son, or any member of his family?"

"Not really," Zuki replied. "We're dissuaded from any fraternization with our subordinates outside of company-sanctioned functions. It's a professional environment and we like to keep it that way. Personal relationships can, well…let's say complicate matters."

"So you weren't aware then that Guy Hauser is Jewish?"

"No, not at all," Zuki said. "Gentlemen, I don't want to seem rude but I have quite a bit of work to do. Is there something you would like to get at specifically?"

Lyons now had a good feel for Zuki. He was a no-

nonsense type and it was probably better they just handle him with forthrightness. "Doctor, we believe that Hauser and his son may be planning to commit a terrorist act here in Chicago."

"What?" Zuki let out a laugh dripping with disbelief. "That's preposterous! I realize that these are precarious times, gentlemen, and that we must all act with patriotic fervor. However, I believe you've made an error in judgment. I may not know that much personally about Guy, but what I *do* know is that he's a red-blooded American if there ever was one, and I cannot fathom him capable of doing anything to harm anyone. I certainly do not believe he would use his skills to commit a terrorist act, if that's where you're going with this."

"We'd like to believe it, too, Doctor," Lyons said. "But I'm afraid the evidence is overwhelming in this case. We have undisputed proof that Hauser's son has stolen very highly specialized firearm prototypes from the Naval Air Station at Key West. We also know that his son has consorted with known terrorists belonging to a group that calls themselves the Resurrected Defense League. And we also know that Hauser's son kept the fact his father was even alive a secret from the Navy when he joined."

"And what is this proof?" Zuki asked.

"The proof doesn't really matter at this point," Schwarz replied. "Let me pose a scenario to you, Doctor. Suppose you have a weapon, or a group of weapons, that you can trigger by using solid-state electronics."

"You must be referring to Stormalite Systems," Zuki said.

The men of Able Team didn't repress their surprise. Lyons said, "You know about them?"

"I know enough," Zuki said. "When you work in this business long enough, you develop contacts. I've known about the special weapons they were developing for some time now, although I've never spoken with anyone about it. I was told in confidence, you see."

"So you must know, then, that it's possible to fire these weapons using a wireless network," Gadgets replied.

"Of course."

"Do you think it's possible Hauser has enough skill to rig up a makeshift firing system based on wireless technology?"

"That, sir, would be an understatement. Understanding network and telecommunications concepts is a requirement in the first year of almost any degree in the field of technology today. The concepts of the Internet, which in and of itself could be viewed as a network in macrocosm, albeit complicated in its structural framework, is now taught to seventh graders. It's estimated that by the age of eight, most children in American homes can use a computer with a greater degree of efficiency and expertise than the adults living in the same house. In fact, the government has realized the value of teaching its future computer programmers to start programming at as young an age as possible, and there are some studies that show anywhere from five to seven is the best place."

"So somewhere in all of that, you're saying yes?" Lyons cut in.

"Yes, that's what I'm saying, sir." Zuki paused a moment, then added, "But even though Guy possesses the consummate skills to wire these weapons, it certainly doesn't mean he has the mental capacity to do it."

"Maybe he doesn't," Blancanales said, "but the men he's working for do. The Resurrected Defense League has already been responsible for a number of actions in the past forty-eight hours."

"You mean, the massacre in New York City?" Zuki asked with a surprise in his tone.

"Could be," Lyons replied noncommittally. "The point here, Doctor, is that we need to find Hauser. If he's innocent, then he has nothing to worry about, but if he's working with the terrorists then he's got plenty to hide, and it would explain why we've been unable to find him."

"Did he report for work this morning?" Gadgets asked.

"Yes, but I gave him the afternoon off."

"Why?"

"He didn't say. Just told me he wanted to take some personal time, and so I approved it. Egads! You think he's going to network these weapons?"

"It's a pretty good bet," Lyons replied. "And I'm sure you'll understand it when I tell you that we're here to prevent that. And we've been authorized to do so by whatever means are at our disposal."

"You mean, you're here to kill him," Zuki said in a

voice that was as nonchalant as it would have been had he just given them the recipe for pumpkin pie.

"Let's hope it won't come to that," Blancanales said with a smile that warned Zuki it was better not to discuss the matter in that light.

"What we aren't going to do is negotiate with terrorists," Lyons said. "We're troubleshooters, plain and simple, and we're here to avert a disaster if at all possible. So if you know anything about Hauser, or if you have some idea of where he might be hiding, it would go better if you tell us."

"I'm not sure I can help you beyond what I've already said," Zuki replied. "I just don't know what else I might be able to tell you that would help."

"Anything at all might make the difference between us nipping this in the bud before it becomes a problem versus having to resort to a solution of permanence," Blancanales said.

"Well, there is one thing that might help you," Zuki said. "I once heard Guy mention that he'd purchased a small piece of property on the North Side."

"What kind of property?" Lyons asked.

"Just a small parcel in one of the commercial areas," he said. "He told me he opened it to run server connections for a club he belonged to. Something about setting it up to provide Internet access and Web page hosting."

"Did he ever get more specific than that? Maybe give you an address?"

"No, but I *do* know that he got it from a real-estate agent that has quite a number of clients here at the base. She specializes in find affordable housing for the civilian workers and military personnel who prefer to live off base because housing isn't always readily available. She comes highly recommended."

"Do you have a name?"

"I've never used her personally, mind you," Zuki replied, sitting forward in his chair and typing information into his computer. "But I happen to have her electronic business card right here in my system."

CHAPTER TWENTY

Tel Aviv, Israel

Just as Brognola had promised, Anthony Scheffler met Phoenix Force at the Tel Aviv Ben-Gurion International Airport.

The intelligence Stony Man had on the Australian was sketchy. Scheffler had started as a customization engineer with Heckler & Koch in the late 1980s after graduating from the University of Brisbane with a degree in industrial engineering with a concentration in metallurgy. After working in both their framing and R&D labs for a number of years, Scheffler returned to Australia where he met the owner and founder of Stormalite Systems, Limited. As soon as he heard of the man's vision, he accepted a position as first junior engineer, then engineering lead, and was finally promoted to director of engineer operations for the Brisbane office of the company. He'd also vested in some stock options, so he'd attributed a considerable amount of wealth in the prospect.

Scheffler was pleasant-looking enough, a young man in his late thirties. He didn't seem cocky or arrogant despite his upbringing and education, but his attitude betrayed his personality as more akin to that of a very curious teenager with an overactive imagination. He was tall and lean, built much like Calvin James, with a ruddy complexion, a birthmark above his right eye and reddish-brown hair. A thick mustache matching his hair color covered his upper lip and mouth, and flared downward, terminating in bushy tufts around his chin.

As soon as they had secured travel arrangements, Scheffler rode with them to an abandoned gravel pit about five miles south of the city. It had been the perfect place to set up a demonstration of the capabilities of the weapons developed by Stormalite, and simultaneously they wouldn't attract attention to themselves. McCarter didn't really like the setup, but he hadn't been given much choice in the matter. This was the one place where they could work without interference.

Scheffler started with a brief explanation of each weapon, several models of each that he had set up in rank and file. Phoenix Force immediately observed some targets that looked to be made of painted wood about fifty yards downrange. Scheffler had provided several different levels of weaponry in a variety of calibers.

"I wasn't exactly sure what you fellows would be comfortable with." Scheffler's Australian accent was heavy, and it took some getting used to when trying to understand him. "They were kind of vague when I asked about your backgrounds in firearms. However, I can now see you gentlemen have handled a gun or two in your time."

This produced various levels of laughter from each of them, and very quickly the members of Phoenix Force shared a silent moment of agreement between one another: Scheffler was a likable character.

"So I'll skip the boring details and give you the straight story on this," Scheffler continued. He picked up the pistol and held it high for them to see. "This is the SS-925 autopistol. It's a variant on the 9 mm, and is equipped for up to five barrels with a stacked set of seven rounds per barrel."

"Excuse me, mate," McCarter said. "Sorry to interrupt, but what in bloody hell do you mean by 'stacked set'?"

Scheffler grinned. "Hello, I suppose that *does* sound kind of funny. Last stacked set you probably saw was in a South London pub."

This time the laughter from Phoenix Force was uproarious, and Hawkins couldn't resist delivering a light punch to McCarter's arm when he noticed the Briton's face go slightly red. Still, he took the joke well enough and the laughter was actually a relief.

"Fair enough," Scheffler said. "Something you probably need to understand up front is that these weapons have no moving parts."

"None?" Hawkins interjected. "Not even extractors?"

"There are no shells, so there's no need for a bolt-carrying system of any kind, mate. The ammunition is stacked in the barrel." He looked at McCarter, winked and said, "That's what I meant by a stack set. Since each round is expelled in hundredths of a second, we can add a number of barrels to a single pistol and trigger them one or more at any given time. For example, each barrel holds seven rounds, but the cyclic rate of fire per barrel is just over 830 rounds per second. That would convert to fifty-one thousand rounds per minute."

"And if you multiply that by five barrels, your actual cyclic rate of fire is around the quarter-million mark," Manning concluded.

"Now you have it, mate," Scheffler said. "And that brings me to a bit about the nomenclature of these weapons. Like the design, we've tried to keep the naming convention simple, so every one of them follows a logical sequence based on a numeric system. All of our weapons begin with the 'SS' to denote we're the manufacturer. The first number then denotes the caliber. The second digit is the leading numeral for the respective cyclic rate of fire measured in hundred thousands, and the last digit is the number of barrels required to achieve that rate if a pistol, or the last two digits if a submachine gun or assault rifle."

"Doesn't sound simple," Hawkins commented.

"It is actually. Take the SS-925 here. It's three digits, so you know immediately it's a pistol. The nine denotes 9 mm, the two indicates its cyclic rate of fire is two-hundred-fifty thousand rounds per minute, and the five indicates the number of barrels required to achieve that cyclic rate."

He pointed to one of the submachine guns and said, "This one here is the SS-5510, and that rifle there is the SS-7608."

"So the subgun fires 5.56 mm ammunition, at five hundred thousand per minute through ten barrels," James recited mechanically.

"You're spot-on, mate," Scheffler said. "Now another thing you have to understand about such a system is that it doesn't take much to empty these weapons. You can reload them rather fast, but the secret will be to hold low and validate your target before firing."

"Does the trigger pull control the rate of fire like in a conventional pistol?" James asked.

"To a lesser degree, yes, but it's still dependent on the skill of the user. In a normal gas-operated firearm, you hold the trigger down for a sustained shot, but you're still limited by the speed of the bolt. After all, the thing can only move so fast. Such moving parts are hard on the equipment, and they not only reduce the amount of firepower that you can direct at the target, they also make it difficult to control the weapon. Here, you have no such limitations. Even a quick squeeze of the trigger will discharge quite a number of rounds, and the effect of the fire is that much greater in a shorter period of time."

"We've seen these things and what they can do firsthand," Manning said. "So speaking for myself, I can believe what you're telling us."

Scheffler nodded. "These weapons are unlike any you've ever fired before. What I'm about to show you is going to knock your knickers off."

Scheffler turned, aimed the weapon at the nearest target and squeezed the trigger. The weapon recoiled only once, and the report was loud, but it was nothing compared to the target. Most of the wood had disintegrated under the first shot, and there was a gaping hole the size of a basketball in the center. Scheffler turned and looked at the men of Phoenix Force who were all now standing with their mouths agape.

"Santa Maria," Encizo said, crossing himself.

"Judas Priest, that was some shit," Hawkins added quickly. He turned to McCarter and said, "I'm beginning to understand the RDL's interest in these weapons."

"Oh, yes," Scheffler said. "Make no mistake about it, gentlemen. A couple dozen men, each equipped with a pistol and rifle of this kind, could easily level a small village here on the West Bank in under an hour using little more than small arms fire."

"Well, that's why we're here," McCarter said. "We need to make sure that doesn't happen. What about the rest of these toys?"

"Let's start slowly," Scheffler said.

The Aussie reached into a square bag of metal framed around leather, and extracted a small set of five plastic sleeves connected to a metal bar. He fit the sleeves into the barrels and then lightly slapped the back of the bar with his palm. There was light popping noise followed by an audible click, then Scheffler removed the plastic sleeves. He flipped a switch at the base of the handle and a whining sound could be heard that was similar to that of a flashbulb camera being primed for the next picture.

Scheffler handed the weapon to McCarter to handle first, with the barrels pointed downrange. "Go ahead. Give it a try."

McCarter took the weapon gingerly. It was simple but a little boxy in design and yet the thing couldn't have weight more than a pound. The Briton studied the handle, which was comfortable with a rubbery substance coating the entire exterior of it with the exception of a black lens on the thumb rest. McCarter noticed that as soon as he wrapped his hand around the grip that a red light lit up beneath his thumb, emitted from the lens.

He squeezed the trigger but nothing happened. He tried again; still nothing. "There's something wrong with this thing."

"Not at all," Scheffler said. "All of Stormalite's weapons are user smart. What I mean is that only a specific user is qualified to fire the weapon. There are sensors in the handle that detect certain distinguishable chemicals, and the sensor beneath your thumb takes a digital fingerprint. Unless the owner is programmed in, the weapon won't fire."

"It's too bad you didn't have that feature in place at the weapons conference," Encizo remarked.

"We were still perfecting the process, friend," Scheffler said in a slightly defensive tone. "My people are very safety conscious. We would never have allowed those weapons to be demonstrated if we'd known someone would actually attempt to steal them. I feel badly enough about it. Why do you think I'm here?"

"Nobody's blaming you, guy," McCarter said. "Why don't we all just get back to business?"

Encizo nodded at McCarter and then extended his hand to Scheffler. "Sorry."

"No worries," Scheffler said, accepting the offer warmly. He then gestured for McCarter to hand him the weapon. He reached up and flipped out a plate that was recessed under the rear of the weapon just above the handle. He inserted a miniature key into an opening beneath the plate and twisted it a quarter turn, then punched a button and handed the weapon back to McCarter.

"Hold it naturally for five seconds or until you hear a beep."

McCarter did as instructed until the weapon emitted its signal and then he returned it to Scheffler. The Aussie repeated his motions with the key and button and then handed the weapon to McCarter.

"One more time, try to fire," he told the Briton. "And this time, let's do this with some feeling."

McCarter took a deep breath, let out half, aligned the three-dot sights on the next target in line and squeezed the trigger. At first, nothing seemed as though it had happened, but then the weapon suddenly bucked in his hand and his ears began to ring with the report. McCarter lowered the pistol and stared at the target in shock. Very similar to Scheffler's target, this one was also torn and tattered, with very little left of the first board worth mentioning and very little to see of the six behind that one.

"Damned bloodiest thing I've ever seen," McCarter said quietly.

"That's nothing," Scheffler said. "Wait until I show you the subgun and assault rifle."

WITHIN A FEW HOURS of completing their training, Phoenix Force was on its way to the West Bank via a government Land Rover that was being driven by an agent of Mossad. It had taken some considerable doing, but Stony Man finally managed to get word to Ilia Yasso inside the special intelligence arm of the Israeli government. When she heard that friends of Bolan needed assistance, she'd used her influence to secure a trustworthy guide and transportation to get them to where they suspected the RDL terrorists were headed.

Yasso had first come to the attention of Stony Man when Mack Bolan was assigned to insure the transfer of a special encrypted computer chip went off between a Special Forces detachment and Israeli troops. The Kach-Kahane Chai had also had a play in that situation. Yasso was a tough go-getter with Mossad who planned to insure that the transfer came off without a hitch, but things went south when the Kahane Chai terrorists infiltrated Fort Carson, Colorado, and massacred the Special Forces detachment, then stole the chips and tried to smuggle them out of the country. Mack Bolan had other plans, and with Yasso's help, he neutralized the plot and decimated the terrorist army. His actions saved Yasso and her people, and apparently she hadn't forgotten.

"So what do you think?" Brognola asked McCarter.

"I think we need to stop these buggers and quick-like," McCarter replied as the Land Rover bounced along the back road from Jenin.

"Well, it looks like we finally figured out where the terrorists are headed, although we spent nearly fifty thousand in bribes."

"Yes, we got your message. They're headed for the village called Arabeh?"

"Yes," Brognola replied. "I want you to get a feel for the present situation so you know what you could be walking into. A few days ago, the Israeli government had to go in and put down a small coup being instigated by one of the village leaders. The security is tight going in or out, and there's only one road leading to the village. The Israelis control it, so we think the first thing they'll do is hit the roadblocks."

"Makes sense," McCarter replied. "They'll want free bloody access in and out of the village."

"What concerns me is that they plan to go in and massacre everyone," Brognola said. "I don't think they're going to be sparing of either side. Remember, they hate the Palestinians, so any blood spilled there will be no loss. The key, though, will be eliminating any Israelis, as well as anyone who could testify the guards were attacked by their own people."

"They can always use propaganda and the media to get the story out the way they want to."

"And they probably will," Brognola replied. "Just remember that you cannot let them succeed. We've done everything we can at this end to support your efforts as best as possible. It's up to Phoenix Force now, David. We're depending on you."

"We won't disappoint," McCarter replied. "See you soon."

McCarter disconnected the call and then started to check the action on his SS-5510. He stopped himself, chalking it up to habit. He wasn't entirely comfortable using these weapons against the terrorists, but he was convinced they would give them the upper advantage. The prototypes the terrorists were carrying weren't anywhere near as stable as the weapons Scheffler had given the Stony Man warriors. Scheffler had personally tested every single one of these weapons, and even the idea that the terrorists were limited in ammunition and accessories was a comfort, however small.

Along with McCarter, Hawkins was also carrying an SS-5510, and the rest of the Phoenix Force warriors had elected to try the SS-7608s, although these particular models only had four barrels, which reduced the cyclic rate to 300,000 rounds per minute. Only McCarter wore the SS-925, although he'd gone with a single barrel only. In any case, every one of the men had retained their pistols in shoulder leather, and Manning had held on to one of the MP-5s—old habits died hard.

Their Israeli driver tapped on McCarter's shoulder and held up five dusty fingers. The Briton nodded and then signaled to the others with a twirling finger that they should be ready to go EVA. The road that approached Arabeh was filled with ruts, gravel and sand. Even a high-quality vehicle like the Land Rover could become easily stuck in the precarious ditches along the side of the narrow road. But their driver seemed to know his way along this route pretty well, and he handled the vehicle like an old pro.

The five minutes elapsed quickly and as the vehicle topped a rise in the road, McCarter could see that the battle was joined. Dammit! He could only hope they weren't too late. If the RDL managed to seize control of the village and get dug into the terrain, they'd have a significant foothold on not just the village but also the surrounding territory; it would prove a much more difficult and terrible task to flush them out. Not to mention that it would probably start the IDF moving in this direction en masse, and that would have long-standing consequences to the region.

"Stop here!" McCarter ordered the driver.

The agent obeyed and Phoenix Force bailed out.

James and Manning immediately headed for an outcropping on a nearby hill, and McCarter rushed the makeshift guard station, which was now collapsed and providing very ineffective cover for the three Israeli troops huddled behind it. Encizo and Hawkins took up positions behind a large boulder near the roadway and swept the hill above them for targets. They didn't appear immediately, but it had obviously taken the terrorists time to figure out that reinforcements had arrived.

McCarter skidded to a halt as the Israelis trained the

muzzles of their weapons on him. "Hold up. I'm British, mates."

The Israeli soldiers cocked their heads and looked at one another, then back at McCarter.

"Why you here?" one of them asked in relatively broken English.

"To save your bloody hides," McCarter said. He threw himself to the ground and crawled the rest of the way to their position. Only an ally would have made such a gesture, so a quick appraisal was all McCarter needed to pass inspection.

"Ambush," the one closest to McCarter said. "Arab guerrillas."

McCarter shook his head. "Wrong, bloke. Those are Israelis attacking you. Israeli terrorists. Like the Kach-Kahane."

"No, not Kach-Kahane Chai," the IDF trooper replied.

"*Yes,*" McCarter said. "They are terrorists, and I should bloody well know because I followed them here."

The Israeli soldiers exchanged more glances and then began to conduct a conversation among themselves. McCarter studied them a moment longer and then shook his head and turned eyes front, searching for the enemy. What he would have given at that moment for a terrorist or two to kill was bordering on the X-rated. He keyed up the microphone of his VOX.

"Hey, any of you buggers see our old friends?" he asked.

"They're on that ridge directly ahead," Encizo's

voice answered, "although I'm not sure why they haven't attacked."

"Maybe we need to—"

McCarter decided that living was better than finishing his statement. He heard a brief popping sound and knew that they had only a few seconds before they became lunch for desert carrion. He began to yell at the Israelis, grabbing a handful of the closest man's collar near his shoulder, jumping to his feet and retreating from their position. There was an eerie silence in the next moment and then the ground beneath him suddenly shook with tremendous violence.

He felt the sensation of his back burning.

His feet left the ground, and he felt the rush of hot wind against his face as he sailed through the air. Another moment passed, then his face hit the ground and the air rushed from his lungs.

McCarter remembered looking down and seeing that he still had hold of the Israeli soldier's shirt near the shoulder.

The only problem, all he was holding was the man's shoulder.

And then the world faded to black.

"MCCARTER'S DOWN! McCarter's down!" Hawkins looked at Encizo. "I think he's dead!"

"I see it," Encizo replied calmly. "Don't jump to conclusions. Hold your position and open fire on that grenade launcher."

The Phoenix Force commandos aimed their new arsenal in the direction of terrorists who were now seemingly focused on celebrating their first major victory, and triggered the weapons. It sounded as though there were only four shots, but in actuality they hit the position with a total of one hundred sixty-eight 5.56 mm and 7.62 mm rounds. Screams resounded through the air as the first blast decimated equipment and flesh.

"We could use about six more of these," Hawkins said triumphantly as he yanked a reload pack from his bandolier and carefully inserted the sleeves into the weapon.

"Yeah," Encizo replied. He reloaded his own weapon and then keyed up the VOX. "Calvin? See if you can get to David. We'll cover you."

"Roger," James replied.

"On my mark, guys," Encizo told them.

The Phoenix Force warriors aligned their weapons on the enemy's position once more and braced themselves for another volley. The Cuban insured he had the target sighted correctly, then he gave the order. Once more there were three reports but more than a hundred rounds were sent into the enemy's position. There was a short delay from the moment they confirmed the rounds had hit, then a large plume of dust, followed by a vicious explosion. They had taken out the grenade launcher!

James reached McCarter fairly quickly and delivered a status report. "He's alive. He's unconscious, but the tough bastard's alive."

"Treat him for injuries and get him to the vehicle. We'll sweep into the village and mop up."

"Acknowledged," James replied.

Manning met up with Encizo and James and, after a quick reload, the trio jogged down the main road and into the village. People didn't appear shocked to see them as they moved up the street in cover-and-maneuver fashion. Such a sight wasn't anything new to these people. They had spent all of their lives in a country at war, so it didn't make much difference to them that these particular invaders looked or dressed a little different. It didn't really matter to them if was Israelis or Palestinians or Americans because ultimately it only spelled one thing: death.

The Phoenix Force warriors kept to the sides of the street, using the irregular framework of the modest buildings to provide cover. They were all cognizant of the positions of their teammates. The weapons they held were powerful, but they weren't discretionary, and when unleashing that many rounds it was a good idea to know it was at the right target. The new weapons had already served as invaluable tools—much more than Encizo would have believed possible.

"Keep your eyes open," the little Cuban whispered into the microphone. "We don't know how many or where."

They both acknowledged the message and then continued on mission. They were here in one capacity and one capacity only: to search and destroy. Encizo thought of it now, envisioning how easy it would have been to simply let these things rip on a full-auto burn and just level the place. But these weren't just a bunch of dilapidated buildings clustered together. These comprised the homes and businesses of the villagers that lived here, and he didn't have a right to take that away from them any more than the RDL did. He was here on more than just a search-and-destroy mission; he was here on a mission of freedom.

"Trouble at high noon," Hawkins called.

Encizo looked up and watched the terrorists coming straight for them. They had the Stormalite weapons leveled and their gait said they were determined to unleash hell on their enemies. There were only a dozen or so, and Encizo knew that he was looking at the remainder of the RDL force here in Israel.

"Down!" he roared.

They dropped to the ground even as the familiar popping noises echoed through the hot, desert air. The air above their heads was filled with a firestorm of the unique ammunition, and Encizo could actually feel the heat and pressure changes in air density as the area immediately above them was suddenly filled with thousands of rounds. He heard the crumbling of walls and sensed the horrific scene that had to have transpired as men, women and children began to scream. He felt something warm and wet smack his hand, and he looked in the direction in time to see the lifeless eyes of a head staring back at him. A head that was no longer attached to its owner's body.

"Take them," Encizo said quietly.

The trio took aim. The terrorists—who had stopped to reload—realized that their enemies weren't holding conventional weapons, but instead they were about to unleash a firestorm of their own. At that point, there

was little more they could do and the Phoenix Force
warriors knew it as well as their opponents did.

There were three loud reports followed by twelve
terrorists falling under a hail of bullets. Some had
limbs torn from their bodies, others literally lost their
heads, and still others were simply cut in two. Blood,
bone and brain matter sprayed in every direction and
a few were knocked off their feet by the impact. It was
almost surreal to Encizo; it was as if he were watching the carnage unfold in slow motion. It was like
nothing he'd ever seen before. The desert sands on that
part of the street were red with blood, littered with the
corpses of what remained of the Resurrected Defense
League. It was a grueling reminder of the kind of destruction that man's mind could devise.

And in the last moments, in the aftermath of the
maelstrom, there was only death.

But in some small way, there was also victory.

CHAPTER TWENTY-ONE

Chicago, Illinois

Wallace Davidia watched the activity of the city streets with interest as he drove south out of Wheeling and entered the Chicago city limits.

Getting into the country hadn't been that difficult. He'd flown to Canada on a passport that stated he was an Israeli citizen. Once that was accomplished, he'd procured forged documents for entry to the United States, including a Michigan driver's license and a birth certificate. Little had changed, and it was much easier being that he looked like an American, spoke like an American—the New York accent had stuck with him—and carried himself like an American.

Between jet lag and the drive from Toronto to Chicago, Davidia was experiencing a significant amount of physical weariness. Still, he also felt rejuvenated at the thought that his plans would soon come to fruition. He wondered how things were going in Arabeh.

Rasham was late in reporting status, but he imagined they were busy preparing for the news of rioting on the streets of this city. He'd turned on the radio sporadically during his trip, hoping for some news, but aside from a brief on new peace initiatives being proposed by the U.S. ambassador to Israel, there wasn't word one. Not that it truly mattered. It would take the media some time to inform the general public.

And only twelve hours remained before the news of total anarchy right here spread like wildfire. The law and order in America, their false sense of security, would be crushed underfoot as the Jewish and Arab communities picked up arms and waged war against each other. Mayhem would spread quickly, and the events here and those in New York City would be enough to spark a conflict long overdue. Neighborhood would rise against neighborhood, and then city against city, and soon there would be a body count in America that was unmatched since the Civil War. Simultaneously, Rasham would begin the propaganda campaign in Israel. It would take long for the IDF to respond when they learned of the massacre of the guard placed outside Arabeh, blaming the Palestinians of the area. The days of ethnic cleansing would return and the Arabs would finally suffer their own genocide.

There were many who had questioned Davidia's motives through the years. A number of the members within the Kach-Kahane Chai, including those he considered friends, had said that Davidia had no real wish to fight for the rights of Jews, but rather was using the anti-Semitic movement to resolve a personal vendetta.

But Davidia didn't care what they thought. He knew where he came from. His father had taught him that, ultimately, whether it was a fight for the Jews or some other call, there was always a political element at the core—always. Groups like the Kach-Kahane Chai weren't fighting a war for the rights of Jews in the purest sense. They were fighting a political war, and that meant the chances of them producing any results above the purely political were unlikely.

It was this view that had caused him to move away from the movement and start his own. The Resurrected Defense League didn't stand for Jewish rights by the political definition. He chose to represent the common Jew, the human being that had to live in fear every day of his life. He fought for the Jew that couldn't get ahead, or find a job, or send their children off to school without worrying that it would be for the last time. Davidia most represented those who had been the victim, or stood to be a victim, of the jihad that the Arabs had declared on the Israelis. This wasn't the same kind of war they had declared on the Americans; that was entirely different. They had declared war on Americans because they resented the vile forms of living that clearly violated their religious convictions. But the Arab war against Israel was about land and ethnic cleansing. They were bent on making the Jewish people and their way of life extinct. Davidia planned to make sure that the enemy suffered their own fate first.

Within twenty minutes Davidia arrived at the small commercial building where Hauser had secretly established his lab. Davidia parked his car in a nearby garage and, as he exited, a meter mounted to the concrete wall caught his attention. He didn't want to do anything that might attract the attention of the police. Then again, it was sometimes the law-abiding citizens that were the most suspicious. Still, Davidia had always believed discretion was the better part of valor, so he dropped some coins into the meter and then headed for Hauser's lab.

When he reached the front door, Davidia looked both ways, then removed the key from his pocket and put it in the lock. He did another quick check of the area around the building exterior before pushing the door open and moving inside. He closed and secured it behind him, then waited and listened. The downstairs interior was old, dusty and bare. There were no lights on, and the sun was quickly setting, the crimson light of dusk casting an eerie glow throughout the room.

And then Davidia heard the voices. They were faint at first, inconsistent, but they were present all the same. Davidia couldn't tell whose voices, and despite the fact that Hauser had agreed to meet him here, he'd understood the man would be alone. Davidia had recently had too many surprises, and he had purposed in his mind that there wouldn't be any more. He was ready for anything.

Davidia reached inside his jacket and withdrew the compact .380 pistol he'd carried right into the country under the noses of the U.S. Border Patrol. He quietly ascended the stairwell he found at the back of the building and peered over the top of the second-floor landing. The loftlike area was well lit and there were computer processing units spread throughout the room, a few of them with accompanying terminals. A long table hugged one wall, and spread across the table was a group of very familiar-looking weapons.

Davidia was puzzled at first, but then it became clear what was going on when he noticed the men bent over the table and working on weapons with focused precision. Davidia immediately recognized Guy Hauser, but the other man had his back to Davidia. The RDL leader considered his options. It didn't look as though Hauser was doing anything to sabotage the material, but he was concerned to see the guns here because his men were to have brought them from the Key West naval base.

"Good evening, Guy," Davidia said, keeping his pistol leveled in the direction of the unidentified second man.

Davidia nearly dropped his weapon when he saw the face that turned and looked at him. There were many people Davidia might have expected to see, but his childhood friend and companion wasn't one of them. It had been at least seven years since he'd seen Delmar Paxton, and he hadn't really planned to ever see him again after he left the country. Naturally, he knew that Hauser had remained in contact with Paxton—and that Paxton had been instrumental in getting Davidia's men onto the installation at Key West so they could smuggle the Stormalite prototypes off the base and eliminate the U.S. government agent sent to work with Remar. But he had never expected to see Paxton again.

"Wallace," Paxton greeted him.

Davidia studied the man's face carefully. There was nothing sinister in Paxton's expression. In fact, he seemed genuinely happy to see Davidia. The terrorist leader holstered his weapon and stepped forward to embrace each of the men. These men were all that really remained of his family, and he saw no reason to treat them any differently than he always had.

"It's truly great to see you alive and well," Paxton told him. "We weren't sure of your survival after we received word of the defeat in Israel."

Davidia felt a cold knot settle in his stomach. "What defeat is this?"

Hauser and Paxton exchanged looks, each unsure if the other was planning to deliver the bad news. Davidia didn't really need to hear it, because he already knew what it meant. Somehow, Rasham's force had been defeated.

Finally, Hauser said, "I'm sorry, Wallace, but the news came to us about a half hour ago. I'd hacked into a satellite linkup that monitored military communications of the Israeli Defense Forces. We thought that if you had arrived early that you would want to hear how they were responding. There was an alert for mobilization, and they were ready to send more than a thousand troops to repel what they thought was another coup under way at Arabeh."

"What happened?" Davidia asked.

"It seems the alert was canceled and they only sent a small force. Apparently they're calling it a terrorist action, probably initiated by the Kach-Kahane Chai movement, which was mysteriously put down by an unknown force. Preliminary reports indicate that perhaps the attack was repelled by an IDF unit that happened to be in the area training when guards near the village sent a distress signal. A few others say it was a group of mercenaries, and some of them were Americans."

Davidia wanted to break something, but he could only stand there and clutch his fists tightly. He brought them to his eyes, fighting back the tears. He was angrier than he'd ever been, and it was a purely emotional response now. He'd lost his people to that force of devils who had blocked his path every step of the way. And he couldn't stand the guilt and anguish when he thought of his brother and friend, who was now most likely dead. Rasham had warned him that this would happen, and because of his need for justice and revenge he had allowed himself to be blinded to the plight of his own people. Rasham had tried to warn him; Davidia just hadn't listened.

"Wallace?" Paxton's voice snatched Davidia back to the cold, hard reality of their present situation. "What do you want to do?"

"Nothing," Davidia said.

"What do you mean 'nothing'?" Hauser asked.

"I simply mean that we're going to move forward with our plans as if nothing has happened. You have the weapons, and you can still rig them to be triggered by wireless network, correct?"

Hauser nodded.

"And my men are nearby?"

"What's left of them," Paxton said. "I brought three of them with me, and the others have been arriving throughout the day."

"We've been getting regular calls from them. They simply call here, leave us a number and then hang up."

"And how many do we have?"

"The last count we received was about twenty-five," Paxton said.

Davidia nodded, some of his strength and fervor returning. "That will be more than enough to enact our plans while still providing us security. Perhaps we can even strike at another city. We *must* move forward, otherwise my people will have died in vain. This force of Americans chipped away at our forces at every turn."

"These must be the same men I encountered down in Key West."

"What men?"

"Three men from the U.S. Marshals Service, or at least that's where they said they were from. Quite frankly, I didn't believe them."

Davidia looked at Hauser and said, "I thought you told my people there was only one man there."

"There was," Paxton said, jumping to the defense of his father. "At least, at the beginning. But then when your men failed to assassinate him, someone from Washington sent three more down. And these guys were definitely different. They claimed to be a special detachment to the Office of Homeland Security, but they were clearly not standard government material. They defeated more than eight of your men, and discovered the weapons cache they were to bring here to aid in our support. They were consummate professionals, and while there were only three of them, they fought like a force of thirty."

"It doesn't make any difference," Davidia snapped. He turned to Paxton and said, "What are you doing here in Chicago then? And if my men are dead, how did these weapons get here?"

"I brought them myself," Paxton replied with a haughty expression. "I decided that if my dad was going to succeed then I needed to step up and take charge of this operation. The men you sent were obviously incapable of handling this on their own."

"They weren't my best," Davidia said, a bit irritated at his longtime friend. He was even more irritated with himself, though, because he knew Paxton was speaking the truth. "My best were in Israel, and even they were defeated. But I won't be dissuaded from my mission. We're going to accomplish our objectives and it doesn't matter if we die in the process. I don't care anything about living now. All I care about is accomplishing what we set out to do now. We can only hope that what we do today will be enough to sound the battle cry for others."

"Wallace, it might be better to rethink this," Hauser told him.

Davidia considered the words of his father's friend. They echoed with the sentiments that Rasham had tried to impart to him and he wondered if there was a lesson to be learned. Of course, the situation had been much different there. The SOG that had ruined their operations in Spain and Israel couldn't be anywhere near Chicago, and whoever it was that had repelled his people in Key West would have returned to Washington, D.C. or still be tied up with bureaucratic red tape in Florida.

"The operation will proceed as planned," Davidia finally said. "How long before the weapons are ready?"

"We've been working on them all afternoon," Hauser said with a sigh. "I'm configuring the last one now."

"Good," Davidia said. "Finish you work, then you can show me how they work. Within the hour, gentlemen, we're going to make history. And the world as we know it will never be the same."

ONCE ABLE TEAM had the name of the real-estate agent who had sold the commercial space in north Chicago to Guy Hauser, it didn't take much to convince the agent they were investors and interested in buying the property. Was it possible for her to get them the exact location of the building? Why, yes, of course she'd be happy to give them any information on it that they needed. But she wasn't sure if Mr. Hauser was really willing to sell, and since she was the original sales agent she'd be happy to talk to them about serving as a buyer agent and intermediary in any negotiations they might like to conduct if they decided to name a price.

Blancanales thanked her for the information and disconnected the call. "We're set."

Schwarz was at the wheel, so he gave Lyons, who

was riding shotgun with a map that had been provided to them courtesy of the Chicago tourist's bureau, the address.

"The only question now is whether or not we contact Grebe," Blancanales noted.

"What, and bring half the Chicago P.D. into this?" Lyons asked sarcastically. "No, thanks. We came here to do this on our own and that's exactly what we're going to do."

"By the way," Blancanales said, "I noticed while I was talking to the real-estate agent that you got a call from Hal."

Lyons nodded, not taking his eyes off the map. "Yeah, he called to say that Phoenix Force was successful in putting down the crew in Israel. I guess David took some serious burns to his back, and some shrapnel, but he was awake by the time they took off from Tel Aviv and bitching that there wasn't any Coke on board."

"If there's a sure sign that damn Limey's wounds aren't fatal, it's that he's found something to bitch about."

"Well, the RDL was apparently planning to create a media spectacle by wasting a bunch of their own people in some small village held under Palestinian control."

"Wouldn't be the first time that's happened," Blancanales replied.

Lyons shook his head and said, "Yeah, the slaughter of innocent people in the Middle East is about as commonplace as homicides in Wonderland. It's probably one of the only events in the world you could set your watch by."

"Triggering a political nuke like an all-out war between the Arabs and Israelis seems contrary to the normal aims of groups like the RDL," Schwarz observed.

"Well, whoever said this Wallace Davidia was normal?" Lyons quipped.

"What do you think we can expect to find at this place?" Blancanales asked.

"Probably a whole bunch of nothing," Lyons said. He instructed Schwarz to turn right at the next intersection, then removed his pistol and checked the action. "But I like to think chance favors the prepared mind."

"What…are you Yoda now?" Blancanales asked, ribbing his friend.

"No, because the only force I know of with any substantive value is Smith & Wesson."

"Just don't let yourself succumb to the dark side," Schwarz said, getting in on the banter.

"Too late," Blancanales cut in before Lyons could conjure a reply.

"We're here," Schwarz said, but he continued past the building and parked a half block down in front of a ceramics shop that was closing for the night.

As he and the others went EVA, Lyons saw a silver-haired black woman coming out of the pottery store. He grinned broadly at her. "Good evening, ma'am."

"What do you want?" she said, quickly locking the

door tightly behind her and using a cane to draw a heavy aluminum gate over the storefront. She turned to look him in the eye and said, "Listen, young man, if you're planning to rob or rape me, you should know I've got a .38 in my purse and I know how to use it."

Lyons put his hands up and said, "Whoa, slow down there, ma'am. I'm sure you do. My name's Carl, and I'm with the Chicago Commercial Planning and Zoning Board. We're doing a survey of local business owners, trying to solicit opinions on the current state of the north side commercial areas."

She looked at him out the corner of her eye. "Well, you either really aren't planning on raping me, or this is just a stall tactic, but either way I know just by looking at you that you're full of bullshit, mister."

"Fine, ma'am," Lyons said with an exasperated sigh. "Would you believe that all three of us work for the Department of Homeland Security and we're searching for international terrorists that want to blow up half the city?"

"Honey, that's not terrorism, that's heroism. Depending of course on where they do it. But I'd believe that story over the original line of crap you fed me."

Blancanales decided to try his own brand of diplomacy. "What we'd like to know, ma'am, is if you've seen any unusual activity going on in that building down there?"

The woman squinted in the direction Blancanales pointed and said, "Oh, Henderson's Hardware? Well, it used to be Henderson's place, but after the old man died about a year ago and then his wife ended up in rehab for—"

"Uh, yes…that's all very interesting," Lyons said. "But what about unusual activity?"

The woman wrinkled her nose, thought about it a moment and then said, "Nah, that old flea-trap's been boarded up for more than a year. Although there was that time, maybe a few nights ago, that I had to come down here because my security alarm went off by accident, and I noticed a light coming from an upstairs window. I thought that was strange, because other nights I've had to come down here I didn't notice it."

"And you're sure the place is supposed to be abandoned?" Lyons pressed.

"That's what I said, ain't it? What's the matter, you don't hear too good?"

"I guess not."

Lyons nodded at the others and they headed down the street, leaving the woman to bitch about the alarm company as if it had been the central topic of discussion for some time. As they approached the building, Lyons began to experience a tingling in his spine and the sensation of hair rising on the back of his neck. Something wasn't quite right about this place.

He could feel it.

"YOU'RE ALL SET, my friend," Hauser said, closing the last suitcase. He handed Davidia a device that was about fifteen by fifteen inches.

"What's this?" the RDL leader asked.

"It's a PC Tablet with a command line version of

the UNIX operating system on it. You push that button right there to turn it on, and when you finish the boot sequence, you'll be in a command line interface." He reached into his breast pocket and removed a small piece of partially crumpled paper that contained a series of digits separated by periods. "These are the IP addresses you'll need to connect to each system. I've tested the wireless connections, and you're pretty hackproof. I doubt anyone could interfere with the codes in time to shut the system down."

Davidia looked at Hauser with a bit of suspicion. "You don't sound convincing, Guy. I need to know this thing is foolproof. It has to work, or we're finished."

"It will work, Wallace," Hauser said. "You're just going to have to trust me."

"It seems these days that putting your trust in others is overrated."

"Hey, Wallace," Paxton said with an edge in his tone. "If Dad says it'll work, then you can be sure it'll work. We're not your lackeys, guy. We're family, and we've risked our asses to help you make this happen. So don't throw it back in our faces now."

Davidia locked eyes with Paxton and he saw something there that told him the man was being truthful. If there was anything Davidia could remember about Paxton that left him with a sense of admiration, it was his sincerity. And he was right, of course. Both of them had risked everything to help Davidia accomplish his mission. The ties that bound them were as strong as the ties that had bound Hauser and his father. If he couldn't trust these men then he couldn't trust anyone.

"What will you do once it's over?" Hauser asked him.

"Probably die," Davidia said, and he meant it. "Because this will never be over for me until I take my last breath. What about you?"

"I've saved enough to get out of here. There's no way I'll be able to go back to my job and pretend like nothing's happened." He looked at Paxton and said, "Besides, I realized today that I have a bit of catching up to do. With my son."

Davidia shook Hauser's hand, then Paxton's, and then picked up the three suitcases and headed for the stairwell. As he started down the stairs, Paxton called to him.

"You take care of yourself, Wallace. Try to slow down long enough that you have an opportunity to grow old."

Davidia decided not to reply. There was an off chance that he was headed to his death today, rather than victory, and they all knew it. It was just that nobody was willing to say it. Davidia was halfway down the stairs when he heard movement below. He paused on the stairs, listening carefully. It was definitely the sound of the front door hinges creaking. He remembered how they had creaked when he'd opened the door earlier, and in that moment he realized he'd closed it but hadn't bothered to relock it.

Davidia went back up the steps quietly. When he reached the top, he set down the suitcases. Paxton and Hauser noticed him and with a surprised expression they started to open their mouths, but Davidia put his finger to his lips then pointed to the floor to indicate someone had made entry. He gestured for them to come and retrieve the suitcases, and they wordlessly did as instructed. That handled, Davidia pulled his pistol and crouched to wait for his enemy.

CHAPTER TWENTY-TWO

Schwarz wondered if they could have made any more damn noise coming through the front door. The squeaking of the hinges and creaking of floorboards under their weight, could just as well have been a herd of stampeding elephants. As far as he was concerned, they had already announced themselves to the enemy, so there was little point in continuing with a soft probe. Except that they wouldn't have heard the barely perceptible shuffle of feet above their heads. There were no voices, no indication of desperate activities, just the faintest hint of noise: humans trying to be quiet.

Schwarz had point, so he moved to the right of the interior that was lit solely by the streetlights. He pointed to his eyes and then upward at the ceiling. His teammates nodded in acknowledgment and then Schwarz waved them into positions against the walls that would provide adequate fields of fire. Once they had the room covered, they waited patiently, each wondering what they could expect above them.

Schwarz crossed the room quietly, no longer concerned about where he stepped. He managed to get across the room and edge closer to a door that was just ajar, visible only because of the sliver of light now visibly spilling from it. Whoever awaited them was probably beyond that door, which Schwarz assumed led to the upper level since there seemed no other visible means of getting there.

He steeled himself, reaffirmed his grip on the pistol and then started to move toward the door. He was about to reach forward and open it when the night outside came alive with flashing red and blue strobes, spotlights in the windows and the sounds of car doors slamming. A moment later the heavy pounding of boots slapping the pavement and clatter of weaponry echoed through the vast lower floor of the empty store, and the door that they had left slightly open was kicked inward with such force that Lyons had to jump aside to keep from having it embedded in his shoulder.

The room was suddenly filled with SWAT officers, their bodies covered in black fatigues, body armor and load-bearing equipment, their weapons held high and at the ready.

"Put 'em down!" one screamed.

"Police officers!" said another. "Drop your weapons! You're under arrest!"

The members of Able Team slowly lowered their pistols as they exchanged furious looks with one another. Lyons opened his mouth to chew them out, but Schwarz quieted him abruptly. The room got silent and there was the faintest sound of something bouncing around inside the wall on the other side of the door. Schwarz realized it was a grenade even before the thing suddenly bounced off the landing and rolled through the small opening in the door.

"Grenade!"

Lyons threw his entire body weight into the two closest officers and used the impetus to force them toward the door. The SWAT team members had cloistered together, so taking out the frontline also enforced some protection for the others. Blancanales went the only place he could: flat on the filthy floor. A cloud of dust rose from the impact. The Able Team warrior threw his arms over his head and opened his mouth, preparing for the eventuality the grenade was a flashbang.

Schwarz dived for a heavy oak table, which also happened to be the only piece of furniture in the room, and overturned it. He threw his body down and away, his feet pointing toward the blast, which came a moment later.

The floorboards shook with the power of the blast and flame exploded into a funnel shape around the oak table, but it was high enough and far enough away that Gadgets was protected adequately from the major effects of the blast. One of the officers wasn't so lucky. The man's expression went from surprise to anticipation to shock all in the seconds leading up to the blast. The majority of the officers had either gone down of their own accord or because of Lyons's lightning reflexes, but this man hadn't accounted for flying projectiles. A piece of the cheap wooden window frame tore away with the force of the blast, turning a harmless piece of wood into a sharp missile.

The officer took the force of the jagged wood square on the center of his forehead. The velocity was too much for the skull to withstand and the wood violated the cranial cavity and lodged in the officer's brain. The man staggered backward and collapsed.

The scene outside went from what seemed like a fairly controlled situation to complete and utter disaster. First there was the sound of breaking glass, followed by a loud popping sound. A moment later, a rear door on one of the police cruisers crumpled, and both the front and rear door windows on the driver's side shattered. Paint bubbled on the door and superheated shards of metal flew through the interior, scarring the plastic seats and spiderwebbing the rear window.

Lyons saw the damage and his jaw fell open. "Holy shit! What the hell was that?"

His teammates exchanged a knowing glance and then looked toward the door leading to the upstairs— or what was left of it. The blast from the HE grenade had blown the door off its hinges and scarred the walls. The heat had ignited a small section of the wall where the cheap wallpaper had apparently been peeling and was ignited, but the fire wasn't anything that couldn't be handled by a half-decent fire extinguisher.

Lyons took one last look at the damage done by the terrorists and then got to his feet. "Screw that. If I've got to risk buying the farm, I'd rather go against one round than a hundred."

He headed for the stairwell. His teammates joined him, and the threesome went through the shattered frame and ascended the stairs. Someone was shooting from the upper window, which meant that's where the attention would be focused. They reached the top of the stairs and Lyons missed the top step. He tripped, Schwarz and Blancanales falling on top of him, only their weight keeping him from sliding down the stairs on his stomach.

His misstep saved their lives as the air above their heads suddenly heated. A millisecond later they were choking on dust and plaster, with wood slivers and pieces of plasterboard pelting their faces and hands. Schwarz raised his head and turned toward the wall, only to discover it wasn't there. It had been replaced by a gaping hole, one that would have been large enough to cleanly divide his upper and lower torsos if he hadn't tripped on Lyons.

The men were on their feet and moving into the landing within seconds. Blancanales and Schwarz acquired the same target simultaneously. It was Paxton, and he'd tossed the Stormalite pistol aside and traded it for a standard-issue Beretta 92-SB. He was still raising the weapon, but the Able Team commandos had him easily beat. There was no choice, so they did the necessary thing. The pair triggered their weapons less than a second apart. Schwarz's round punched through Paxton's chin, shattered his jaw and severed the first and second vertebra of his spinal column. He was probably dead before Blancanales's round took him in the sternum. The impact of two bullets tossed his body against the wall and it collapsed to the floor and rolled twice before coming to a stop.

Lyons spotted Hauser in the corner. The man was visibly trembling, his hands up in front of his face. He kept looking from Lyons to Paxton, then back at Lyons, and then back at his son. Abruptly his expression changed from fear and shock to hate and rage.

"Don't do it," Lyons told him.

But it seemed Hauser was no longer hearing him. The man let out a blood-curdling scream and with a speed that was surprising for a man of his years, launched himself out of the corner and charged Lyons. The Able Team warrior would normally have engaged the man in combat, but it was abundantly clear in that fleeting moment that there would be only one way of neutralizing the aggression, and Lyons fully exercised it.

He raised his pistol and shot Hauser point-blank in the skull. The man's body arched backward, suddenly off balance, and then he fell to the ground in an almost slow and purposefully deliberate fashion. A suddenly wicked and eerie silence followed, and the three Able Team warriors realized that the shooting had ceased outside. They looked toward the front of the second-floor loft and noticed the casement-style window mounted to the front of the A-frame-like roof was wide open.

Lyons rushed to the window and looked at the scene below. The carnage was unreal. Two huge holes had been torn in the side of the SWAT vehicle. Bodies were strewed everywhere, and it looked like a scene straight out of hell.

"God help us." Lyons cursed under his breath and then turned to look at his comrades. "We better get down there."

Schwarz led them down the stairs and when they reached the first floor they noticed one lone officer seated just inside the door with his back against the wall. His face was a ghastly pale color, visible even in the poor lighting, and he had his MP-5 cradled in his arms more like a baby than a weapon.

Schwarz stopped and looked down at him. "Get on your feet, man."

The SWAT officer looked up at the sound of the warrior's strong voice, but the look in his eyes was devoid of emotion. He'd just seen his friends and colleagues shot down in a heartbeat. But somehow they had missed this one man. That was a case of survivor's guilt that Schwarz could see the cop might never get over. He looked upon the scene with a sinking feeling, and the thing he noticed most was the amount of blood that puddled in the street. Sirens wailed in the distance.

"Gadgets, we better go," Lyons told him.

The Able Team warrior looked at his friend, nodded and then crouched in front of the officer. "Look, son, you're going to look back on this some day and it will be easier. I know it doesn't seem like it, but believe me when I say it *will* get easier. Until then, you've got to stay hard and take it one day at a time. But whatever you do, you can't give up. You hear me?"

The officer stared blankly at him for a while but then finally he nodded. And while Schwarz wasn't comfortable with leaving the guy here on his own, he took solace in the fact that he was getting through—at least it seemed like he was.

As the trio started toward their car, Lyons told them, "We got Paxton and Hauser, but we're still missing Davidia."

They were about halfway down the block when an unmarked sedan with a blue-and-red flasher in the window screeched to a halt at the curb and Grebe jumped out with three detectives.

"What the hell is going on?" he demanded.

"Maybe you can tell us," Lyons said, stepping forward and getting nose-to-nose with the man. "We told you not to attempt apprehension, and so you go and do exactly the opposite of what we asked you to."

"Yeah, well, I don't take orders from you, pal!" Grebe snapped.

"Before the night's over, you won't have to take orders ever again," Lyons said.

"Yeah, and just what the hell is that supposed to mean?"

"Whatever you want it to mean, prick!" Lyons jammed his finger in Grebe's chest and said, "Because of your dumb fuck pigheadedness, you've got at least seven or eight dead cops over there, and another who's probably going to have collect bennies for the rest of his life because he won't be able to pull a car over without thinking about how some bureaucrat with a hard-on got a bunch of his buddies wasted!"

"Go easy, Ironman," Blancanales said, reaching for Lyons's shoulder.

"You stay out of our faces, Grebe. I see you anywhere near this case, and I'll pop a cap in your ass just for the pleasure of expending the bullet."

"Is that a threat, Irons?" The radio suddenly squawked with a flurry of traffic. Grebe turned to one of the detectives and said, "Find out what's going on."

The man reached inside the squad and yanked the microphone from its holder. "One-Bravo-One to dispatch... Would you ten-nine your last traffic?"

There was as paused before the dispatcher answered, "Suspicious vehicle was spotted leaving the quarantine area. Suspect is a white male, tall, average build, with dark hair, and was seen leaving an underground garage in a blue sedan with rental tags. Make and model is unknown, but RP states that suspect was brandishing what looked like a pistol and carrying two large suitcases."

Another voice broke through the transmission before the detective could respond. "Two-David-Seventeen to dispatch. Be advised I have the vehicle in sight, suspect matches description, we're traveling southbound on Lakeshore Drive."

Schwarz looked at Lyons and said, "Davidia?"

Lyons nodded, and then Able Team whirled and rushed for their vehicle. Grebe started to shout protests, even a few obscenities, but they ignored him. Schwarz got behind the wheel and Lyons took shotgun...literally. The urban soldier jacked the pump on an AS-3 combat shotgun he'd stowed in the front seat, and verified he was loaded with No. 2 and double-aught. Blancanales prepared an MP-5 A-3 for himself and then checked the action on an FNC for Gadgets.

"How far is Lakeshore Drive?" Schwarz asked.

"Close," Lyons replied, and he directed his teammate down a road that would take them straight to it.

Soon they were speeding south and trying to catch up with the squad car. There was a good chance that the cops would attempt to make a traffic stop on Davidia, and there was no way the terrorist leader was going to halt for them. After all, he'd spent a number of years as a Brooklyn cop, so he was well trained in escape and evasion driving tactics *and* police procedure. The other troubling thing were the weapons he carried. The devastation he'd unleashed on those SWAT officers had been catastrophic.

"We can't afford a repeat of what happened back there," Blancanales announced suddenly, almost as if he'd been reading Schwarz's mind. "It's do or die time, guys."

"Agreed," Lyons growled.

Schwarz shifted into fourth and gunned the accelerator as their first traffic light turned yellow. He wasn't planning to stop for anything if he didn't have to, red light or no, and if they got backed up in traffic, he'd get out and jog. He was in complete agreement with Lyons and Blancanales. They couldn't give Davidia, or whoever it was they were chasing, another opportunity to use those weapons, particularly not against the civilian population.

"There!" Lyons said, pointing out the windshield. There was still only a single squad car following the blue Chevy, and that was one too many. "You think you can take out that car in this traffic?"

"Piece of cake," Schwarz replied, and he eased into the right lane. The officer hadn't chosen to turn on his lights, probably for fear of losing the suspect until he could solicit additional units to help participate in the chase. Schwarz meant to insure that no further cops got killed this day, and he was going to start by saving this guy's life without his even knowing it. Schwarz stayed in the right lane, keeping his vehicle just far enough back that his front grille remained parallel with the fender on the squad car. They continued down the busy drive. Schwarz waited patiently, driving with the speed of traffic until he spotted the concrete medians in a construction zone ahead.

"Hang tight," he announced, and then he turned into the cop's right fender. He dropped his vehicle into a lower gear and then alternated between accelerator and brake. The cop tried to get out of the maneuver, but in true fashion he spun out and his vehicle broadsided the median, spinning to a halt and facing oncoming traffic. As he regained control of the vehicle, Schwarz risked a glance in the cop's direction. He looked surprised but he was unharmed.

Schwarz took the position behind Davidia and the RDL leader immediately increased speed. The speeds slowly increased as traffic lessened and then suddenly Davidia turned off the exit for Soldier Field.

"What the hell is he doing?" Lyons said. "Going to a football game?"

"Of course," Blancanales said. "Think about it. They needed someplace they could be secure for a very short time. They probably had to find a way they could house a cache of men and weapons. What better place than a football stadium in off season?"

"How would they have avoided being seen by the groundskeeper?" Lyons asked.

"You think someone working here during the summer wouldn't give them a key? Now you're being naive, Ironman. They could have used anything from threats to blackmail to gain access."

"Well, in a very short time, it won't matter," Lyons said.

Schwarz negotiated the maze of cones and other barricades, some of which it looked as though Davidia had simply driven through, and arrived at the entrance to the stadium in short order. The vehicle was parked there but it was empty, the driver's-side door still standing wide open. Able Team went EVA as soon as Schwarz got their rental stopped, and approached the broad arches of the stadium with extreme caution. The danger of the weapons in Davidia's possession was his ability to trigger them by remote access and wireless networking protocols. That meant he could set up the weapons anywhere and use them against Able Team without putting himself in harm's way.

The trio met their first opposition on the stairwell leading into the stadium proper. Two terrorists appeared at the landing and trained their mini-Uzis on them, unleashing a fusillade of 9 mm hell. Schwarz and Blancanales pressed themselves to the side of the railing, Lyons went flat, and then all three of them opened up simultaneously. The first terrorist was shocked to see his belly stitched open and his intestines spill out of his stomach. He dropped to his knees and Blancanales ended the play with a shot to head. The second terrorist took rounds to the chest and a shotgun blast to the belly. The impact lifted him off his feet and dumped him on the landing with a loud thump.

Lyons got to his feet and took up the center position between his teammates. They got to the top of the steps, then stepped into the stadium itself. Rounds began ricocheting off the metal poles and seats and tearing gouges in the steps. The Stony Man soldiers fanned out, intent on putting a quick end to the battle. Terrorists had taken up firing positions, some of them from considerable distance, and Able Team had mutually but silently agreed that the key to victory was taking the fight to the enemy.

Blancanales began picking off the terrorists on his left, catching two of them with good clean head shots.

Lyons knew the shotgun would be ineffective against the terrorists at that range, so he left the matter to Pol and Gadgets. Besides, he had a matter of his own that needed attending. He abandoned the shotgun for his .357 Magnum Colt Python Elite revolver and went in search of Davidia.

WALLACE DAVIDIA knew his cause was lost, and he felt personally responsible for the deaths of his colleagues and faithful followers.

Davidia knew there was nothing he could do to bring back the dead, but he could at least insure that those responsible suffered some casualties of their own. After abandoning the car, Davidia took the weapons and headed for the field. From the center of the stadium, he could position the guns to fire in every direction and he would be completely out of sight. He took one look at the activities in the stands and knew he could set up quickly at minimal risk. The men and women of the Resurrected Defense League had sworn to protect him, the cause and each other with their lives, and in this they had achieved a major victory.

The attacks from his forces continued, although they were rapidly running out of time and bodies. There wasn't much use Davidia could see in prolonging the suffering. The weapons were already loaded, so it was just a matter of waiting and watching. He primed the devices, then sprinted to the nearest exit sign. Once beneath the relative safety of the stadium, Davidia turned on the PC tablet and watched the system carry through its bootstrap. As soon as he was at the command line interface, he began to type in the codes that Hauser had developed for him. One by one, Davidia watched with excitement as the weapons seemed to come alive. The servos and vertical-horizontal balances moved by a simple electromechanical association. But it was the fact that they were responding under nothing more than simple networking signals.

Davidia then punched in one of the pointers to the assault rifle and used a mouse ball and tracker built into the PC tablet to control the movement. He swung the muzzle in the direction of one of the men who was moving along the stands and shooting down his people like it was child's play. Davidia waited until the laser sight locked on to the target and the red lettering on the LCD turned to green, then engaged the firing mechanism. The weapon chugged away and sent a total of two hundred rounds in the enemy's direction.

The stands around the man erupted in a cloud of dust and metal, and when it cleared a moment later, Davidia no longer saw the man. The only thing visible was the destruction left in the wake of the weapon. Two hundred rounds of 7.62 mm ammunition fired at that velocity had literally disintegrated the six middle seats of the twenty-fifth row. And with those seats had also fallen the enemy agent that had been targeting his people.

There was the sudden, unmistakable clicking of a hammer being drawn back and Davidia felt the cold barrel of a pistol at the back of his head.

"Put it down," a cold voice ordered.

Davidia did as instructed, then under further command turned to face the gunman. He was tall, blond, muscular and had eyes that were as blue and cold as gunmetal.

"Who are you?" Davidia asked.

"Does it matter?" the man asked.

Davidia shrugged. "Not really. I guess there was some point in my life where I suspected it would end this way for me. I just didn't think it would be this soon."

"People like you usually don't, Davidia," the man replied.

"You know my name. How nice."

"Yeah, but there's some people who know your name who are wishing they hadn't. You've caused the death of more innocent people today than I care to count."

Behind him, Davidia could hear the shooting continue as his people fought to maintain control of the situation. The sound of police sirens in the distance began to grind on his nerves. They were already clearly outnumbered. The cops would only finish what these men had started.

"You were once a cop," Davidia said.

The man looked genuinely surprised. "How do you know that?"

"I see it in your eyes, hear it in your voice. You don't demand service and loyalty and obedience from others, you command it. And there are only two kinds of people I know that can do that—cops and soldiers."

"And I suppose you view yourself as a soldier?"

He shrugged. "Maybe once, but no longer. Now, though, I welcome death. In fact, I beg for death. My existence no longer matters because someone will eventually show up to replace me. It's inevitable. For now, all I want is death."

And the man with the blond hair and cold eyes gave it to him.

EPILOGUE

Stony Man Farm, Virginia

On the West Bank, Israeli officials were still questioning civilians as to exactly what had happened. Damage assessments were being made of the buildings in the village of Arebah, but investigators were dumbfounded by the sheer number of rounds they were finding lodged in the strangest places. They were also convinced that the Kach-Kahane Chai terrorists that the Palestinians swear were shot down by Americans, couldn't have possibly been fired upon with small arms only, and so while there was not yet evidence to support the claim, they were ruling the destruction as being caused by an explosive compound "of indeterminate origin."

In Chicago, the funerals for the police officers were under way. The mayor fired Grebe—true to Lyons's prediction—the same evening he received a call from the head of the Justice Department on behalf of the

President, wanting to know why agents from the Department of Homeland Security didn't receive full cooperation from the Chicago Police Department as promised. Oddly, the police were still baffled by what had actually caused such massive destruction to police equipment during a SWAT operation in the north part of the city, and equally disturbing damage to Soldier Field in the south. Not to mention the inordinate number of unidentified bodies that one police spokesman said "looked like they'd gone through a cheese grater...or maybe the other way around."

It was a tired and weary crew that gathered in the War Room for their debriefing. David McCarter had even elected to be present, despite the fact he was under doctor's orders to get bed rest and plenty of it.

"Yeah, right," James said. "That's about a three-day prescription, max, and it's not refillable."

"That's what *you* think," Price told him.

"Listen up, because I know you're all anxious to get out of here," Brognola said. "The President asked me to pass on a very special thanks to each of you. I know this was a tough job, and you guys performed remarkably."

"Just our usual high standards," McCarter said, flashing him a smile.

"I'm glad to see you're in good spirits," Brognola replied. "It means you can get back to work."

"Oh...really?" McCarter groaned some, adjusted his body in the chair and said, "Maybe I shouldn't rush it, you know? This could turn out to be more serious than the doctors thought."

"Doubtful," Carl Lyons replied. "Only part that really got hurt was your ass."

"In your case, that would have a deleterious effect on your thinking, mate," McCarter shot back.

Lyons sat back, folded his arms and said, "And they wonder why I drink."

James Axler
Outlanders

CERBERUS STORM

SPOILS OF VICTORY

The baronial machine ruling post-apocalyptic America is no more, yet even as settlers leave the fortressed cities and attempt to build new lives in the untamed outlands, a deadly new struggle is born. The hybrid barons have evolved into their new forms, their avaricious scope expanding to encompass the entire world. Though the war has changed, the struggle for the Cerberus rebels remains the same: save humanity from its slavers.

DARK TERRITORY

Amidst the sacred Indian lands in Wyoming's Bighorn Mountains, a consortium with roots in preDark secrets is engaged in the excavation of ancient artifacts, turning the newly liberated outlands into a hellzone. Kane and the Cerberus warriors organize a strike against the outlaws, only to find themselves navigating a twisted maze of legend, manipulation and the fury of a woman warrior. Driven by power, hatred and revenge, she's now on the verge of uncovering and releasing a force of unfathomable evil....

Available November 2005 at your favorite retailer.

TAKE 'EM FREE

2 action-packed novels plus a mystery bonus

NO RISK
NO OBLIGATION TO BUY